The Bournemouth Library
Tel (01202) 454848

Praise for Maria Duffy

'As funny and frank a portrayal of a close-knit Dublin
community as I've read since Roddy Doyle's Barrytown
trilogy. Unputdownable' Niamh Greene

'Fresh, zany and, at times, laugh-out-loud funny'
Irish Examiner

'A funny, heartwarming novel which sparkles with
rich Dublin wit throughout'
Off the Shelf

D1333478

BOURNEMOUTH

410078066

Born in Dublin, Maria Duffy knew from an early age that she loved writing, but it never occurred to her that she could pursue the craft as a career. Instead, she began working at a bank after completing a business course. Maria went on to have four children with husband Paddy and became a stay-at-home mum. She had never stopped writing and when her youngest started school, she decided to dust off the book she had once started. Once she began to write again, she knew it was what she wanted to do for the rest of her life. Her debut novel, *Any Dream Will Do*, was published in 2011. *The Letter* is Maria's third novel.

www.mariaduffy.ie
@mduffywriter

Also by Maria Duffy
The Terrace
Any Dream Will Do

The Letter

MARIA DUFFY

HACHETTE
BOOKS
IRELAND

First published in 2013 by Hachette Books Ireland

Copyright © Maria Duffy 2013

The right of Maria Duffy to be identified as the Author of the Work
has been asserted by her in accordance with the Copyright, Designs
and Patents Act 1988.

All rights reserved. No part of this publication may be reproduced, stored in
a retrieval system, or transmitted, in any form or by any means without the
prior written permission of the publisher, nor be otherwise circulated in any
form of binding or cover other than that in which it is published and without
a similar condition being imposed on the subsequent purchaser.

All characters in this publication, other than those clearly in the public
domain, are fictitious. All events and incidents are the product of the
author's imagination. Any resemblance to real life or real persons,
living or dead, is purely coincidental.

A CIP catalogue record for this title is available from the British Library.

ISBN 978 1444 743 661

Typeset in Book Antiqua by Bookends Publishing Services.
Printed and bound by Clays, St Ives plc.

Hachette Books Ireland policy is to use papers that are natural, renewable
and recyclable products and made from wood grown in sustainable forests.
The logging and manufacturing processes are expected to conform to the
environmental regulations of the country of origin.

Hachette Books Ireland
8 Castlecourt Centre
Castleknock
Dublin 15, Ireland

A division of Hachette UK Ltd.
338 Euston Road
London NW1 3BH

www.hachette.ie

For Gerry, Denyse, Ciarán, Aoife and Siobhán.
With love.

ONE

'Matt James Patrick Smellie, do you take Ellie Marie Concepta Duggan to be your lawfully wedded wife?'

Matt nodded solemnly. 'I do.'

'And Ellie Marie Concepta Duggan, do you take Matt James Patrick Smellie to be your ...'

'Objection! I object to this farce of a wedding.' Lara, the loose-tongued bridesmaid, threw herself between the couple, grabbing Matt in a headlock. 'He's mine and you're not going to take him away from me. He doesn't love you, Ellie. He's only after your fortune.'

'For fuck's sake,' giggled Ellie. 'This isn't an episode of *Dallas*, you know!'

'Well, I'm just trying to prepare you for every possible scenario.' Lara sniffed. 'A great catch like Matt could have lots of women ready to snatch him from the arms of his betrothed.'

'Chance would be a fine thing,' said Matt, wrestling his way out of Lara's grip and at the same time ducking from the slap his fiancée aimed in his direction.

Sharon, who'd taken her priestly role very seriously, sat down on the sofa and sighed. 'I suppose there was no point in trying to do a practice run while you lot were tanked up on wine.'

Lara flopped down beside her. 'Aw, sorry, Shaz. It must be no fun watching a bunch of drunks when you're sober as a judge. Would you not even have *one* glass?'

'Not tonight, Lara. I'm in at six in the morning and you know what I'm like with even a few sips.'

'Right. That's our cue to go,' said Matt, reaching unsteadily to retrieve his jumper from the back of the armchair. 'Come on, Lara, we can share a taxi.'

'Aw, do I have to? It's still early.' Lara burrowed further into the sofa, her tiny frame almost disappearing in the expanse of feather cushions.

Sharon looked mortified. 'God, I didn't mean I want you to go. At least stay and have a coffee.'

'Yes, come on,' added Ellie. 'We have cake and everything. I'll stick the kettle on.'

Matt shook his head. 'No, honestly. I was about to head

anyway. I have a guy coming in for a training session at seven so I'll need to be bright and breezy in the morning.'

Ellie pouted. 'I probably won't see you for a few days now. My shifts are all over the place this week.'

Matt pulled her into a hug. 'Well, in less than seven weeks' time, you'll be sick of the sight of me when we're living together as Mr and Mrs Smellie!'

'Let's get this straight once and for all,'snapped Ellie, pulling away from him. 'I can't wait to be your wife, but I'll never, *ever* be Ellie Smellie.'

'Ah, g'wan, you know you want to be really.' Matt grabbed her bum and pulled her back to him.

'Eh ... sorry to interrupt this beautiful moment, but I think we might have an overnight guest if we don't get Lara up from here soon.' Sharon indicated her friend, who was beginning to snore, head tilted to the side, mouth wide open.

Ellie laughed. 'She's such a lightweight. Come on, Lara. Time to go.'

Lara reluctantly opened one eye. 'Oh, but it's *soooo* comfy here. Could I not just stay and have a little snooze? Knowing my luck, Ethan will be awake when I get home and Peter will probably pass him over to me.'

Ellie felt sorry for her friend. Being a mother didn't come naturally to her and, although she loved her little three-year-old, the sleep deprivation was killing her. 'I'm sure Peter will have worn him out and he'll be fast asleep by now.'

'I hope you're right,' said Lara, dragging herself up from the sofa, 'because if I have to get through another sleepless night, I won't be responsible for my actions.'

'You've been saying that for the last three years,' Sharon told her. 'It seems to me you're getting through it just fine.'

Lara sighed. 'It's a case of having to. Right, I'll love you and leave you. I'll give you both a buzz during the week and maybe we'll have a night in The Gardens.'

'Sounds good to me,' said Ellie, walking her guests to the door. She gave Matt a final smooch on the lips before pushing him and Lara out into the night. 'I won't keep the door open, if you don't mind. I wouldn't want to let the cold in.'

Lara drew in a sharp breath as the chill hit her. 'Yes, you go on in and leave us out here, like a couple of dogs!'

'Night, Lara. Talk to you during the week.' Ellie was still giggling as she joined Sharon in the kitchen.

Sharon was already pouring tea. 'I really am sorry to have broken up the party, Ellie. I should have just slipped off to bed and left you all to it.'

'Don't be silly. None of us wants to face Monday morning with the hangover from hell so I'm glad we finished up when we did.' She sat down and wrapped both hands gratefully around the steaming mug. 'You know, I still can't believe I'll be married and moved out of here in a matter of weeks. It doesn't seem real.'

Sharon nodded. 'I know what you mean. It's been great,

hasn't it? I mean, us sharing a house. I did worry about it at first, with us working together too. I thought we'd get on each other's nerves but it's all been fine.'

'It's been great. And, honestly, I don't know how I'd have got through the last few years without you. You've been my rock.'

'Ah, God, Ellie, don't! You'll have me in tears. We're good for each other. I'd never have lost all that weight without you encouraging me.'

'Of course you would have, you big eejit. I didn't do it *for* you. *You* were the one out running at the crack of dawn and counting the calories in everything you ate.'

'But you know how hard it was for me at home, Ellie. I'd never have done it if I still lived there, with Mam piling the calories into me as though I was going to fade away. That's what got me to this size in the first place!'

'To *that* size, Sharon – not *this* size. It's a thing of the past. You're looking amazing these days – positively glowing.'

'Ah, thanks,' said Sharon, blushing. 'I still have some way to go but I'm confident now that I'll get there.'

Ellie drained the last of the tea. 'By the way, have you thought any more about getting someone in to share with you? It's going to be very expensive to stay here on your own.'

'I'll survive for the moment. I have a bit put away and can dip into that if I need to. Don't you be worried about me.'

'But I do worry, Sharon. We've been friends since we were in our prams, for God's sake – you're like a sister to me. Only a few months ago you were saying you dreaded being left here on your own. How come you're not so worried about it now?'

Sharon shifted uncomfortably in the chair. 'Well, I'm not saying I'm not worried … it's just … well, I'm heading for thirty and it's about time I acted my age. I went straight from living with Mam to living here with you. I've got to get used to standing on my own two feet and not being so reliant on others.'

Sharon was a new woman, Ellie thought. The old Sharon would have wallowed in the fact that she was the last of the three friends to be single. She would have moaned about being left on her own. Maybe her weight loss had given her confidence at last – and she had every right to feel smug about it. Or maybe it was something else. Either way, she was looking fantastic and had worked really hard for it.

Sharon was still talking: 'So a bit of time here on my own won't do me a bit of harm. And, besides, you'll be just down the road if I need someone to make my dinner for me.'

'Feck off. You're welcome over any time, but you should have learned by now that my chef skills remain firmly in the hotel kitchen.'

'Ah, but you wouldn't see your friend going hungry, would you? The friend you abandoned to go and live the dream elsewhere.' Sharon had a mischievous glint in her eye.

'Well, there'll always be food in the fridge so you can come on over and help yourself whenever you like.'

'Okay, deal,' said Sharon, standing up from the table. 'I think I'll call it a night, though. I bloody hate these early shifts. You're so lucky you don't have to be in until twelve.'

'Ah, but you'll have half your day done by the time I get in. You go on up – I'll look after these.'

'Thanks, Ellie. I'll see you tomorrow at work. Try and get in ten minutes early and I'll take a quick break with you if I can.'

'I'll do that. Night, Sharon.'

Ellie's heart felt as though it was about to burst with happiness as she busied herself cleaning the kitchen. The dried-up remains of their dinner sat on the counter, which didn't faze her at all. As a hotel chef, she was used to keeping her kitchen spick and span. She scraped the bits into the bin and began loading the dishwasher.

She'd lived with Sharon in their little rented house just off Doyle's Corner for the last two years and had loved every minute of it. They worked at the same hotel in the city centre and it was an ideal location for them to hop on a bus or walk to work. As Sharon was on Reception, they were rarely in at the same time, but they'd often spend hours at home discussing the other staff and sharing snippets of gossip. Ellie was a tiny bit sad that that particular era was coming to an end, but she was also looking forward to new beginnings.

With everything tidied away nicely, she doused the surfaces with anti-bacterial spray. When Sharon did the shopping, she always came back with those fresh-smelling sprays – the ones that made your kitchen smell like a garden – but Ellie put them at the back of the cupboard under the sink, trusting only those that claimed to kill 99.9 per cent of all germs.

Just seven weeks to her wedding. She could barely believe it. Matt was the most gorgeous, wonderful man and she was the luckiest woman in the world to be marrying him. He was kind and considerate and never lost his temper with her, even when she was having one of her 'mini-fits'. Every now and again when things got on top of Ellie, whether it was work, wedding plans or anything else, she'd go off on a rant about stuff (usually unrelated to whatever was stressing her) and end up having a little cry. The first time he'd seen her like that was when they'd been together about three months. Her mother had been nagging her incessantly about visiting her auntie Joan because all the other nieces and nephews were perfect specimens of humanity and went to see her in her lonely, spinster flat. Everyone except Ellie. Matt had called in just after her mother had had another go at her, then gone to bingo. No sooner had he walked through the door than Ellie's rant had started. Didn't her mother realise how busy she was? Didn't she know how hard chefs worked, getting up so early and going on till late? And next door's cat was keeping her awake by sitting on her windowsill and miaowing all night. And her brother was a lazy sod and did nothing in the house. The mini-fit was born and Matt suffered through them with a ready ear and a comforting hug when she was done. Ellie was a lucky girl and she knew it.

She checked the gleaming kitchen one last time and wiped a smudge off a tap with a tea towel. She turned off the lights and headed up the stairs to her bedroom. The house was small but cosy and Ellie dreamed of owning one just like it. She loved the character of the old red-brick front, and although it was a terraced house, not a sound got through those thick old walls. In contrast, the apartment she'd bought with Matt was modern, and the thin walls didn't allow much privacy between neighbours. It had come onto the market at a knock-down price and was all they could afford at the time.

Matt had moved in, and she'd been tempted to join him, but her mother had persuaded her that it was so close to the wedding, she might as well stay put for now. If it had been a few months earlier, she'd definitely have moved in, but with only a few weeks to go, she'd been happy enough to concede.

She glanced around the bedroom as she snuggled down under her well-worn feather duvet. It was beginning to look very bare – she'd been bringing stuff bit by bit to the new place. Her mam had been nagging her to tackle her room at home, claiming they wanted to redecorate it as a guest room. Ellie really wasn't looking forward to that task.

Two years ago, when she'd left to live with Sharon, it somehow hadn't seemed like she was leaving for ever. She wasn't going far and her mother had seemed to think she'd be back. Ellie had never really understood why, but maybe it was just her way of coping with her daughter flying the nest. Now that she was getting married, everything seemed more final. She'd never go back to live in her family home and the thought of moving all her things out was daunting. But she owed it to her parents to do as they asked. Although she argued constantly with her mother, she couldn't have asked for better parents than Jean and Andy Duggan. She'd had a very happy childhood and had plenty of great memories to cherish.

She'd pay them a visit next weekend. Lately, juggling work and wedding preparations, she hadn't made much time for them. And, in fairness, her mam was doing a lot of the organising for the wedding. Ellie and Matt had originally thought of going abroad to get married but on seeing the look of disbelief and shock on her mother's face when they had mentioned the possibility, they'd decided it wouldn't be worth the hassle. So it had gone from a foreign wedding to a small registry office do to a full-on church ceremony with a hundred-plus guests and a fancy hotel reception. Ellie's parents had insisted on paying so she and

Matt had gone along with it. As long as they were getting married, nothing else really mattered.

Ellie was happy that the wedding was helping to take her mother's mind off her grief. It had been a difficult few years, but it was true what people said – time really did ease the pain. It never went away but day by day it felt more manageable. She was suddenly overwhelmed with sadness as thoughts she'd buried began to surface. Tears pricked her eyes and she turned her face into the pillow. She hadn't allowed herself to cry in a long time for fear she'd never stop. But maybe she needed to let it all out instead of bottling it up. Her chest heaved as the tears fell. She cried silently into her pillow for what seemed like hours until she didn't have another tear left in her.

Just then her phone beeped, making her jump. Ten past midnight. There was only one person who'd be texting her at that time. She grabbed the phone from the bedside locker and glanced at the message:

You're such a strong, wonderful person and I can't wait for us to be married. I love you loads. Xx

She closed her eyes and gave thanks to God for giving her a soulmate – someone who could sense her every thought, hope and dream. She couldn't wait for 15 March. It was going to be the happiest day of her life.

TWO

Sharon yawned as she sat at the reception desk in the hotel. It had been a busy morning with check-ins and check-outs, but it had quietened a lot since ten. She hated the early shifts and today was no exception. She'd much prefer to get up and go out for a run in the morning, then be at work at a reasonable time. But she loved her job so she had to take the bad with the good.

She sat up straight and smoothed her skirt as an elderly couple approached the desk. 'I'll take this,' she said to the other receptionist, who was busy filing her nails. 'How are you today, Mr and Mrs Ackerman?'

'I'm plum worn out, darlin', to be honest. But it's good to

keep going. And how's about your good self?' Mr Ackerman took off his Stetson and held it to his chest as he spoke.

'I'm good, thanks – just a bit tired too. What can I help you with this morning?'

'Well, me and Mrs A were plannin' on a good ole walk when we noticed the toad choker out there. We were just wonderin' if you'd have an um-bear-ella we could borra?'

The Ackermans, who were from Texas, had been staying at the hotel for the last two weeks and Sharon was proud to have got to know some of their dialect. The first day she'd met them, she'd thought they were talking a different language altogether, but after a few days and a lesson or two from Mr Ackerman, she'd begun to understand them.

'Here we go,' she said, producing a large golf umbrella from under the desk. 'The forecast is for heavier rain later so I wouldn't go walking too far if I were you.'

'Don't you be worryin', darlin'. Sure I'm all hat and no cattle. We'll probably be back in ten minutes.'

'Well, have a good day, whatever you do.'

He slipped his hat back on and tipped it by way of saying goodbye. His wife barely ever spoke, and Sharon suspected that she was used to him doing the talking for both of them.

It was almost eleven. Three more hours and she could go home to bed. She usually made it her business to be in bed on a Sunday night before ten, especially if she was on the early shift, but with Matt and Lara coming over last night, her routine had been scuppered. Still, they'd had a good night. Matt was such a nice guy – Ellie was lucky to have found him. In fact, they were lucky to have found each other because Ellie was a pretty good catch too. They made a handsome couple, Matt with his muscular frame and Keith Duffy good looks, and Ellie stood almost six feet tall, like an Amazon beauty. Six months ago, Sharon had felt pangs of jealousy when she'd seen them, but now she was happier in herself. She looked forward to letting everyone see her new figure in the shapely bridesmaid's dress Ellie had picked out for her and Lara. She'd had to have it taken in at almost every fitting over the last few months and she was hoping for a couple more adjustments before the big day.

Her handbag, which she'd left underneath the desk, suddenly vibrated, stirring her out of her reverie. They weren't supposed to keep their mobile phones with them on Reception but Sharon hated to be without hers. She usually put it on silent and would steal the odd peep to make sure she wasn't missing anything. A quick glance around to make sure none of the management was hovering, and she whipped it out. Just what she needed. It was from him:

Are we on for tonight? Same place 8 o'clock? I can't wait until we tell her about us. All this sneaking around is killing me! See ya later! Xx

'Sharon Young! Don't you have work to do? And how many times? No mobile phones while you're on Reception.'

'Sorry, Pauline. I – I was just checking something … you know, for an emergency or …' Pauline Burke, the general manager, scared the living daylights out of Sharon and she'd often be reduced to a quivering mess when she was around.

'Well, put it away. You can take your break soon and you can do all the checking you want on your own time.' Pauline fixed Sharon with her trademark death stare before click-clacking her way across the marble tiles.

Everyone in Toolin's Hotel lived in fear of Pauline, and Sharon and Ellie spent hours talking about her. They often compared her to some of the hated contestants on *Big Brother* – you loved to hate them, but if they were gone, you'd miss them. There'd certainly be a big dent in the hotel gossip if Pauline were to leave.

When she was sure Pauline had gone to annoy someone else, she grabbed her bag again and made a dash to the toilets. She hated quiet days like this, but a five-minute visit to the Ladies would break the monotony. There was nobody else in there so she opened up her makeup bag and touched up her lipstick. She stared at herself in the mirror and was pleased to see that her cheekbones seemed even more defined than they had been last week. When she'd had all the weight on, her face had been round and sunk in her numerous chins. Now her green eyes had never looked so big, and even her long chestnut hair was benefiting from her new healthier diet. She knew she'd never be as gorgeous as Ellie, with her Mediterranean good looks, but she was aware that she was beginning to turn heads. She pumped out a generous quantity of Molton Brown hand cream from the wall dispenser and headed back out, rubbing it in. She dumped her bag back under the desk and almost jumped out of her skin when a voice rang in her ear. 'Slacking again, I see!'

'No, I was just– Jesus, Ellie! You scared the living daylights out of me. I've just had Pauline on my back for looking at my phone. I thought you were her on my case again.'

'I thought I'd get in a bit early like you suggested and have a quick drink with you before the lunch rush. Can you take your break now?'

Sharon looked at Dawn, her fellow receptionist. 'Is that okay with you?'

'Off you go,' said Dawn. 'It's not as if we're out the door here.'

'Thanks. I won't be long.'

'She's a bit of a strange one,' said Ellie as they headed towards the bar. 'She seems nice enough, but her face never changes from that deadpan look.'

'She's okay, but she wouldn't win Personality of the Year. I've given up trying to get any conversation out of her.'

'Well, enough about her.' Ellie ordered a couple of diet

cokes at the counter and perched her bum on one of the bar stools. 'I've been mulling over the situation with Lara.'

'What situation?' Sharon was intrigued.

'Didn't you think she seemed out of sorts last night? I can't quite put my finger on it but I got the impression that everything wasn't okay at home.'

'No! Really? I thought Lara and Peter were rock solid. Do you think they're having problems? Did she say something to you?' Sharon was usually the one to notice if there was something amiss with her friends and she felt immediately worried that she'd missed something.

'Relax, Sharon. It's just a gut feeling. Lara was hitting the drink pretty hard last night and she didn't seem herself. She kept talking about not wanting to go home and how she's not getting any sleep. I suppose I was reading between the lines.'

Sharon gave a little laugh. 'But, as I said to her, she's been moaning about that since Ethan was born. I'm sure it's nothing out of the ordinary.'

'Well, I can't help thinking there's more to it.' Ellie was insistent and Sharon had to acknowledge that her friend's gut feelings were seldom wrong.

'So what do we do? Should we ask her outright if something's wrong?'

Ellie shook her head. 'We're long overdue a night in The Gardens – just you, me and Lara. If she has something to say, she'll say it in there. Let's do it one night during the week.'

'Right, you're on,' said Sharon, retrieving the slice of lemon from the bottom of her glass and wincing as she sucked the bitter juice. 'How about Thursday night? I can check if it suits Lara.'

'That's fine by me. I'm on earlies on Thursday so I won't be rushing when I get home. But you'd better get a wriggle on. Someone seems to be missing you.'

Sharon followed Ellie's stare to Reception, where Pauline was standing like a referee, her left elbow bent at a right angle displaying her man-sized watch. 'You can't be serious! She's actually feckin' timing me. Bloody bitch. I'd better run. Have a good one and I'll see you at home later.'

'That's my *ten* minutes done, Dawn,' said Sharon pointedly as she arrived back at her post. 'Why don't you go for your break while we're quiet?'

Pauline tutted loudly and, with nobody to berate, clacked off to find another poor soul who might be slacking.

Sharon thought of what Ellie had said about Lara, and had to admit that Lara had seemed unhappy lately. She hoped it was nothing more than a build-up of sleepless nights. She knew only too well how lack of sleep could send a person mad. When she'd been seriously overweight, her breathing had been bad and she'd suffered from insomnia. Well, hopefully she'd find out if there was a problem on Thursday night. The Gardens had been a regular meeting place for the three women since they'd been in their late teens. If the walls had had ears, they would have heard some amazing stories and shocking secrets over the years. It was their place of truth. Now, Sharon hoped they wouldn't hear anything shocking on Thursday. For the first time in years, things were going well for all of them. Lara had her little family, Ellie was about to get married and Sharon was the happiest she'd been in a long, long time.

○

'Here you go, Ethan. You can have your lunch in front of the telly just this once, okay?' It made Lara feel better to say 'just this once' even though meals in front of the telly were a regular occurrence. It was the only way she could get any work done. The article she was writing about emigration had to be in by six p.m. and she'd barely started it. She'd tweeted for people who'd be willing to talk to her about their experiences of emigration and had a few lined up to ring that afternoon. Hopefully her little boy would go for a nap after lunch and she'd use that opportunity to make the calls. She was exhausted and a little hung-over from last night and was finding it hard to juggle work and her son.

She sighed as she sat in her little office space in the corner of the kitchen. She hated the fact that she now spent most days in slouchy tracksuits, usually with dried-in Weetabix on the bum or milk down the front. She missed power dressing for the office. She missed the cut and thrust of the working environment and the constant stream of new blood keeping her on her toes.

Lara had worked on a national newspaper since she was twenty and loved everything about that world. At just five foot two, she'd often been overlooked for promotions or jobs but had made it her business to prove that though she was small, she was fierce too. If there was a story to be had, Lara had been the one to get it. If it meant sitting in the car and staking out a doorway for hours until the person she was looking for appeared, she'd be there. She was tenacious and resilient – nothing got in her way. The office had been largely male-dominated and she'd earned the respect of every single colleague. That was why it had been such a hard decision to leave.

She and Peter had looked at their options when she was pregnant and had thought long and hard about things. They'd come to the conclusion that it would be better for one of them to stay at home and, unfortunately for Lara, she'd drawn the short straw. Peter was a principal officer in the civil service, a good pensionable job, while her post was precarious. There'd been whispers about redundancies and she knew that she could well be targeted. Imagine if Peter had been the one to give up and then she was made redundant. Where would they have been then, with a mortgage to pay and a child to support? And Peter had pointed out that she could still get some freelance work to fit in around her time at home.

She'd balked at the idea of becoming a stay-at-home mam, but she'd lost a lot of her fight in the months after the birth, when she'd been feeling low and miserable. Anyway, she knew that Peter never would have agreed to be a stay-at-home dad, no matter what the circumstances. He loved Ethan but would be appalled at the thought of spending every day at home with him. He liked to think he was liberal but, in truth, he was an old-fashioned guy at heart and believed in the man being the main breadwinner. He'd hardly been able to contain his delight the day she'd handed in her notice and had just stopped short of throwing a party.

But Peter was a good guy. He'd realised she felt a huge sense of loss after the decision was made and he'd encouraged her to find some freelance work. She hadn't bothered initially – it wasn't what she'd wanted to do – but he'd gently persuaded her that she'd feel a whole lot better if she was doing something she loved. And what she loved to do was write. Yes, she'd enjoyed the buzz of the office environment and the social events that went with it, but she was a writer at heart, and when she was writing, she felt alive.

Once she'd secured that first job to write an article for one of the big nationals, she'd felt a whole lot better. She wasn't exactly elated by her new status, but it was better than making Lego castles, eating rubbish and watching daytime telly. At least now she was reclaiming a bit of herself.

'*Maaaaammy!* Can you come and do Lego with me? I want to make Peppa Pig but I haven't got any pink.'

Fuck! She'd never get anything done at this rate. Roll on September when she'd be able to enrol him in a pre-school and at least have a few hours to herself every day. 'Just a minute, love. Or how about I give you a lolly and you can watch a *Peppa Pig* DVD instead?'

'Yay! Can I have a pink one like Peppa Pig?'

'Of course you can.' Lara sighed and stared at the blank computer screen. She had to stop daydreaming and get on with the writing when she had the opportunity. The luxury of having endless time to write was gone for ever. She had to accept the way things were and take her opportunities when they arose.

She settled Ethan on the sofa with his lolly and beloved *Peppa Pig* DVD and sat back at the computer. The article could wait until Ethan went down for his nap. There was something else she'd been working on for the last six months and she'd been putting off doing anything about it. Somehow the time felt right now and, although she was nervous about it, she knew she was doing the right thing.

Her hands shook as she typed the words of the covering letter, but she didn't stop until she'd finished. She glanced over it, and when she was happy with what she'd written, she added the attachment. After checking it once more, she took a deep breath and pressed send. With a bit of luck, this email would mark a change in her life – for the better.

THREE

Ellie pulled her Calvin Klein skinny jeans over her hips and was alarmed at how snug they'd become. She'd only worn them last week and they definitely hadn't been so tight. She'd have to watch her diet over the next few weeks if she didn't want to have her wedding dress let out. The trouble was that she was surrounded by food all day and it was too easy to grab a slice of cheesecake when she was on a break or a plate of buttery pasta for lunch. The food at the hotel was delicious and very hard to resist.

She'd already done an early shift but had promised her mam she'd go into town with her for a couple of hours. She was tired and wasn't looking forward to it, but Jean

Duggan had pulled out her trump card last night on the phone.

'Agnes Larkin was saying the other day how her daughter takes her into town of a Saturday, hail, rain or shine. It breaks my heart that you can't be bothered to spare me a couple of hours.'

Ellie loved her mam but she drove her mad. The last thing she wanted to do when she had a few hours free was spend them traipsing around the shops with her. She'd planned to invite herself to her parents' house for Sunday dinner this week, but since it was only Tuesday and her mother had given her an earful, she'd agreed to the trip to town.

She completed her outfit with a gold-embellished Guess T-shirt and slipped her feet into a pair of purple Converse. Ellie was a very down-to-earth girl in many respects but a self-confessed snob when it came to clothes. Her friends' jaws dropped when she told them how much she'd paid for an item of clothing – they could stock their summer wardrobes in Penneys for the same amount. But Ellie would never dream of shopping in Penneys. It was the cause of many arguments between her and the girls, who mostly favoured cheap and cheerful. She told them that the more expensive brands lasted longer, but they argued that trends changed often and longevity no longer mattered. She had to admit that they had a point. She had a wardrobe of top-quality clothes in great condition, but they were just too last-season to wear. Still, she worked hard for her money and was frugal in every other part of her life so she continued to indulge herself whenever the mood took her.

This was the main reason she'd booked the trip to New York. In a fortnight, she'd be jetting off with Lara and Sharon to one of the fashion capitals of the world. She got tingles down her spine just thinking of all those designer shops and her empty suitcases just waiting to be filled. She planned on bringing out two large cases with very little in them and hoped to haul them back bulging at the seams.

Taking their role as bridesmaids seriously, Lara and Sharon had sat down with Ellie a few months ago to organise the hen party. They'd been thinking of pushing the boat out and having a couple of days down in Galway, complete with tacky veils, fluffy pink garters and L signs for the bride-to-be. When Ellie had blown that idea out of the water with her plan for a long weekend in the Big Apple, they'd hopped on board straight away. It would be good for the three of them to get away. They'd been friends for so long and had been on many holidays together, until a few years ago.

Her phone beeped, startling her, and she realised she'd begun to drift off. She jumped up, feeling a bit disoriented, and checked the message.

Ellie. Where are you? You said you'd be here at three. Mam.

Shit! It was already ten past. She could do without getting on the wrong side of her mother today. She tied her mass of black curls into a bunch at the top of her head. A quick dusting of Bare Minerals foundation and a touch of lip-gloss and she was out the door in a flash. She'd planned to walk the twenty minutes to her mam's because they were getting the bus together but she jumped into the car instead. The buses were frequent enough so she'd leave the car at her mother's.

○

'Well, it's about bloody time,' said Jean Duggan, when Ellie rolled up ten minutes later. She was standing at the door in her best mauve cardigan over grey slacks. 'There's an eighty-three due in a few minutes so if we hurry we should catch it. If not, we'll be waiting another half-hour.'

'Sorry, Mam. There was an emergency in work and I had to talk them through some stuff on the phone.' She hated lying but, in the interest of peace and her sanity, she'd had to come up with an acceptable excuse.

Her mother locked the front door and hurried them along to the bus stop. 'They work you too hard in that place, Ellie. Sure we've barely seen you these last few weeks.'

'I know, Mam, but with the wedding coming up and me taking a few weeks off, I have to put in the extra hours.'

'I suppose. And, speaking of the wedding, we have loads

to discuss. I've brought my notebook so we can sit down at some point and go over everything.'

Ellie's heart sank. She was excited about her big day, but when her mother got into full wedding mode, her head almost exploded. 'Great, Mam. I can't wait.'

Minutes later they were sitting in a stifling bus on the way into the city centre. Thankfully the journey would only take ten or fifteen minutes – Ellie could already feel trickles of sweat down the back of her neck. As her mother seemed happy enough to look out of the window, she pulled out her iPhone. She tapped on the Twitter icon and typed:

@EllieDuggan On way into town with de mammy. This may not end well! #mammyduggansdayout

She sat back and waited for a response. Ellie loved the social networking site and had found a lot of friends on it. A few were even coming to the wedding. But she wasn't stupid: she hadn't tweeted a general invitation.

@marshamooney Oooh I can't wait to hear all about it. Your mammy stories are always brilliant.

@chefsarahb Ha! I thought you were planning to relax after work today. Looks like Mammy Duggan had other ideas.

@EllieDuggan Mammy Duggan isn't so bad really – but I may have to accidentally lose her if she steers me towards the sensible shoe section.

@marshamooney Ha! My mam is always going on about me ruining my feet in heels too. Like I'm going to wear Hush Puppies with my little black number!

'Ellie, can you not leave that thing for five minutes? How did we survive in our day without a mobile phone? Could you not just have left it at home for one afternoon?'

Ellie logged out of Twitter in case her mother demanded to have a look. God, if she could see some of the things her daughter had tweeted about her. But it was all in good fun. People on Twitter loved to hear her Mammy Duggan stories, even if she did exaggerate them to get more laughs.

'Sorry, Mam. I'll put it away now. I only wanted to answer an email I forgot about. I'll even stick it on silent so it won't disturb us for the rest of the day.'

'Right so.' Jean seemed satisfied with her grand gesture. Ellie didn't tell her she still had it on vibrate – just in case.

They stepped off the bus on O'Connell Street and Jean immediately took charge. 'Right, I was thinking we'd head to Roches Stores first to look at the makeup. If you're insisting on doing your own face for the wedding, you should at least buy some decent stuff. Then maybe we'll cross back over O'Connell Street to Clerys. I want to get a bit of new bedding for when the visitors come.'

Ellie hated this side of the city. She much preferred the opulence of Grafton Street, with its designer brands and little coffee shops. 'I was thinking we'd head over the south side, Mam. I'd love to check out the makeup in Brown Thomas. They do MAC stuff and you can't get it here.'

Jean crinkled her nose in the way only mothers can. 'Well, it was far from Grafton Street you were reared, Ellie Duggan. Why would we traipse all the way over there when we have the best of shops here? If you don't like the stuff in Roches, sure can't you get what you want in Clerys?'

'Well, it's just that —'

'Right, that's settled. I might even take you up to Clerys Rooftop Restaurant for a bite to eat and we can go through all the wedding stuff there.'

There was no arguing with her. She'd just have to suck it up. It was only a few hours after all and she owed it to her mam. It had been tough for her when Ellie had moved out, even though it was only down the road. The new apartment was even closer to her Glasnevin home so when she moved in there after the wedding she'd make it her business to visit her parents more often.

'… and your auntie Breda, your auntie Anne and uncle Fred, Sandra O'Brien and her husband from around the corner and …'

Ellie smiled to herself as they walked into Roches Stores. She didn't have a clue what her mother was going on about but it was most likely something to do with the wedding. It was all that was talked about, these days. Well, roll on 15 March.

○

'Howareya, love? It's good to see you. Are you staying for your tea?' Andy Duggan was relaxing in his armchair when Ellie and her mam came back from town.

Ellie bent down to hug him. 'Thanks, but I won't stay this evening. I only came back to get my car.'

'Early shift?'

'Yes, mostly earlies this week. I'm exhausted.'

'I keep telling her she'd want to mind herself,' said Jean, appearing in the sitting room, dragging a load of Clerys bags behind her. 'If she runs herself into the ground, she won't enjoy the wedding one bit.'

'Your mam's right, love. You work way too hard. You should give yourself a break and relax a bit.'

Ellie took that as her cue. 'Why don't I come over on Sunday so you can feed me one of your famous roasts? I'll even eat all my veggies so you know I'm getting enough nutrition.'

'Oh, you see that, Andy? I can't do right for doing wrong. When *I* told her she was working too hard I got the head bitten off me but *you* say it and she's suddenly turning into Daughter of the Year!'

'Jean!' Andy was shocked by his wife's venom.

'Mam, don't be like that. I'd been planning on asking you if I could come over on Sunday anyway. Haven't you been asking me to clear out the room? I thought I could do that after dinner.'

'Ah, I'm sorry, love. I don't know what came over me. It's just all this wedding stuff. It feels like the time is getting so close and there's still so much to do.'

'Listen, Mam, I told you me and Matt can do whatever needs to be done.'

Jean sighed. 'It's not just that, love. It's … you know … with all the preparations and everything, sometimes I get angry that she's not here. She should be part of all the celebrations. She should be your bridesmaid.'

Ellie winced at the mention of her sister. Caroline's untimely death wasn't something they spoke about very often, these days.

'And I know you don't like to talk about it much, Ellie love, but I'm sure you're thinking about her too – especially at the moment.'

'Of course I'm thinking about her, Mam. I think about her all the time. But talking about her won't bring her back.'

That comment hung in the air until Jean spoke again. 'We could go to that grief counsellor again if you thought it might help. I know you weren't into it back then, but maybe now that some time has passed ...'

'Mam! I'm absolutely fine. I don't need counselling and I don't need to talk about anything. It is what it is and we just have to get on with it.'

'Your mam is only trying to help, love,' said Ellie's dad, who'd been quiet during the exchange. 'None of this is easy on any of us.'

Ellie was ashamed of her outburst. 'I know, Dad. And I'm sorry, Mam. I just don't want you stressing over anything.'

'Who's stressing over what?' A boxers-clad vision of lankiness appeared in the doorway, his unkempt hair and red eyes suggesting he'd just dragged himself out of bed.

'The state of you, Mikey. What have you been up to?' Ellie smiled at her younger brother, glad of an opportunity to change the subject.

'We had a midnight gig with the band last night and one thing led to another. Let's just say it was a late one.'

'Michael Duggan. Go and put some clothes on you. You're a disgrace.' Jean was appalled at her son's appearance. 'One of these days you'll get a proper job and stop your flitting about playing music.'

'I *do* have a proper job, Ma. Don't I work in a music shop as well as in a band? So I have two jobs. That's more than most.'

Ellie chuckled to herself. He knew how to wind his

mother up. Ellie did it unintentionally, but Mikey was constantly trying to get a rise out of her.

'And anyway,' continued Mikey, 'you didn't say – who's stressing?'

'Oh, it's just wedding stuff,' said Andy. 'You know how the women get stressed over everything. I'd keep well out of it, if I were you.'

Mikey nodded. 'Enough said. I'm out of here. Are you hanging around, sis?'

'No, but I'll be back on Sunday so I'll see you then if you're here.'

'I wouldn't miss one of Ma's famous roasts, now, would I?' He winked cheekily at his mother and, although she shook her head, Ellie could see that Jean loved the banter with her son.

'Right, I'm off,' Ellie said. 'Mam, I'll give you a ring during the week and I'll see you all on Sunday.'

''Bye, love,' said her dad, without moving off his chair. 'And maybe you'd bring us one of those lemon cheesecakes from the hotel for dessert.'

'Andy! You can't ask her to do that. Sorry, love. But if you are bringing something, their Black Forest is much nicer. Only if you are, though.'

Ellie laughed. Her parents were like a comedy duo and they didn't even know it. She went outside and hopped into her old Mazda to head home. The whole idea of leaving her childhood house to go *home* still seemed strange to her, even though she'd been doing it for two years now. But she hoped that, as the years moved on, she and Matt would make a new life for themselves, and home would be wherever Matt was. Didn't they say, 'Home is where the heart is'?

Ellie felt a rush of guilt as she drove off down the road. She knew her mother had wanted to talk about Caroline but she hadn't been able to face it. Her life was good at the moment, and if she allowed herself to remember, things would begin to crumble.

She also had mixed feelings about Sunday and doing the final clear-out of the room she'd grown up in. She hadn't yet delved into the lifetime of bits and pieces that lay inside the big chest of drawers. It was going to be emotional – she knew that much – because just as she hadn't cleared out her stuff completely, neither had they cleared out Caroline's. It was three years now since Ellie had lost her sister and sorting through things in the room they'd shared would be the hardest thing she would ever do.

FOUR

Sharon pulled her scarf tightly around her neck as she walked past Phibsboro Shopping Centre on her way to her mam's. She'd briefly thought about driving but since she hadn't managed to fit in much exercise over the last week, she'd decided to brave the elements and walk instead. Her new Skechers tone-up boots promised to give her the shapely legs she craved, and as those last pounds were proving hard to shift, she reckoned anything was worth a try.

Tonight was the girls' night out in The Gardens and she was really looking forward to it. She'd come home from work knackered and had planned to catch up on *Operation Transformation* on her Sky box and have a long soak in the bath afterwards. But a phone call to her mam had changed all that.

Deirdre Young hadn't said much, but Sharon could tell she wasn't herself. Having grown up in a house with only the two of them, Sharon knew her mother inside out. Her dad had walked out when she was only two and had made a new life for himself on the other side of the world. He had a new family now in Australia and didn't want to know about his old one. Sharon could always tell when her mother was having a down day and felt a huge responsibility to make sure she was okay. Today was no different. Whatever plans she'd made, Sharon was always ready to drop everything if her mother needed her.

Her anxiety eased a little as she passed the Botanic Gardens. She smiled to herself, remembering many happy hours spent there with Ellie and Lara when they were kids. It was only two minutes away from their street and it was like having the best garden ever. It was hard to believe they were all grown-up now and that, in a few weeks' time, she'd be the only one not married. It didn't bother her the way it used to because she was in a much happier place, but she still dreamed of walking down the aisle to meet her Prince Charming at the altar. Ever since she'd watched William and Kate's wedding, she'd dreamed of wearing her own wedding dress, not like Kate's but like Pippa's bridesmaid's dress. It had been a pipe-dream back then because, at size twenty-four, she'd never have been able to wear a dress like that. But now, with her size-fourteen figure and a new love in her life, that dream wedding might not be entirely out of the question.

She turned into the estate where she'd lived most of her life and the old feeling of dread rose into her throat, threatening to choke her. She'd hated coming home from school when she knew her mam was having one of her episodes. She'd often find the breakfast things still on the table, the curtains shut and her mam lying under a blanket on the sofa. It had been tough for a child to deal with but it hadn't happened too often. Her episodes were even less frequent these days, but Sharon was always on high alert for any sign of a downward spiral.

She rang the bell, not really expecting an answer, and rooted in her pocket for the key. But just as she pulled it out, the door swung open.

'Howareya, love? Come in quickly. It's freezing out there.'

'Mam! Y-you're up and about. That's great.' Sharon couldn't contain her surprise.

'Of course I'm up. What did you expect?'

'I ... em ... I just thought ...'

'Well, I've got to keep moving, love. That's what they keep saying on *Operation Transformation*.'

Sharon was gob-smacked. The mere mention of any weight-loss show in the past, and her mother would go crazy.

'Well, don't just stand there with your mouth open! Come on in and have a cuppa and I'll tell you all about it.' Her mother slowly led the way down the hall into the kitchen, leaning on her walking stick for support. At twenty-two stone, she'd developed all sorts of health problems over the years and walking was difficult.

'You sit down, Mam. I'll make the tea. So what's all this about, you watching *crap* stuff like that on telly?'

Deirdre lowered herself into a chair and dropped her stick beside her on the floor. 'It's not really crap when you get into it. Some of the stuff on there is quite enlightening.'

Sharon shook her head in disbelief. 'Haven't I been telling you that for years? So, go on. Tell me what's been happening. I haven't seen you look so positive in ages.'

'I thought it was time, Sharon. I know I've resisted doing anything about my weight for years, but something just clicked in my head the other day.'

'Well, thank God for that,' said Sharon, placing two mugs of tea on the table and sitting down opposite her mother. 'What was it that got you thinking?'

'Well, there was nothing else on and I flicked over to one of those weight-loss programmes and they were showing a woman in the States who was morbidly obese. Oh, it was awful, Sharon. She was bedridden and couldn't move at all. Her son had to wash her and everything. Imagine the humiliation. And there I was, sitting on the sofa with a bowl of nachos, right after I'd polished off a big plate of bolognese. I just saw my life flash before my eyes. I don't want to be her, Sharon. I really don't.' She burst into tears and Sharon jumped up to comfort her.

'Mam, don't get upset. You won't be like her. I'll make sure of it. You know I'll help you. I've been trying to do it for years but you wouldn't let me. If you're willing now, we can fix this. I promise.'

'I'm s-so sorry for how I've been, Sharon.' She grabbed a tissue from the box on the table. 'And the damage I've done to you too. You would never have put on all that weight if it wasn't for me.'

Sharon sat down again, but kept her mam's hand firmly in hers. 'Mam, you weren't well. You couldn't help suffering with depression. And look at me now – I'm absolutely fine. So don't be worrying yourself about things.'

'Thanks, love. I don't deserve you. You've always been so good to me.'

'Well, there were only the two of us, Mam. We looked after each other. But on the phone earlier, you sounded really down. I thought I'd come over to find you in bed with the curtains closed.'

'God, no. For the first time in ages, I feel excited about life. I can't think why you thought I was depressed.'

'But your voice was barely a whisper and you sounded as though you were crying.'

'Ah, sure that was me trying to get my breath back. I'd just come in from my walk when you rang and –'

'Your *walk*?' Just when Sharon had thought she couldn't be surprised any more, her mother had come out with that nugget. The most Deirdre Young had walked in years was from her house to the car in the driveway, which she was still able to drive – just about.

'Yes, I went out for a little walk. I thought the fresh air would do me good. Just to the entrance of the estate and back. I have to say, I was fairly winded afterwards but it's a start.'

'Mam, that's brilliant. I'm so proud of you.'

'And apparently exercise can help with depression too. I'm less likely to be in the doldrums if I get out for a bit of fresh air and a walk every day.'

Sharon had never seen her mam so animated and her heart soared to hear her speak like that.

'My Superquinn shopping arrived this morning too,' continued her mother. 'I've ordered loads of fruit and veg this time. I'm determined to make it work, Sharon. You've inspired me, you know. You've lost all that weight despite me trying to sabotage your efforts.'

'Ah, Mam, it wasn't like that. You were—'

'It was *exactly* like that, love. When you were living here, I made no effort to support you in your weight loss. I suppose a part of me felt jealous that you could do it and I couldn't. But that's all changed now. There's no way I'm leaving you yet – I've still got plenty of years left in me.'

Sharon welled up at this because she'd feared her mother

would die young of some weight-related complication. 'Of course you have, Mam. I want you to walk me down that aisle when the time comes and to bring your grandchildren to the park and to—'

'Weddings? Grandchildren? Is there something you're not telling me, Sharon Young?' Deirdre's eyes twinkled in a way Sharon hadn't seen in years.

'Well …' said Sharon, a glint in her own eye. 'There *is* this guy …'

○

'Just one more story, Mammy, *pleeeeease!*'

Lara smiled but inwardly she was screaming. She'd already read three stories to her son but it was as though he sensed her rush to get away. Peter was downstairs watching football, oblivious to the fact that she was already late. Men! She loved her husband but sometimes she wanted to bloody strangle him. He was one of the good guys but he was a real man's man. If there was football on the telly, nothing else mattered. She could strip naked and dance an Argentinian tango in the living room and he'd strain his neck to see the screen.

'Just two pages of a new story, then Mammy has to go, okay?' But in truth, there wasn't much chance of her stripping naked these days. Since they'd had Ethan, everything had changed. They'd always had a healthy and adventurous sex life but a colicky baby had put paid to that. Ethan had spent the first year of his life in bed between them. Lara had laughed when she'd been asked at one of her post-natal checks if she'd considered contraception. 'Yes.' She'd smiled. 'And he's called Ethan.'

'Just one more page, Mammy, just one …'

'No, Ethan, you've had enough. Mammy has to go out and Daddy will be up to you in a minute.' She kissed her son on the top of his head, tucked the duvet up around his neck and headed downstairs. Lara was a no-nonsense mother. She was loving and caring and gave a lot to her family, but she also recognised the need to take time for herself. She'd seen so many people fall into the trap of giving everything to their families and it didn't end well.

'I'm off, Peter.' She popped her head into the sitting room where he was sprawled on the sofa, eyes glued to the football. 'Ethan is waiting for his goodnight kiss. I'm going to have a few drinks so I won't take the car.'

'Right, love. Enjoy yourself. And say hello to the girls for me.' His eyes didn't leave the screen.

The sharp cold hit as soon as she was outside the front door and she pulled her Dunnes Stores *faux*-leather jacket tighter around her neck. If it was this cold here, imagine what it would be like in New York. She'd heard it was freezing at this time of year. Maybe they'd get snowed in and would be able to grab an extra few days over there. Ha! Chance would be a fine thing! She'd been disappointed that the girls hadn't wanted to go for more than three nights. Ellie had said she couldn't afford to take any more time off work, with the wedding coming up, and Sharon had been vague, muttering something about commitments. Honestly, she knew Sharon had a hard time with her mother, but she was a grown woman now and should be able to have a life of her own. She had sympathy for her situation, of course, but Deirdre Young had plenty of friends and wasn't exactly bedridden. Sharon was a bit of a home bird and used her mother far too often as an excuse not to do things.

In reality, the trip was one Lara could ill afford, but there was no way she'd have missed out on it. In fairness, Peter hadn't balked when she'd suggested taking a little out of their rainy-day account and she'd been stashing away a bit from her freelance work for the last few months. She was looking on New York as a life-saver. If she hadn't had that to look forward to, she'd have been tearing her hair out.

She checked her watch as she hurried down the road. Half past nine. She wouldn't be far behind the girls, after all. The Gardens was only a stone's throw away. As she walked past the Botanic Gardens she thought how lucky she was to live in such a great area with so many facilities close by. When she and Peter had been looking for a house a couple of years ago, there'd never really been any doubt in their minds that they'd stay local. Peter was from around there too and they both loved it.

And she didn't like to admit it, but she'd have hated

to move too far from her friends. Lara liked to be known as an independent woman and wouldn't want anyone to think she couldn't survive without the girls. But the male-dominated environment she'd worked in for the last ten years had forced her to hide her emotions and appear more confident than she felt. Her colleagues had made it clear that they were waiting for the little woman to fall on her face and confirm that newspaper journalism was a man's job.

The friendly lights of the pub were a welcome sight and she could almost taste that warming glass of red wine as she pushed the door open. The girls were sitting at a table in the corner, already deep in chat. It was exactly what she needed – a good girlie gossip to help her remember how things used to be and forget about the rut she was falling into.

FIVE

Ellie took a big slug from her second glass of wine and winced as the alcohol burned its way down to her stomach, but she was enjoying the buzz from the wine and the company. They were having a right laugh, which made her feel all the more excited about New York. 'So, are we going to make an itinerary for this trip or just play it by ear?'

'I don't know, Ellie,' said Sharon, sipping her Diet Coke. 'I'm the one who's never been there so I'll leave it up to you two. What do you think, Lara?'

'Come on, girls. Are you really asking me that? Don't

you know that I'll have the trip planned with military precision? You can't go to New York for a few days and not have a plan. We don't want to waste one minute of our time there so leave it to me.'

Ellie was quick to jump in: 'That's fine by me as long as you set aside one complete day for shopping. And that doesn't mean a couple of hours – I'm talking about one full, wonderful, morning-to-night shopping day.'

'Oh, sweet Jesus, no!' said Lara, feigning shock. 'No bloody way! Why would you want to waste precious New York time on shopping? I'll factor in an hour or two and that's your lot.'

'Well, if you're going to be like that, I can always go off on my own and leave you two to your own devices.' Ellie hadn't expected such resistance to shopping. Surely the girls knew it was her main reason for going there in the first place. She had to bite her tongue. The last thing she wanted to do was end up arguing with them. And they'd been having such a good night too.

Sharon stifled a giggle. 'I think she's having you on, Ellie.'

Ellie looked at Lara and realised Sharon was right. 'Bitch! You had me going there.'

'I didn't think you'd fall for it,' laughed Lara. 'You're so easy to wind up, Ellie Duggan. Of course we'll do whatever you want to do. This is *your* special weekend – the last one before going over to the dark side.'

'What dark side?' Ellie was confused.

'Marriage, you eejit!'

Ellie caught Sharon's eye. Was that merely a flippant remark or a sign that there was really something wrong, as she'd suspected the other night? She wanted to find out but Lara was a bit tipsy so it might not be the right time for a serious conversation.

But Lara was still talking: 'It's really not what it's cracked up to be, you know.'

'What isn't?' Sharon was watching her carefully, Ellie noted.

Lara sniffed loudly and her mood seemed to change. 'Marriage, Sharon. Fuckin' marriage!'

'What do you mean?' asked Ellie, taken back by her friend's tone. 'Is there something wrong?'

'Us women are in far too much of a hurry to get married and have kids, these days. But what we don't realise until it's too late is that it changes *everything*.'

'God, Lara. I've never heard you talk like that.' Sharon looked as though she was going to cry. 'Are ... are you and Peter having problems or something?'

'Well, not problems as such ... but just stuff ...'

Although Ellie had suspected something was amiss, she hadn't really expected Lara to admit anything. 'What stuff, Lara? Jesus, I've been so caught up with the wedding plans lately. I'm really sorry I haven't been there for you. I thought you and Peter were rock solid.'

'The thing is, we really *do* love each other. That hasn't changed. But it's a whole lot of other factors that impact on our day-to-day lives. There's always fucking something.'

'Like what?' Sharon indicated for the lounge girl to bring another round of drinks. It looked like they were going to need them.

'Well, for starters, we now have a mortgage to pay. It's funny … When you live at home or even when you're renting, you take certain things for granted. But it's a whole different ball game when you have to pay the bills and keep the fridge stocked – and it's amazing how one little extra mouth sends the food bill through the roof. I never realised how much money my parents must have spent just to keep everything ticking over.'

'But Peter has a good job, hasn't he?' said Ellie. 'And you still do some freelance stuff. Surely that's enough to keep the wolf from the door.'

'It's not *just* the money. We're not on the breadline yet. It's more the weight of responsibility. There's nobody to pay the bills if we don't, nobody to look after Ethan if we want to head off somewhere. It's just us.'

Ellie felt a bit unsettled by the bleak picture Lara was painting. 'But surely that's exciting too, Lara. Isn't it exciting to be in control of your own life, not to have your parents breathing down your neck and not having to conform to someone else's schedule? And as for having nobody, what about your friends? We're always here for you. You know you only have to ask and we'll be glad to babysit if you and Peter want to get away.'

'Ellie, you're missing the point. I'm very lucky and I know I have a lot of support, but what I'm saying is that the buck stops with us – me and Peter. We have to be responsible for our family. We can't make rash decisions any more and we can't do whatever we want to do.'

Sharon had been quiet but piped up now: 'God, isn't it funny that we always want what we can't have? I *want* that responsibility. I'm envious of you two being so secure in your relationships, and especially you, Lara, having Ethan. I want to feel empowered and know that the decisions I make will have a huge impact on others.'

'I know what you're saying, Sharon, and I should be grateful for everything I have, but I can't help feeling trapped.'

'Jesus, Lara. Is it that serious? ' This was getting way too heavy and Ellie was sorry they'd started the conversation.

Lara seemed to pick up on her friend's anxiety and her tone softened. 'Don't get me wrong. We're not talking divorce courts or anything. I only want to make some changes. You know me, I'm a career girl at heart, and much as I love Ethan, being home with him all day is turning my mind to jelly.'

Sharon nodded. 'I know where you're coming from now, Lara. When my mam had me, she had to give up her job and I think that was the start of her depression. I'd hate to see you go down the same route. You need to make changes now if that's how you're feeling.'

Tears formed in Lara's eyes. 'That's what I've been thinking. I can't say I'm depressed, but I'm afraid that if some things don't change, that's what's going to happen.'

Ellie moved closer to her friend and put an arm around her. It wasn't like Lara to cry so she must really be feeling fed up. 'Can you talk to Peter about it? Maybe he could take on more of the responsibility with Ethan so that you can get more involved in your freelance stuff.'

'The funny thing about it is,' sniffed Lara, wiping her eyes, 'that if Peter knew how I was feeling, he'd do everything he could to sort it out. I've been bottling it all up, I suppose. I didn't want to be a failure as a mother.'

'God, Lara. You're not a failure.' Sharon pushed into the alcove on Lara's other side, so she'd feel surrounded by her friends. 'You're brilliant with Ethan and he adores the ground you walk on. I just hope I can be like you when I'm your age.'

'Fuck off, you bitch!' Lara laughed and gave Sharon a friendly dig in the ribs. 'Just because you're still in your twenties! You'll be joining us in the thirties club at the end of the year.'

Ellie was glad the mood had lightened. 'Just let us know what we can do to help, Lara. Any time you need us, we're here.'

'Thanks, girls. I don't know what I'd do without you.'

'And changing the subject for a minute,' said Ellie, 'tell us about your secret lover, Sharon.'

'Wh-what?' Sharon turned bright pink.

'Aha! I'm right, amn't I? I knew it!'

Sharon recovered quickly. 'Chance would be a fine thing. And if I had a lover, don't you think I'd be shouting it from the rooftops rather than keeping him a secret?'

'Hm! I'm not convinced.'

'Anyway,' continued Sharon, 'what makes you think I have one?'

'Because I've heard a few whispered conversations on the phone at home and you always hang up quickly when I come into the room. And you've been disappearing a lot in the evening and I know you're not always going for a walk because you have makeup on and are dressed far too nicely for walking.'

'A right little detective you are, aren't you?' laughed Lara. 'Next you'll be following her to see where she's going.'

Sharon looked shocked. 'Jesus, Lara, don't be putting ideas into her head! I can't think of the phone calls you're talking about, Ellie, but I sometimes head down to Mam in the evenings.'

Ellie giggled. 'Relax, will you? I'm only teasing you. Maybe we'll find you a nice man at the wedding. I know the tradition is the bridesmaid gets with the best man but Matt's brothers are both taken so there'll be no shenanigans there.'

'I'll find my own man, thank you very much,' said Sharon. 'I can't think of anything worse than being fixed up with somebody.'

'We'll see!' Ellie winked at Lara. 'I'm just slipping to the loo. Will I get one for the road on the way back? I don't know about you two but I'm done in at this stage.'

'Ah, go on, then,' said Lara, draining the last of the wine in her glass. 'Sure we'll have one more.'

'Right, won't be a minute.' Ellie headed towards the toilets and realised she was unsteady on her feet. God, she'd only had three glasses of wine. There was a time when it would have taken a couple of bottles to get her drunk. That had been after Caroline's death. Drink had been her friend for a while. It had been the only way to numb the pain. Well, thank God she'd moved on and the future was looking bright. Maybe she'd pop down to the cemetery at the weekend and pay a visit to the grave. It was about time she had a chat with her sister and filled her in on all the wedding plans. A lump formed in her throat: Caroline wouldn't be there on her big day. She pushed the thought aside. She'd promised herself she wasn't going to get upset about it. This was an exciting and important time in her life and she had to allow herself to be happy.

◎

'I don't understand why you won't tell her,' said Lara, as soon as Ellie was out of earshot. 'It's not like you're doing anything wrong.'

Sharon sighed. 'I know, I know. It's stupid, really, but she's going to think it's really weird.'

'Well, it is a bit, but each to their own.'

Sharon was about to snap at Lara, then saw the grin on her face. 'But, seriously, it's so close to the wedding, I don't want anything upsetting her.'

'It's hardly the scandal of the decade now, is it? So what if there's six years between you? Who cares? If you were eighteen and he was twelve, there might be a few eyebrows raised, but you're almost thirty and he's twenty-four, for God's sake.'

Sharon knew Lara was right. She'd been seeing Ellie's brother, Mikey, for the last four and a half months and they'd become very close, despite the age gap. She'd known him practically all his life and it had been a surprise to her when she'd felt the first bolt of electricity. It had happened at Ellie's thirtieth birthday party last October in the local GAA club. They'd all had a lot to drink and Sharon, who got drunk at the sniff of a glass of red, had pulled Mikey onto the floor to dance with her. Little Mikey, they used to call him. He'd never been any more to her than Ellie's baby brother. But as they'd twirled and kicked their legs to 'Jail House Rock', something had stirred inside her. She'd suddenly stopped seeing him as little Mikey. She could tell he felt something too and they'd sobered up fairly quickly. A chat later in the night had led to a date and things had moved on from there.

'So are you going to?' Lara was staring at Sharon, waiting for an answer.

'Going to what?'

'For fuck's sake, Sharon. Were you not listening to a word I said? Are you going to tell Ellie? I think you should. She'd hate that you're keeping it from her.'

'I will tell her – I promise. But not just yet. I know we're not twelve and eighteen any more but we were once, Lara. When we all left school, Mikey was just going into secondary. If I can't get my head around that myself, how is Ellie going to feel? You know how protective she is of him – especially after Caroline.'

The two fell silent for a minute. They hadn't spoken much to Ellie about Caroline lately, for fear it would make her too sad. It had taken her a long time to get to where she was now and Sharon, for one, didn't want to burst her bubble by making her think unhappy thoughts. She knew that if Ellie wanted to speak about her sister, she would.

'I suppose,' said Lara reluctantly. 'But if you two are going to keep the relationship going, she'll have to know.'

Sharon perked up. 'Maybe I'll tell her when we're in New York. At least over there she'll have lots of things to distract her and it may not seem like such a big deal.'

'Good idea. And how are things going with you two anyway?'

Sharon felt herself blush furiously as she remembered their liaison the previous day in the flat when Ellie was at work. 'Really good, Lara. Honestly, I've never met anyone like him. He's so kind and loving and really considerate when it comes to … well, em, you know!'

'Urgh! Too much information. But I'm glad you're happy. And I know Ellie would feel the same once she was used to the idea.'

'Right, here she is. Change the subject.' Sharon laughed hysterically in an effort to throw Ellie off the scent but realised she must look like a mad woman. Acting had never been her strong suit. Ellie raised a quizzical eyebrow from the bar and Lara just shrugged her shoulders.

Sharon smiled to herself. She'd come a long way this last year. They said good things came in threes and it was certainly true for her – her weight loss, finding her soulmate (because that was what Mikey was) and now her mam's new-found optimism. Life was good, and at that moment she felt like one of the luckiest girls alive.

SIX

'This is delicious, Mam,' said Ellie, tucking into her roast beef with gusto. 'I have to hand it to you. Nobody makes Sunday roasts like you.'

'Thanks, love. That means a lot coming from a chef. And I know you make all that fancy stuff in the hotel, but I still say you can't beat the old favourites.'

Mikey piled as much as he could fit onto his fork and paused before stuffing it into his mouth. 'Ah, that arty-farty stuff is a joke. It's usually gone in a few mouthfuls and you're left starving afterwards.'

Ellie felt the need to defend her craft. 'But have you

ever tasted *haute cuisine*, Mikey? You can't just condemn it for how it looks. A lot of what we make in the hotel looks fabulous but it's wholesome and there's plenty of it.'

'You can't convince me. Fitzer won a voucher in a raffle for that new posh restaurant in Finglas. Four of us had a meal there and ended up going to the chipper after.'

'Jesus,' said Ellie. 'Life just isn't fair. You put away about ten times as much food as me and you're still a lanky streak of misery! I'd only have to look at that amount of food for my hips to expand by a few inches.'

Ellie's dad had been listening to the banter. 'You look gorgeous, love. Your mam and I were just saying that you'll make such a beautiful bride. I can't wait to walk you up that aisle.'

'Thanks, Dad.' Ellie felt choked up. Andy Duggan was a very quiet man. He never had much to say so when he said something as profound as that it really made an impact.

'Your dad's right, Ellie. You don't need to lose any more weight – except maybe an inch or so off your waist so that the dress will sculpt you nicely.'

Ellie caught Mikey's eye and they both had to stifle a giggle. It was the standing joke between them that their mother couldn't give a compliment without a sting in the tail. She'd regularly say to Ellie, 'Your hair looks lovely like that – but you'd look ten years younger if you didn't sweep it off your face.' Or 'That dress suits you really well – the stripy one you had on the other day made you look fat around the middle.' She didn't even realise she was doing it and Ellie was well able to brush it off.

'And speaking of dresses,' continued Jean, 'when is your next fitting? Monique must be almost finished by now.'

'We've a fitting the Wednesday after we come back from New York. It'll give us the incentive not to indulge in the huge portions you get over there.'

'Well, you know Monique. She'll be on your backs if you upset her sizing. It's easier to take a dress in than let it out.'

'Don't worry, Mam. We wouldn't dream of upsetting the very highly strung Monique!' The girls loved their regular fittings with the French dressmaker. She was hilarious – although she never intended to be. Her broken English always sounded funny to them and she'd get wildly upset by the slightest thing. At the last fitting, Sharon had hitched her dress up around her boobs and Monique almost lost her life, screaming: 'For love of ze God! Ze boobies should be placed *gently* in ze dress. We do not *pull* ze fine silks.' They'd all had to swallow their giggles and nod in agreement but it had given them a good week of laughs.

'So what did you bring us for dessert?' asked Mikey. 'Whatever about the fancy dinners in the hotel, they do a bloody good dessert.'

'There's lemon cheesecake and an apple pie.' Ellie didn't mention that she'd whipped up the cheesecake herself the previous night and the apple pie was from Eurospar. Her family seemed to think she could take whatever food she wanted from the hotel just because she worked in the kitchen.

Jean got up. 'I'll get this table cleaned up and then I'll bring them out.'

'I'll give you a hand, Mam.' Ellie began to gather the plates together.

'No, love, honestly. Mikey and your dad will give me a hand. Why don't you go up and get a start on your room?' Her mother's voice was gentle but firm and brooked no argument. 'There's loads of stuff in that chest of drawers and your daddy's going to paint it so he wants it empty. I'll give you a shout when the desserts are out.'

Ellie sighed. It had been inevitable, but she wasn't looking forward to going through that stuff. She planned on moving back into the house for the few days before the wedding and her mam was nagging her dad to give the room a complete overhaul for the occasion. Ellie had pleaded that it wasn't necessary but Jean's mind was made up. With a heavy heart, she went up to the bedroom where she'd slept for twenty-eight years of her life.

The room looked bleak and a chill ran down Ellie's spine as soon as she stepped inside. After Caroline's death, there'd been talk of getting a double bed to replace the two singles. 'It would be far more comfortable for you,' her mother had said. 'And we could redecorate and replace that dusky pink on the walls with something more mature.'

But Ellie had point-blank refused. *How could her mother*

think of changing things so soon after her sister's death? How could she want to wipe away Caroline's memory? How could she be so cruel?

She sat down on the end of her old bed and let herself flop backwards. She looked over at the identically dressed bed across the room. She and Caroline would spend hours just lying there, gossiping and moaning about their love-lives and their spotty skin. They'd chat about their hopes and dreams, and giggle at how they'd played yet another practical joke on their annoying little brother. They'd shared that room until Caroline had moved into a flat, a few years before she had died.

Caroline had been two years older than Ellie and the pair had been best friends as well as sisters. Even after Caroline had moved out, they'd still spent a lot of time together. They'd often say that some of their best holidays were the ones they went on together – just like that last year …

The crash of something falling to the floor and smashing downstairs in the kitchen brought Ellie back to the here and now. Her mother would be calling her down any minute, wanting an update on her progress. She sat up and looked across at the old pine chest of drawers that had been in the room for as long as she could remember. Well, she'd better make a start on going through her stuff. She knew for a fact that the big bottom drawer was full of old pictures so she braced herself for an emotional few hours ahead.

The first she came across were of her debs. God, how

could she have let herself be seen in a dress like that? And, even more importantly, how could she have let herself bring a guy like Jamie O'Brien with her? He'd been such an arsehole, getting drunk before the dinner and falling asleep with his head in his food. Then there were pictures of her, Lara and Sharon in Mallorca. It was hard to believe that that holiday had been ten years ago. She was happy to note that she didn't look much different now from what she had then. Maybe she was a size or two larger.

'How are you getting on up there, love? I've just put the desserts out if you want to come down and grab some before they're all gone.'

Ellie knew she'd have to stop getting caught up with pictures or she'd never get the job done. 'Right, Mam. I'll be down in a few minutes.'

She smiled at the memories of years gone by as she gathered up the rest of the pictures. She was about to place them in one of the cardboard boxes her mam had left out for her when another photo fell to the floor. She picked it up and tears sprang to her eyes. It was of her and Caroline in New York five years ago. They were standing in front of the ice rink at the Rockefeller Center, both making silly faces at the camera. Caroline had won the flights in a charity raffle and had asked Ellie to come along with her. They'd had a brilliant time shopping and doing all the touristy things and had vowed to go back again some day when they'd saved up enough money.

She ran her thumb over her sister's face in the picture and blinked away the tears. She'd want to cop on to herself because if she fell to pieces at every reminder of Caroline she'd be there until next week. She placed the picture carefully into the box and headed downstairs for a break.

'How are you getting on, love?' asked her dad, lifting a big slice of cheesecake onto his plate. 'I tell you, there's some amount of stuff in that chest of drawers.'

Ellie sighed. 'It's going to take a while but I'll get through it.'

'Do you want a hand, sis? I'm great at de-cluttering – a few bin-bags and a grim determination is all you need!' Mikey was already on his second slice of cheesecake and didn't look as if he'd stop at that: his eyes were checking out the apple pie.

'Ah, you're all right, Mikey. I'll manage. Actually, Mam, I don't really feel like having dessert yet. Do you mind if I get back up there? There's a lot of stuff to go through.'

'Go on, love. Just give me a shout if you fancy a cuppa and I can bring one up to you with a slice of cake, if you like.'

'Are you sure you don't want me to—'

'No, Mikey!' Jean cut him short. 'This is something Ellie needs to do on her own.'

It was all starting to make sense now, Ellie thought. It was another of her mam's little ways of trying to make her talk about Caroline. She just wished she'd stop interfering. No talking in the world was going to bring her sister back.

Ellie went upstairs, closed the bedroom door and took a deep breath. If her mam wanted her to confront things head on, well, that was what she'd do. Caroline was gone and it was unbearably sad, but life had to move on.

With renewed energy, she took out each drawer and laid them on the floor. Bit by bit, she began to go through the stuff. Mikey had been sort of right about the bin-bags because a lot of stuff had seen better days, like dried-up makeup and stale perfume. Then there were other things, like old books that had somehow found their way from the shelves into a drawer, and notebooks full of doodles drawn by her and Caroline. One of the drawers was full of soaps, none of which smelt of anything now.

Ellie lifted it and tipped its contents into one of the boxes. She'd ask her mother what she wanted to do with them. She was just about to replace the empty drawer in the unit when she saw an opened envelope stuck to the base. It was addressed to Caroline. She felt torn as to whether or not she should look inside. Maybe it was something personal. Should she really be looking at her dead sister's personal stuff? But, on the other hand, what harm could it do? The envelope was open and inside was another smaller one, containing a folded piece of paper. Ellie pulled it out and sat on the end of the bed.

She unfolded it, smoothed it and began to read.

SEVEN

'Ellie, quick! The pan!'

'Oh, fuck!' Ellie turned to see smoke billowing from the steak she was cooking. Shit. The order had specified well done, not black and charred. She'd have to pull herself together. It was the second she'd burned during lunch and two fillet steaks in the bin wouldn't make the boss happy.

'What's up with you?' asked Sarah, her sous chef, grabbing another steak for Ellie to start again. 'You've been miles away all day.'

'I know. I'm sorry. It's all the wedding stuff. It has me exhausted. '

'I'm still waiting for a well-done fillet steak for table four and risotto for table eight.' The high-pitched voice of Julien, the maître d', echoed through the kitchen and both girls got their heads down to fulfil the orders quickly. Ellie finished her dish, dropped it onto the pass and breathed a sigh of relief.

She cleaned the work surfaces, washed her pots and pans, and when she was sure everything was sparkling, she took off her apron and left the sweltering kitchen. Thank God that shift was over. She hadn't slept a wink last night and she was almost dizzy with exhaustion. She'd grab a cup of tea in the bar to wake herself up before heading to the bus stop.

She found herself a quiet table in the corner and gratefully took the weight off her feet. Her head was in a spin from the emotion of the previous day.

'What are you doing relaxing in here? I thought you'd be up to your eyes with the lunch rush.' Sharon plonked herself down in the seat opposite.

'I'm just finished,' said Ellie, wishing Sharon hadn't seen her because she wasn't feeling very sociable. 'Actually, I was just having a quick cuppa before heading off. You're working until later, aren't you?'

'Yep, here until six. I didn't want to take my break yet, to be honest. It makes the afternoon too long. But the lovely Pauline insisted I go now because there's a coachload checking in shortly.'

'Ha! Glad I don't have her breathing down my neck. So

how did it go with your mam last night? Is she still making progress?'

'God, Ellie, it's unbelievable. It's like she's a new person. It's going to take a long time to get her healthy again, but she's watching her food and cooking up healthy meals and she's been out walking every day. I'm so proud of her.'

'That's brilliant, Sharon. I'm delighted for her – and for you. And with all you've learned about healthy eating and exercise this last year, you'll be a great help to her.'

'Thanks. That's what I'm hoping – if she'll listen to me. And that reminds me – how did the big clear-out go in your house yesterday? I saw the boxes in the sitting room when I came home last night but you were in bed.'

'It was fine, I suppose.' Ellie couldn't muster the energy to say any more.

'Oh? I'm sensing a tone. Was your mam being a pain?'

'She was okay, actually. And for once we didn't go through all the wedding plans in minute detail.'

'Well, what's up then? You don't seem yourself.'

'It's nothing. It's just … it's just …' To Ellie's surprise, tears sprang to her eyes and she just couldn't help them falling – big fat tears dripping onto the table.

'Jesus, Ellie. What's wrong? What is it?' Sharon grabbed a tissue from her pocket and thrust it at her friend.

Ellie wiped her eyes and tried to catch her breath.

'You're scaring me now,' said Sharon, concern showing on her face. 'Is it something really bad?'

'Oh, Sharon, it's just everything. There's so much to do for the wedding, and I don't know half the people who are coming because my mam keeps adding to the list, and I'm sure I've put up a few pounds since the last fitting of my dress, and I burned the steaks at lunch and – and –' Sharon was trying to hide a smile but Ellie noticed. 'It's not funny, Sharon. I'm having a crisis here. It's like my world is going into meltdown.'

'Well, you know what Matt would say if he was here,' said Sharon, her eyes twinkling.

Ellie looked at her and couldn't help laughing through her tears.

'Mini-fit!' they said in unison.

'I'm sorry, Sharon. I suppose this is what they call pre-wedding jitters. I just realised how much I still have to do, and on top of that, I didn't get much sleep last night so I'm exhausted.'

'That's understandable.' Sharon leaned across the table and lowered her voice. 'But there's nothing else, is there? You and Matt are okay, aren't you?'

'Of course we are. No, there's nothing else. Well, except … it's just that …' Ellie shook her head. She was still trying to digest the contents of the letter. She didn't know what to do with it. Should she show it to her mother or to Matt? 'Clearing out that room with all its memories has made me a bit emotional, that's all.'

'Ah, Ellie, it's bound to be hard. I'm sure Caroline is

looking down on you and cheering you on. I know she'll be with you on your big day.'

Ellie cleared her throat. 'Yes, you're right. I'm sure she'll be with me. And I know she'd be happy for me.'

'Of course she would. And with the wedding coming up, she must be on your mind all the time, but you haven't spoken about her much lately.'

'I haven't had time to dwell on the past.' Ellie frowned. 'It's not as though I made a conscious decision not to talk about her.'

'I know,' said Sharon, watching her friend carefully. 'But me and Lara are always there for you if you want to talk about anything. Better out than in, as my mother always said.'

Ellie laughed, drying her eyes. 'She was referring to you getting sick when she said that, if I remember correctly.'

'Well, that's true. But it works for feelings too.'

'I'll remember that – for both scenarios!'

Sharon checked her watch. 'Jesus, I'd better fly. I'm well over the ten minutes for my break. If that coachload of guests is here already, there'll be hell to pay.'

'I'll see you at home later,' said Ellie, glad that she didn't have to rush back to work herself. 'And thanks for the chat.'

'Any time. See you later.'

Ellie watched her friend rush off. She was looking forward to their time in New York. It would give her a chance to relax before the wedding and to have some quality girlie time together. It would be good to get away from everything and just concentrate on having a good time. Her mood lightened at the thought.

But then she remembered again the events of the previous day and the letter. How could she not have known such a huge secret about her sister? She'd thought they told each other everything. Although she'd been tempted, she hadn't shown the letter to her mother. It would only have dragged up all sorts of memories – memories Ellie had buried for the past three years. And there was the wedding to think about.

She reached into her bag and took out the letter. She scanned the contents again. Tears pricked her eyes but she wiped them away quickly before folding up the letter and stuffing it deep into the pocket of her bag. Nothing would be gained by dredging up old emotions. Some things were better left in the past and this was one of them.

She had a sudden urge to talk to Matt. She wished he was there to put his arms around her, but hearing his voice would be the next best thing. It was after two so he'd probably be on his way home from the gym. She grabbed her phone and went straight to her favourites, where his number was at the top of the list.

'Hi, Matt. I'm just leaving work so thought I'd give you a buzz. Are you home?'

'Just on the bus,' he whispered. 'Are you okay?'

'I'm fine but I'd love to see you tonight. Will I come over?'

'Well, there's an offer I can't refuse. Yes – will I make dinner?'

'No, don't bother. I'll grab something at home. I have boxes of stuff I took from my mam's yesterday so I'll bring those over.'

'Old pictures?'

'Yep, among other things.'

'I knew it. I can't wait to have a look at them.'

Ellie laughed. 'And who says I'm going to let you? They might be private, you know.'

'Ah, go on. I bet you were a gorgeous child – all hair and no teeth!'

'Shut up, you! I won the Bonny Baby contest two years running in the summer project, you know.'

'Well, you'll just have to prove it by showing me the pictures then, won't you?'

'We'll see. It depends on what you have to offer as a swap.' She was teasing him now and smiled to herself as she thought of him on a packed bus, trying not to let anyone hear what he was saying.

'Get over here by seven and I'll show you what I have. I promise you'll like it.'

'Oooh, cocky, aren't you?' giggled Ellie. 'Right, I'll be there. Looking forward to it.'

Ellie stood up and buttoned her coat, bracing herself for the transition from the warm hotel to the cold outside. She felt lighter after talking to Matt. He always managed to cheer her up. He'd never known Caroline so it wasn't something they talked about much and Ellie liked it that way. Matt was her future and she needed to concentrate on that. Thank God for the day she'd met him – otherwise her life would have been very different now.

○

Sharon saw her bus pulling into the bus stop on O'Connell Street just as she crossed O'Connell Bridge. Feck! She was knackered after a busy shift, but couldn't face a half-hour standing in the rain, waiting for another. She mustered all the energy she could and sprinted down the street. Thankfully there was a queue so she made it in time to hop on.

The damp smell of rain-soaked coats mixed with the hot air blowing from the vents made her stomach lurch and she pushed her way down to the back where she squeezed into a seat, proud that she was barely out of breath. Six months ago, she wouldn't have attempted it but now, a seasoned runner, she was well able for it.

Sharon was a born worrier and the chat she'd had with Ellie earlier had unsettled her. She'd worried over the last few months that Ellie had barely made reference to Caroline. Lara had said it was probably just that she was too busy with the wedding stuff to think about it, but Sharon thought differently: maybe Ellie was blocking out the pain of not having her sister around, which couldn't be good for her.

'Oh, for fuck's sake,' Lara had said, when Sharon mentioned it. 'Do you have to psychoanalyse everything and everyone? I know you're into all that mind stuff, but sometimes things are straightforward and don't need to be analysed.'

Sharon had backed off and decided not to say anything, but she'd been keeping a close eye on Ellie and today had just confirmed her suspicions. Caroline had played such a big part in Ellie's life that it was only natural she'd think about her even more coming up to such an important event. But now it was as though everything she'd suppressed over the last few months had shot to the front of her mind and she was having trouble dealing with it. At least there were still a few weeks to the wedding so there was time for Ellie to get her thoughts together. As far as Sharon was concerned, she needed to talk about her sister. If she didn't, she was likely to implode.

The truth was, when Caroline had died, something had seemed to die inside Ellie. When she'd been given the terrible news, she hadn't cried. Instead she'd taken charge and looked after her parents, who were falling to pieces. As the eldest remaining child, she had launched into organising the funeral. Sharon had watched her during those early days and felt she was trying to block out the pain – if she was looking after others, she'd no time to wallow in her own grief. When a few months had passed and her parents and brother hadn't needed her as much, she'd gone a bit off the rails. She had turned to alcohol to blot out the pain and become a real party girl. Her friends had tried to calm her down, but she'd been determined to go out most nights of the week and have a wild time. It had lasted for about six months; then, after some gentle persuasion from Sharon and Lara, she'd copped on to herself. But still, she'd barely acknowledged Caroline's death. Sharon would never forget how scared she'd felt for her friend during that time. Life was good for Ellie now and she hated the thought of anything spoiling that.

The bus was already trundling past the Mater Hospital and Sharon stood up to get off. If Ellie was home, she'd have a chat with her. Maybe she'd suggest a night in with a bottle of wine and a movie, even if it was only Monday. They usually asked Lara over when they were having a movie night but Sharon didn't want to include her this time. Lara had a big heart but hated getting deep about stuff.

The rain had stopped but there were still big puddles at the side of the road and Sharon tried to dodge the splashes from the cars as they whizzed past. She crossed the road, went up the path and turned her key in the lock. Living on a main road, she missed the community spirit of the housing estate she'd grown up in, but there were advantages to living close to the bus and shops.

'Hiya, Sharon,' said Ellie, coming down the stairs with a towel wrapped around her head like a turban. 'You're soaked. I'd say you can't wait to get into a nice hot shower.

You might need to give the water twenty minutes or so to heat up again, though.'

Sharon shrugged out of her wet coat and threw it onto the banisters. 'It's grand. I'd prefer to just kick off my shoes and get a cup of tea first.'

'Great. I'll stick the kettle on and join you for a quick one. Then I'm heading out to Matt's for a while so the shower and the telly are all yours.' Ellie went into the kitchen, and Sharon heard the tap running.

'Oh! More wedding plans?' Sharon was disappointed that her heart-to-heart with her friend would have to wait.

'I think he has a plan for me but not a wedding one.' Ellie had a glint in her eye and Sharon laughed.

'Oh, *that* sort of plan. Lucky you!'

'I know! It's exactly what I need at the moment. You have the house free if you want to do any entertaining yourself.'

'Sure what entertaining would I be doing?'

'Well, just if … you know … if there was anyone you wanted to ask around.'

'I wish,' said Sharon, watching Ellie carefully. 'I think it'll be just me, a glass of wine and reruns of *Friends*.'

'I'll probably stay over with Matt tonight because I'm not in until twelve tomorrow. There'll be nobody interrupting your *movie*. Just so you know.'

Shit! Did Ellie suspect something? Maybe she already knew about Sharon and Mikey but was waiting for Sharon to tell her. She definitely suspected something. Sharon would need to have a chat with Mikey and decide what they were going to do. Mikey had wanted to tell Ellie all along but Sharon had worried that people would be against them. If Ellie or Mrs Duggan disapproved, it could mark the end of their relationship and Sharon hated the thought of that. It seemed very early days still, but she loved Mikey. She knew he loved her too, even though he hadn't exactly said so. She'd never have believed it could happen like that and so quickly, but for them it had. For the first time in her life she could see her future mapped out for her, and Mikey was the biggest part.

'Right, I'm off to get ready,' said Ellie, jumping up from the table and startling Sharon out of her reverie. 'I'll probably catch you in work tomorrow, but if I miss you, I'll see you tomorrow night.'

Sharon watched Ellie bound out of the kitchen door and realised that Matt was the reason for the change in her mood. He was good for her. He made her happy and that was all Sharon wanted for her friend. Maybe Lara was right and she shouldn't psychoanalyse everything. Ellie was marrying the man of her dreams and had a wonderful life stretched out in front of her. Maybe Sharon should forget about her for tonight and concentrate on the man of her own dreams.

When she heard Ellie put the hairdryer on upstairs, she grabbed her mobile and dialled.

'Hi, Mikey. Fancy joining me for a *movie* night?'

EIGHT

'Brace yourself.' Ellie opened the door to Matt with a scowl on her face. 'She's in full wedding mode – turbo-charged and ready to launch at you!' It was the Sunday before the girls were due to head off to New York and Ellie had reluctantly agreed to spend a few hours with her mother, going over the wedding plans.

Matt kissed his fiancée full on the lips as he stepped inside. 'I can handle your mother. I'll tell her I'm taking you out for a drive to Howth to de-stress you. She'll love that.'

'Oh, and that's exactly what I need – fresh air and a walk to shed a few pounds at the same time.' Ellie took Matt's hand and led him into the kitchen where her mother was poring over lists and wedding magazines.

Matt didn't wait for her to turn but came from behind and planted a kiss on her cheek. 'How's it going, Jean? Glad to see Ellie's keeping you busy.'

'Ah, howareya, Matt love? Well, you know me. I like to keep on top of things. Ellie, why don't you make a pot of tea and we can all look at this stuff?'

'Mam, me and Matt were going to—'

'That would be lovely, Jean, wouldn't it, Ellie?' He shot her a mischievous grin and Ellie wanted to throttle him. She'd been subjected to Jean for the last couple of hours – even her dad and Mikey had disappeared, claiming they had to go to Woodies for some gardening tool or other. She needed to get out for a while.

'Well, maybe we'll have a quick cup, then,' she muttered. 'But didn't you suggest heading out for a bit of fresh air, Matt?'

Matt was nodding at some pictures of flowers Jean was pointing to. 'Yes, I was thinking maybe Howth. There's nothing like a walk on the pier to blow off the cobwebs.'

'Well, I won't keep you,' said Jean, pushing some magazines in front of Matt. 'I only wanted to show you what I was thinking about for the buttonholes. Rather than just a boring single rose, I was thinking maybe an orange rose with a white freesia, like in these pictures. It's nice to be a bit different. What do you think?'

Ellie rolled her eyes as she placed the mugs of tea on the table. 'Mam, we don't need to be different. Why can't we just leave things as they are?'

'It's a great idea, Jean,' said Matt, looking as though he was really interested when Ellie knew full well he didn't give a toss about the flowers. He was a charmer for sure.

'You see, Ellie? I'm glad someone has good taste. If the wedding was left up to you, it'd be steak and chips down at The Gardens.'

'Don't knock it, Mam. A wedding in The Gardens with a plate of their lovely food would be brilliant. Imagine the *craic* we'd have!'

Jean gave her daughter a friendly jab with her elbow. 'You're gas, Ellie. Good job I know you're only joking. Can you imagine what people would say?'

Ellie hadn't been joking. She'd have loved a small affair in her local with only close family and friends. But the whole thing had escalated to the point at which she was almost expecting her mother to suggest a horse and carriage to bring her to the church.

Jean was still talking: 'And I haven't confirmed anything with Uncle Joe yet about the car. I know he offered and I know you said you'd like him to drive you to the church, but I thought you might just have a look at this brochure first.' She pushed a page with pictures of vintage cars under Ellie's nose. 'They look so classy and I thought one of them would suit the occasion better than Uncle Joe's old thing.'

'Mam! I don't want a vintage car and Uncle Joe's old thing, as you call it, is an almost new Audi A6. That's what I'm having!'

'All right, all right, keep your hair on. It was only a suggestion. You'd swear I'd asked you to go in a horse and carriage.'

'Now, there's an idea,' said Matt, kicking Ellie under the table. 'Wouldn't that be something different? It would certainly get everyone talking.'

Jean was surprised but delighted. 'Do you think so? I could just check—'

'No, Mam!' Ellie slapped her hand on the table. She'd had enough. It was all right for Matt, coming in here to have a laugh and wind her up. He didn't have to put up with Jean's incessant phone calls about guest lists and hymns and everything else associated with the wedding. 'Come on, Matt. Let's get that walk in before it starts to rain. I've had enough wedding talk for one day.'

'Sorry, Jean. The boss has spoken. I'd better do as I'm told.'

Ellie was already putting on her coat. She felt bad for being so snappy with her mother but it was all very stressful. A walk by the sea was just the tonic she needed. She had four busy days of work ahead before heading off to New York and she'd be stuck in a sweaty kitchen with no fresh air.

'Just hang on till I grab my coat,' said Jean, standing up from the table and putting the wedding stuff in the dresser drawer. 'I won't be a sec.'

'Y-your coat?' Ellie wanted to cry.

'It'll be nippy out there in Howth today if that wind has anything to do with it. I'd hate to catch a cold when there's so much to be done.'

'Mam ... I ...' It was then she saw the smile forming on her mother's lips.

'Relax, love. I'm only having you on. I may be an annoying mother of the bride but I'm not stupid. I know you two need a bit of time on your own and you wouldn't want your old ma coming with you.'

'It's not that, Mam. It's just that ... well, I haven't seen Matt in a few days and we have a lot to catch up on.'

'I know, Ellie. Honestly, I was only joking with you. Look, I know I can get a bit overpowering about the wedding, and I'm sorry if I'm driving you mad, but it's just so good to have a happy house again.'

Matt put his arm around his soon-to-be-mother-in-law. 'You're not driving us mad, Jean. We're glad of your help, aren't we, Ellie? There's so much to do and it's very generous of you to give so much of your time to organise it.'

'Yes, Mam. We really are grateful. And I'm sorry if I'm a moody cow sometimes.'

'Well, get off out of here and enjoy the rest of your day. It'll do you both good to get a bit of fresh air. And, Matt, drop over next weekend when the girls are away and I'll cook you something. It'll be nice to have a chat ourselves.'

Matt squeezed Ellie's hand as they headed for the front door. 'I'll do that thanks, Jean. Get the baby photos out. I'm looking forward to it already!'

○

'Am I a right cow?' asked Ellie as they strolled along the pier hand in hand. 'I try to indulge my mother as much as possible but sometimes she gets too much.'

'You're not a cow at all. You've been great with her – very patient and understanding. As you said yourself, we would probably have preferred a much smaller affair but we've let your mother make most of the decisions.'

Ellie stopped suddenly and looked at him. 'You're okay with that, though, aren't you? I mean, we discussed it and you said you understood.'

'Relax, Ellie. I'm perfectly fine with whatever way we get married. What's important at the end of the day is that we say those vows and sign that bit of paper. I can't wait for you to be Mrs Smellie.'

'I've told you a million times – dream on!'

'We'll see about that.' Before she knew what was happening, Matt had bent down, grabbed her around the knees and hauled her over his shoulder like a sack of potatoes.

'Let me down! Let me down!' Ellie squealed and pounded on his back as he ran along the pier. 'People are looking at us.'

'They're just jealous.' He put her down and pulled her to him, kissing her hard on the lips. 'I love you, Ellie Smellie. And I can't wait until we can be together all the time.'

This time she didn't object to the name. 'I love you too, Matt ...'

'Uh-oh! Did I sense a "but" at the end of that sentence?' He took her hand and led her to a wall where they could sit down.

'No, not exactly, but I feel ... I know it's silly but I just feel ...'

'What's wrong, Ellie? You're getting me worried now.' He lifted her chin gently with his hand and forced her to look at him.

'It's Caroline. Sometimes I feel it's wrong to be so happy when she's ... when she's ... She was such a lovely person. It's just not fair.' She bit her lip and tried to choke back the tears. If she let one out, there was a good chance that she'd start blubbing and wouldn't be able to stop. And she really didn't want to be doing that on the pier in Howth or in front of her soon-to-be-husband.

'Ah, you poor thing.' Matt wrapped his arms tightly around her. 'Of course it's not fair. Your sister should be here to share your happiness. She should be your bridesmaid and she should be the one to take the brunt of your mam's fussing. I'm so sorry, Ellie. I wish there was something I could do.'

'I miss her so much.'

'I know, love. And I'm glad you've told me. I sometimes don't want to mention her in case I upset you, but I love you being honest with me about how you're feeling.'

Ellie stiffened. If only he knew.

'And I really wish I'd known her,' he continued. 'She sounds like such a lovely girl.'

'She was the best – a far better person than me.' Ellie bit her lip to stop herself crying.

'Now that's not true, Ellie. You're a beautiful person, outside and in. I know it, your family and friends know it, and Caroline knows it. I bet she's looking down on you now, thinking, Will she ever cop on to herself and look at that fine, handsome fella she's landed?'

Despite herself, Ellie had to giggle. She loved that about Matt. He was sensitive and kind, and he knew when to make her laugh and how to lift her out of herself when she was feeling down. 'Well, why don't you take your good-looking self off to that ice-cream van and get me a ninety-nine? It's ages since I had one.'

'Sounds like a plan. But should you really be eating ice-cream if you're to fit into that dress?'

'Feck off, would you? Watch your own waistline. I've noticed a couple of love handles forming there of late.'

'Really? I'll have to get you to show me in the car before we head home!'

'It depends on whether you manage to get those ice-creams before the van heads off.'

Matt saw it start to move and chased after it like a greyhound out of the traps. Ellie's heart filled as she watched him. Not only was he a lovely person but he was totally gorgeous. His job as a personal trainer kept him muscular and toned, and his natural tan set off the blueness of his eyes. She was a lucky girl.

After finding the letter last Sunday and her subsequent mini-fit with Sharon the following day, she'd toyed with the idea of talking to Matt. But when she'd gone over to his place on the Monday night, she'd just wanted to forget about everything and enjoy being with him.

'Here we go – an extra large ninety-nine with sprinkles and raspberry sauce. Don't say I don't look after you.'

Ellie launched herself on the ice-cream. She hadn't allowed herself many treats lately because she was trying to shed a few pounds, but the creaminess on her tongue was divine. 'Ah, you're a good one, Matt. What would I do without you?'

'Well, you'll never have to find out. Now, let's start walking to the car before the rain comes. I've been watching that big grey cloud and it's definitely heading in our direction.'

'Ha, there's not a cloud in the sky, you chancer! I know what's on your mind and I'm not sure I should allow it so close to the wedding.'

'It's almost five weeks to the wedding. Jesus! Do you want to kill me altogether? Besides, there isn't too much we can do here in broad daylight with so many people around.'

Ellie stuffed the last piece of her cone into her mouth as they got to the car. 'If you play your cards right, I might suggest a detour on the way home. I believe there are a few very romantic spots at the back of Dublin Airport where you can watch the planes take off and land. Apparently the earth actually shakes!'

'Ellie Duggan! You're very naughty, do you know that?'

'Let's get going and I'll show you just how naughty I can be.'

Matt didn't have to be asked twice. His old Honda Civic had never seen such speed. Yes, thought Ellie. She was a very lucky girl.

NINE

'You're not going to be watching that for long, are you?' asked Lara, standing at the sitting-room door with Ethan in her arms.

Peter didn't take his eyes off the screen. 'It'll be a while, love. Sure the match has only just started.'

'But – but you do know I'm heading off in the morning, don't you?'

'Of course I do. But I thought you'd be packing and getting yourself organised.'

Lara could feel the blood rising to her cheeks and had to bite her tongue. 'Well, I *am* planning to get myself sorted – right after I finish putting those casseroles I cooked for you into containers, cleaning up after dinner, bathing Ethan and putting him to bed!'

'Grand, love. When you're sorted, maybe we'll have a catch-up. The match should be finished by then.'

Lara stormed up the stairs with tears in her eyes. How fuckin' dare Peter treat her like that? She wasn't a skivvy. She'd killed herself all week trying to get the house organised for her few days away so he wouldn't have to do much. It galled her that he didn't even seem to notice.

Ethan, oblivious to her upset, squealed with delight when she began to run a bath for him. She couldn't help but smile at his enthusiasm, his eyes dancing beneath the fine golden curls.

'Yes, sweetheart. The bath's for you. Will we put lots of bubbles in it?'

'Yay! Bubbles!'

She emptied almost half a bottle of her own Radox bath cream into the water. She wasn't going to see him for four days so she wanted to spoil him a little. She was glad now that Peter hadn't offered to bath him. There was something calming about watching her son dive into the bubbles and hearing him giggle to himself. But, still, it would have been nice if he'd offered. Actually, it would have been nice if he'd offered any help at all.

Her mother always said she was stubborn as a mule and Lara had to admit she was right. Peter wasn't a bad guy – he was just a man. He didn't seem to know what to do around the house. He didn't notice when the dishwasher needed emptying or the bedclothes needed changing. He didn't pick up the broom when bits of cereal crunched beneath his feet and he could sit in a room full of dust without batting an eyelid. Ask him to do any of it and he'd comply with a good heart. But Lara couldn't bring herself to ask. She was well aware that she should never try to change someone, but she really wanted him to notice things and do them of his own accord. They hadn't come naturally to her either when she was a career woman but, faced with the full-time job of looking after Ethan and running a house, she'd had to learn pretty quickly.

She was her own worst enemy, and she knew it. She should have just asked Peter to record the football and give her a hand with a few things but, no, she'd wanted him to make the grand gesture. God, she was turning into one of the whiny, needy housewives she would have sneered at in the past. If she didn't do something about it soon, she'd end up having a breakdown – or, even worse, losing the man she loved.

Because she did love him. Even when she wanted to scratch his eyes out for not noticing how clean the bathrooms were or for leaving his cup and plate on the sitting-room floor, she never stopped loving him.

'Mummy in the bath!' Ethan was holding out his hand for Lara to join him in his world of bubbles.

Much as she'd love to sit in with him and forget about

everything else, she just wasn't in the head space for it. 'Not tonight, sweetie. Let's get you out of there because the water is going cold.'

'No, Mummy! The bubbles is funny.' He slapped his two hands onto his face, covering himself with suds, and Lara had to laugh.

'Okay, five more minutes, then.'

Lara knew it wouldn't take much to make her happy. After all, she had the ingredients for a perfect life – just had to find a way of juggling them all to make it work. And watching her son, his little body covered with bubbles, made her even more determined to find the solution. The few days in New York would be good for her and would give her time to think. She might even have another chat to the girls about it. Their discussion in The Gardens the previous week had got a bit heavy, but this time she'd chat to them about practical things she could do to make her feel more herself again.

'You two look like you're having fun.' Peter leaned against the door-frame, a huge smile on his face.

'Ethan sure is,' said Lara, laughing as he attempted to throw a handful of bubbles at his dad.

'So why don't you go off and do your packing, love? I'll take over here now and put this little man to bed.'

Lara immediately felt guilty for thinking so badly of him. 'Thanks, Peter. I'll take you up on that.'

He took the big fluffy towel from her hands and knelt

down beside the bath. 'Let me know when you're finished the packing and I'll open a bottle of wine. It will be nice to have a couple of hours together. After all, I won't see you for four whole days.'

'Definitely. I'll be done in twenty minutes and Ethan should be in bed by then.' She headed into the bedroom she shared with her husband and sat on the bed. Her mother always said that when you think positive thoughts good things will happen. It was so true. Her heart felt much lighter all of a sudden and she knew without a shadow of a doubt that she and Peter would get through this – once she'd figured out what 'this' was.

○

'Oh, and, Ellie, I sent an invitation today to your auntie Val. I'd hate her to feel left out.'

'Mam, I don't have an auntie Val!' Ellie was a bit fed up with her mam constantly adding to the wedding guest list. Her parents were being very generous in paying for the hotel reception, but Jean felt that gave her the right to invite whoever she wanted.

'Ah, Ellie, you know who I mean – Val, my old friend from school who lives in Finglas. You always called her "Auntie Val" when you were growing up.'

'But I haven't seen her in about fifteen years – and you don't exactly keep in touch with her either!'

'We send each other Christmas cards. It's just that if she heard Ann O'Driscoll got an invite and she didn't, she'd be very upset.'

'And who the hell is Ann O'— Forget it. I really have to head off, Mam. Matt is already back at the house waiting for me and I have to finish my packing.'

Her mam gave one of her trademark sniffs. 'Well, I'm not doing all this for the good of my health, you know, Ellie. This is *your* wedding and I'm just doing what I can to help.'

Ellie had to bite her tongue. It was far from being her wedding with the way it had been taken over by Mammy 'Wedding Planner' Duggan. But it wasn't worth the fight. 'I know, Mam. And thanks – you've been great. We'll sit down and go over some more stuff next week.'

'Okay, love.' Jean's voice was softer. 'I do understand, you know. It's an exciting time but stressful too. If Caroline was here, she'd have us all organised. She was always so calm under pressure.'

'She was,' said Ellie, anxious to get out of there before her mother began reminiscing again. 'Although we're not doing too badly ourselves, are we?'

But Jean's eyes had glazed over. 'Poor Caroline. She'd have loved all this. God, if only she'd stayed calm that day. Things could have been so different. If only she'd thought before she acted.'

Ellie didn't like where this was going. 'We all miss her,

Mam. But for now I really need to get home. I'll have to be up at the crack of dawn for that flight in the morning.'

'Okay.' Jean sighed, walking her to the door. 'Are you sure you don't want your daddy to give you a lift to the airport? It's no bother, you know.'

'Your mam's a great one for volunteering me for stuff,' came her dad's voice from the sitting room.

Jean turned red. 'I thought you were upstairs, Andy. What are you doing hiding in there and scaring the living daylights out of me?'

'Honestly, it's fine, Mam.' Ellie wanted to avoid leaving the two of them having one of their famous spats. 'Matt is bringing us out before he heads to work.'

Andy came into the hall to give Ellie a hug. 'You know I'm only joking, love. I've no problem picking you and the girls up in the morning and taking you to the airport.'

'I know, Dad, but it's all sorted. I'll be back on Tuesday so I'll pop over if I have a chance in the afternoon.'

'Right,' said Jean, still giving her husband filthy looks. 'Have a safe flight and keep in touch.'

Ellie got into her car for the few minutes' drive to her own place. Her suitcases were actually packed and ready in the hall but she hadn't wanted to tell her mother so, in case she'd felt obliged to stay a bit longer. She was looking forward to having an early night with Matt. He didn't stay over too often because they both felt it wouldn't be fair on

Sharon, but as he was giving them a lift early in the morning, it seemed like the sensible thing to do. Her emotions had been all over the place in the last couple of weeks and she was hoping that falling asleep in Matt's arms would make everything seem all right.

'Hiya, love. Come in and sit down. Will I pour you a glass of wine? You look like you need it.' Matt jumped up from the sofa and Ellie smiled. He seemed so much at home there. She was glad that he and Sharon got on brilliantly and were happy to spend time together, even when she herself wasn't in.

'Thanks, Matt.' She kissed him full on the lips. 'I'm completely knackered. And my mother has me worn out with all her wedding talk.'

'It was good of you to go over tonight. I'm sure she was delighted.' He rattled around in the kitchen and came back with two glasses of white wine. 'Will I get us some nibbles to go with this?'

Ellie fell back onto the sofa and stretched. 'No, don't bother. I think I'll have this and head up. I don't want to be grumpy in the morning. You know what I'm like when I don't have enough sleep. Where's Sharon?'

'You called?' said Sharon, appearing at the door.

'Jesus, you're like a white witch. I was just wondering where you were. Are you coming in to join us? Matt has just opened a bottle of white if you fancy it.'

'Not for me, thanks. I'll leave you two lovebirds to it. I'm heading to bed to get my beauty sleep. What time are we going to leave here in the morning?'

Matt rubbed his head. 'Well, the flight is at twenty-five to eight and you'll want to check in two hours early, and it will take us twenty minutes to get there and we have to pick up Lara on the way ...'

'Five, Sharon. We'll leave around five.' Ellie laughed at Matt, who was still trying to work it out. 'Forget it, love. I know maths isn't your strong point.'

He pushed her over playfully on the sofa and began to tickle her.

'*Stooooop!*' screamed Ellie, writhing around.

'I'll leave you two to your, em, games and head to bed. Night. See you in the morning.'

'Night, Sharon,' panted Ellie, finally pulling herself away from Matt's grip. 'Sleep well.'

She turned to her fiancé, who had a glint in his eye, and all she wanted to do at that moment was go to bed. 'Let's forget about the wine, Matt. I can think of better things to do tonight!'

'Sounds good to me.' Matt stood up and held out his hand. He pulled Ellie to her feet and they headed up the stairs.

Minutes later, they were lying in bed, Ellie in the foetal position with Matt's body spooned around her. She felt happy when it was just her and Matt. She felt safe with him.

When he had his arms around her, she was able to forget her worries, and all that mattered in the world was their love for each other.

'What are you thinking about?' Matt whispered in her ear.

Ellie turned to face him, keeping his arms pulled tightly around her. 'I'm just thinking about how happy I feel when we're here together.'

'Me too. I'm going to miss you while you're away, you know.'

'I'll miss you too but it's only for a few days.'

'How was your mam tonight? Anything new on the wedding front?'

'Oh, God, don't talk to me about it. She's driving me mad with the arrangements. You know, I really couldn't give a toss about any of it except that I'm marrying you.'

Matt traced his fingers gently across her face. 'Me too, Ellie. But if it helps your mam to deal with Caroline's death by making an extra fuss of you, that's fine by me.'

Ellie stiffened. 'Do you think that's what she's doing? Using me to get over Caroline?'

'I didn't mean it like that. I just meant that it must be hard for her. She's already lost one girl and now her other one is getting married. It's probably making her feel good to give you a big send-off.'

Ellie sighed. 'It's hard for us all.'

'I can only imagine.' Matt pressed his lips against hers

and kissed her softly. 'But I know Caroline would want you to be happy, love. From what you've told me, she was a very generous and loving person and would want the best for her little sister.'

'She really was, Matt. And I know she's happy for me, wherever she is.' Ellie turned over so she was facing away from Matt again, but she pulled his arms tightly around her. She didn't want him to see her tears. He was hugely supportive but he wouldn't understand the weight of her guilt. Nobody would. She'd never spoken to anyone about that day. She'd tried to push it out of her mind as much as possible so that she could get on with her life. She kept telling herself that she deserved to be happy. But in fact she didn't deserve her happiness: she should have died that day, not Caroline.

TEN

'Oh, God, oh, God, we're going to die! I just have a feeling. I know we are. Jesus, let's just get off this thing!'

'Calm the fuck down, Sharon, will you?' whispered Lara, looking around to see if anyone was watching her friend's hysterics. 'If you'd only had a drink in the bar, like I said you should, you'd have been fine.'

'I'd have been sick if I'd drunk anything. My stomach's in knots. How are you two so calm?'

Ellie, who was in the window seat, took her friend's hand. 'Sharon, you'll be fine. Remember those relaxation techniques we found online last week? Just close your eyes and try to meditate.'

'You're right. It's going to be fine, it's going to be fine, it's going to be fine ...' She closed her eyes and grabbed Lara's hand too.

Lara grimaced. God, it was going to be a long journey if Sharon behaved like this the whole way. She seemed to be getting worse as the years went on. She'd always been afraid of flying but never as bad as this. At least her meditation or whatever it was seemed to be working because she was quiet for the moment. She glanced at Ellie, who seemed a little subdued. Lara had expected her to be buzzing with the excitement of the trip but she had been unusually quiet since they'd arrived at the airport. Maybe she was exhausted, with all the wedding preparations. And judging by the passionate kiss she'd had at the departure gate with Matt, she'd no doubt be missing him too.

Lara felt a pang of guilt as she thought of her husband. He'd come good in the end last night. He'd put Ethan to bed, cleaned up the kitchen and even made some supper for them to have in front of the telly. But she needed this time away from him – away from her humdrum daily life. She hated that her biggest worry, these days, was burning the sauce for dinner or forgetting to buy teabags. She wanted to feel like she used to when she worked in the office: important and respected. She just wanted to feel like Lara again.

'Oh, sweet Jesus, what's that?' Sharon gripped her

friends' hands so tightly they both yelped and even Ellie looked like she'd strangle her.

'Come on now, Sharon. We haven't even left the ground yet. They've just switched on the engines.'

'Here,' said Lara, handing Sharon her iPod. 'There's loads of stuff on it so why don't you stick in the earphones? It'll help you to relax.'

'Thanks, Lara. And I'm sorry I'm such a wimp. I'll be fine once we're up there – when I know the plane is still intact and none of us has been killed.'

Ellie shook her head. 'Lovely! Now you even have me a bit jittery.'

Lara looked at her friends and rolled her eyes. 'Well, you two can stress all you like. This is bliss for me. I can't remember the last time I had a few hours of peace and quiet during the day. I'm going to take full advantage of it and use the time to catch up on my sleep and my reading.'

'Me too,' said Ellie, pulling her Kindle out of her handbag. 'I've downloaded a few books to keep me going. Thank God for technology.'

Lara sat back and closed her eyes as the plane headed towards the runway. At least Sharon was more relaxed now. Hopefully the music would send her to sleep and she'd behave for the rest of the journey.

It was hard to believe they'd be in New York soon. She'd make sure they all had a brilliant time. Both she and Ellie had been there a couple of times so they knew all the best places to go. It was the sort of place where you could lose yourself – forget your troubles and wrap yourself in the colourful, buzzing atmosphere of one of the greatest cities on earth. For the next few days, she was going to claim back a bit of herself. She wouldn't be 'Mammy' or 'Peter's wife'. She'd just be plain old Lara O'Toole.

○

It took Sharon a few seconds to get her bearings when she woke up. Oh, God, the flight! She'd worked herself up into such a frenzy that she'd been exhausted by the time they were up in the air and must have dropped off to sleep. The other two were engrossed in a movie and there was a lovely sense of calm around her.

Jesus, what on earth had come over her earlier? She'd made a right show of herself. She'd never been a big fan of flying but had never lost it like that before. Maybe it was because she hadn't been on a plane in a few years. Or maybe it was because she was seeing a glimpse of happiness sneaking into her life and was scared of something happening to spoil it.

A few years ago, she'd thought she'd never find love. She'd felt that nobody could love someone like her – someone who could barely take two steps without getting out of breath, someone who looked so disgusting, someone who didn't love themselves. But things were a lot different now.

She glanced over at Ellie. She sort of felt silly now that she hadn't told her about Mikey. She'd be happy for them, Sharon was sure of it. But she was also sure that Ellie was bottling up far too much emotion. She liked to give off this air of a strong, independent woman, but it wasn't a sign of weakness to mourn your sister. It didn't mean that Ellie was any less strong if she cried about her now and then.

Sharon knew that Lara would go mad if she tried to make this trip into a soul-searching one, but she felt she owed it to Ellie to talk to her a bit more about Caroline. She needed to face her emotions if she wanted to move on and be truly happy. A few days away together would be just the thing to get her talking. It would be like the old days – the three of them gossiping and laughing. They'd all had a few tough years between one thing and another, and this New York trip was going to mark a positive change in all their lives.

The plane hit an air pocket and dropped suddenly, causing a gasp among the passengers. 'Oh, Jesus, Mary and Joseph, Jesus, Mary and Joseph, Jesus, Mary and Joseph.' Sharon blessed herself, keeping her eyes shut tight.

'You big eejit,' giggled Ellie. 'It's just a bit of turbulence.'

But Sharon wasn't taking any chances. With her eyes still firmly shut, she prayed to God to get them safely to New York.

○

Sharon couldn't contain her excitement as she bounced up and down on the king-sized bed. 'Oh, my God! I've never seen anything like it. It's like something straight out of a movie.'

'It's pretty amazing all right.' Ellie grinned, pulling open the wardrobe doors to reveal fluffy towelling robes. 'What do you say we get into these right now and order some room service?'

'Not a chance,' said Lara, laying out her selection of maps and brochures on the bed. 'We've only got a few days here so we're going to make the most of it.'

Ellie smiled but her heart sank. What she wouldn't give to curl up into one of those beds right now, read a book and have a snooze. But it looked as if Lara was going to have them on the go for the whole time.

Lara was still talking: 'So I was thinking, instead of eating in here, we could head down towards Times Square and pick up something along the way.'

'Where do you get the energy from?' Sharon was now lying completely flat on her back and looked as though she could fall asleep. 'I mean, I thought, out of all of us, you'd be the one looking to have a rest. You're always saying you don't get enough sleep with Ethan.'

'Well, that's true,' said Lara. 'But I don't have enough fun either, these days. And you know what I'm like – I'm an organiser. I just want to make sure we get the most out of this trip.'

'Well, we appreciate it, don't we, Sharon? Are you two girls sure you don't mind me having the other room on my own? I wouldn't mind sharing with either of you, you know.'

'We insist,' said Sharon, sitting up and stretching. 'This is your special weekend so you should have the best room. And, anyway, we'll probably be in that gorgeous sitting room most of the time when we're here. The beds will be solely to put our heads down for a few hours.'

'Right, then. Let's do as Lara says and get out of here. I'll just stick my case into my room and brush my teeth.'

Ellie marvelled at the opulence of the suite as she walked through the living room to get to her bedroom. The décor was beautiful – subtle yellow-striped wallpaper was a lovely backdrop for the dark-wood furniture, and the pale green soft furnishings blended in beautifully. The view from the window was stunning, with the seemingly endless spire of the Chrysler Building rising up into the sky. Ellie was delighted they'd decided to splash out and stay in such an amazing place. Just being there had lifted her spirits.

Her own room was a little smaller because there was only one bed but it had a lovely en-suite. She was glad to have her own space. She'd probably spend most of the trip with Sharon and Lara but it would be nice to get away from them too. She needed some thinking time.

Ten minutes later all three of them were sitting on the sofa in the living room, Lara, pen in hand, making a list. 'So, if we take it easy today, get our bearings and have a look around, we can fill tomorrow with lots of touristy stuff.'

'Oh, please can we go ice-skating at the Rockefeller Center,' said Sharon, who was bursting to see everything. 'It's what always comes to mind when I think of New York.'

Ellie shook her head. 'I don't think it's on at this time of year. I think it's only at Christmas.'

'It *is* on,' said Lara, scribbling. 'I've already checked and I thought we might do that first thing in the morning, then head up to the Top of the Rock. We can get a ticket that covers the whole thing and the price is really good if we do them together.'

Although the thought of ice-skating didn't fill her with joy, Ellie had to admit that without Lara, she and Sharon would probably just wander around for the whole time they were there. 'You're such a brilliant organiser, Lara. So the Rockefeller Center in the morning it is. Why don't we try to fit in all the touristy things tomorrow and go to the outlets on Sunday? We can't come all the way over here without paying them a visit.'

'Sorted,' said Lara, beaming. 'I had a quick word with the concierge when you two nipped to the loo before we checked in. He said there's a private bus that goes from just down the road and comes back in the evening. It's not much more expensive than the public transport and it's a lot more comfortable.'

'That's brilliant.' Ellie was delighted. Shopping was

the thing she was most looking forward to. 'And since we have a few hours on Monday, maybe we can walk around Ground Zero and a few other places before we go.'

Lara nodded. 'That should cover everything. What do you think, Sharon?'

Sharon looked as though she was going to burst with joy. 'Oh, God, it's perfect. Absolutely perfect. I can't believe I'm here. I can't wait to get out there and see the city.'

Ellie smiled at her friend. 'Right, let's get out there and have some fun. We can walk around and get our bearings and find somewhere nice to eat. It may be some time before the three of us have a chance to get away together again so let's make the most of what we have.'

'Don't,' said Sharon, staring at her friend. 'I hate it when you say things like that. I don't want this to mark the end of an era. I know you two are moving on with your own lives but I still want us to stay friends. I want us to be able to spend time and go places together.'

Ellie laughed and threw an arm around her. 'Ah, you big eejit – you're such a worrier. Of course we'll still do things together. I just mean with the wedding and everything, it might be a while before I can afford to go away somewhere like this. As I said to you before, nothing much is going to change except that I'll live five minutes away rather than in the same house.'

But even saying those words, Ellie felt a bit unsettled. Things didn't feel right any more. All the elements were there for her to be completely happy. She had a wonderful family, great friends and was about to get married to one of the most gorgeous and loving men in the world. She should feel over the moon. But she didn't. Ever since that day at her mam's, dealing with memories of the past and finding that letter, something had changed. The stuff she'd been bottling up was beginning to bubble to the surface and she felt powerless to control it. She was praying that she could manage to slap a smile on her face for now and be the usual jolly Ellie everyone expected.

ELEVEN

'God, this view is spectacular!' Sharon ran from window to window, marvelling at what she saw. Ellie felt buoyed up by her enthusiasm. 'Look! Ellie, Lara, did you see this? Look how the sun is shining down on the Hudson. It's just beautiful.'

'Jesus, calm down, will you, Sharon? You're like a kid with a sugar overload!'

'Ah, leave her alone, Lara,' said Ellie, laughing at Lara's description, although she was spot on. 'We were probably like that the first time we saw it too.'

Sharon ran back to the other side and the others trailed behind her, like proud parents. 'I could see this a thousand times and I'd never get sick of it. Oh, God, I love this city. Look at the Chrysler Building. Isn't it amazing? I'm so glad we came to the Top of the Rock instead of the Empire State – I can't imagine anything being better than this.'

'Well, the Empire State Building is pretty amazing too,' said Lara. 'But I'm not sure our schedule will allow for a visit there. We'll just have to see how the time goes.'

Ellie smiled at Lara, thankful once again that one of them had taken charge of the trip. 'You're brilliant at organising, Lara. I think you've missed your calling.'

'Ha! Yes, maybe I should go into the wedding-planning business or something.'

'I was thinking more managerial – I just can't see you as a wedding planner. There's more chance of my mother taking on that role.'

'You're right. I'd hate it. All that pomp and ceremony. But I do love being organised. I'd hate us to be here for a few days and end up just wandering aimlessly.' She nodded towards Sharon. 'But we'd want to drag her away from here pretty soon. Our ice-skating slot is in half an hour and I don't want us to miss a minute of it.'

Ellie sighed. 'I suppose. You do know that me and ice-skates just don't agree, don't you? I'm like a new-born foal as soon as I step onto the ice.'

'Ah, you'll be grand. I'm pretty good at it, if I say so myself, so you can hang onto me.'

Sharon rushed over to them. 'You've got to come over

here. You can see the whole of Central Park. I can't get over it – it's amazing.'

'Right,' said Lara, rolling her eyes at Ellie. 'Let's have a look, then. Now, you've got five more minutes before we have to head down.'

Sharon pouted. 'Aw! Can't we stay a bit longer?'

'Unfortunately not, Sharon. We just don't have the time.'

Ellie smiled at the two – like mother and petulant child. The girls were a good tonic for her. Despite all the stuff going on in her head, she was actually enjoying herself. It was good to be away from everything at home – from the madness of the wedding and the constant reminders of the past. In a small way, it was even good to be away from Matt. While she was here, she didn't have to look at his trusting face and know in her heart that she wasn't being honest with him about everything. He was a good man. He deserved better than that.

'Ellie! Jesus, were you actually falling asleep there?'

Ellie realised she'd closed her eyes while she was lost in thought. 'Of course I wasn't, Lara. I was only resting my eyes.'

'I know that look,' giggled Sharon. 'I've seen it a million times at home when you've come back from a shift knackered and close your eyes for a little doze.'

'I'm telling you, I was *not* asleep.' Ellie was speaking the truth, but if they'd left her another few minutes, she was sure she would have been.

'Right, let's get down there and onto the ice.' Lara was back to organising them. 'It's been ages since I had a skate. I can't wait.'

Sharon blew on her hands to warm them up as they headed for the escalator. 'I went skating for the first time in Liffey Valley Shopping Centre at Christmas. I was actually surprised that I was pretty good.'

'We can put Ellie in the middle of us then,' said Lara. 'Even Bambi needed help from his friends!'

○

At the Rockefeller Center they collected their skates, battled their feet into them and headed out to the ice.

'Come on, Ellie. You can hold onto me until you find your feet.' Lara stood on the ice confidently and held out her hand for Ellie.

'Oh, God, I can't do it!'

'Of course you can,' laughed Sharon, and took off on the ice, winding between skaters and taking the corners like a pro.

Ellie gaped. 'Jesus, would you look at her! You'd think she was born on the ice. I can't believe she's only skated once and is so confident.'

'It just comes naturally to some people, I suppose. Come on, Ellie. Let's at least get you skating along by the wall.'

She tentatively placed one skate on the ice and almost did the splits. 'Fuck! This is just not for me.'

At that moment, two kids glided past. They couldn't have been more than four years old and they were chatting and giggling as they went. Ellie noticed they had different types of skates on – there were two blades on each skate, giving them greater support on the ice.

'That's what I need,' she said, pointing to the children. 'A pair of those. It just doesn't seem natural balancing on one tiny blade.'

Lara laughed. 'I don't think they do them in a size seven, Ellie. Right, that's it. You're getting on now.' She hopped deftly off the ice and pushed Ellie on, causing her to squeal as her legs splayed awkwardly in different directions.

'Bitch!' But she was laughing too.

'Let's get her moving around,' said Sharon, stopping herself with flair right beside them. 'One on each side.'

They linked Ellie's arms and began to skate quickly around the rink, ignoring her high-pitched screams. But slowly she began to find her footing, and after ten minutes with the girls supporting her, she decided to brave it on her own.

Sharon clapped as she stood back and watched her. 'You see? I knew you could do it.'

'Well, she's not exactly Jayne Torvill but it's a start.' Lara ducked to avoid the friendly slap Ellie tried to give her, which resulted in Ellie on her bum on the ice.

'Ouch, ouch, ouch!'

Sharon and Lara collapsed into fits of giggles and Ellie couldn't help joining in although she could feel the bruises forming on her backside.

'Let's go and get some pictures in front of the golden statue,' said Sharon, already heading over to it.

When Ellie caught up with the girls, they already had their phones out and were taking pictures.

Lara called to her. 'Get in there with Sharon, Ellie, and I'll take one of the two of you.'

'Right, hand me that phone,' said Ellie, when Lara had taken a variety of pictures. 'Now you stand with Sharon, and I'll take one of you two.' She tentatively left the safety of the wall to stand in front of the two girls. When she managed to steady herself, she held up the phone to take a picture. The girls cocked their heads to the side, sticking out their tongues and doing their best to look as silly as they could.

Ellie froze. Her hands began to shake and the scene in front of her blurred.

The girls seemed oblivious. 'Come on, Ellie,' moaned Sharon. 'I'm freezing here. I want to get moving again.'

'I – I'm sorry. It's just … it's just …' Tears blinded her and she turned to skate over to the wall.

Lara shouted after her: 'Ellie, what's up? Where are you going?'

She didn't wait to answer but pulled herself along the

wall to the exit and jumped off the ice. She ran inside and sat down heavily on a bench. Ignoring the stares of other skaters, she put her head into her hands and cried. She should have known it was a bad idea. What had she been thinking? She'd been so sure she was on top of things and that she could control her emotions but, God, she couldn't have been more wrong.

'Ellie, what's the matter? Jesus, are you okay?' Sharon sat down beside her.

Lara sat on her other side. 'What happened out there?'

'I ... I'm sorry.' Ellie accepted a tissue from Lara and blew her nose. 'It was just seeing you both there like that. It just reminded me ... I know it's stupid but I just couldn't help thinking about—' She was off again, big tears streaming down her face.

Sharon put an arm around her. 'What is it, Ellie?'

Ellie shook her head and tried to compose herself. A lot of people were staring now and she suddenly felt stupid.

'Come on. Let's get rid of these skates.' Lara was still taking charge and Ellie was grateful. 'We can get ourselves a hot chocolate and have a proper chat.'

Five minutes later they were huddled around a table in the little coffee shop beside the rink, their hands cupped around their steaming mugs.

'So, what happened?' asked Sharon gently. 'I thought you were beginning to enjoy yourself.'

Ellie sighed. 'Do you remember the last time I came

to New York? It was five years go. Remember who I was with?'

The two girls bowed their heads. They both seemed lost for words.

Ellie continued: 'Caroline and I had such a great time over here. And, honestly, I have brilliant memories of the trip and they shouldn't make me sad.'

'So what was it about taking the picture?' Lara still looked puzzled.

'When I did that clear-out in my mam's a couple of weeks ago, I was looking at old pictures. Well, I found one of me and Caroline – it was taken here on the rink, right in front of that gold statue. We didn't want to ask anyone to take it so we held the phone up to take it ourselves, sticking out our tongues and making silly faces.'

Realisation dawned on Sharon. 'Oh you poor thing, Ellie. So Lara and I reminded you of the picture. I'm so sorry. It must be so hard.'

'I'm fine now, honestly. It was just a bit of a shock. When you two were making faces, all I could see was me and Caroline.'

Lara joined in. 'We should be trying to take your mind off Caroline rather than bringing back all those memories. I'm really sorry. I should have known not to bring you here.'

'Don't be sorry. I don't want to forget. The memories I have of me and Caroline here are all good. It was just the bit of *déjà vu* that got to me.'

'Maybe it's a good thing this happened,' said Sharon, spooning the last of her hot chocolate out of the mug. 'I mean, I'm glad you're confronting things, Ellie. The worst thing you can do is bottle everything up.'

'Oh, for fuck's sake, Sharon.' Lara rolled her eyes. 'She doesn't need her emotions analysed and I don't think she wants to spend the holiday talking about her dead sister.'

'Lara!'

Lara looked a little sheepish. 'I didn't mean to be insensitive, Ellie. I just hate it when Sharon goes all Jeremy Kyle on us.'

Sharon looked ready to throttle Lara and Ellie couldn't help laughing. 'Listen, you're both brilliant and it's good to have a balance of opinions. I promise I'll talk about things if I need to but, for now, let's get out of here and enjoy the rest of the day.'

'Good idea,' said Lara, putting her gloves back on. 'If we get a move on, we can be at Ground Zero in half an hour. I know we said we'd leave that until Monday, but we have time today. We can pick up some lunch there too after we do the tour.'

Ellie stood up. 'That sounds good to me.' She was happy to share some of her feelings with the girls – in fact, she was glad to have opened up a little. But she couldn't tell them the extent of how she felt. That was something she'd have to deal with herself.

TWELVE

'I can't believe we're going home already,' said Sharon, closing her case with ease and laughing at the two girls who were wrestling with theirs. 'And I'm glad I didn't go crazy with the shopping yesterday.'

'For fuck's sake, Sharon. Get yourself over here and sit on this, will you?' The veins were popping out on Lara's neck as she strained to move the zip on her case. 'And I didn't actually buy very much. It's the shoes that are extra bulky.'

Ellie giggled. 'You didn't buy much, my arse! You even outdid me on the shoe front – and I *never* thought that would happen.'

Sharon piped up: 'Well, in fairness to Lara, she may have bought more shoes but she didn't pay the ridiculous prices you did.'

'You get what you pay for,' Ellie reminded her. 'I always go for quality rather than quantity.'

'Well, I hope Mr Choo appreciates your custom!' Sharon was delighted to see Ellie in such good form. She'd picked herself up after the tears on Saturday and they'd managed to enjoy the rest of the day.

'There we go – good job you've got a fat bum, Sharon.' Lara ducked, obviously expecting a clatter from her friend, but Sharon just laughed.

'There was a time when I'd have taken offence at that, you know. But not any more. And that's because I know my bum is firm and toned and hasn't been fat in six months or more.'

Lara nodded. 'You're looking pretty hot, all right. I'm going to have to work on myself if I'm to compete with you in those bridesmaids' dresses.'

'That reminds me,' said Sharon. 'We have a fitting with Monique this week.' Sharon loved their fittings with the fiery French dressmaker, even if she did spend her time giving out to them. 'Can you believe it's less than four weeks to the wedding? I'm so excited for you, Ellie.'

'It certainly is hard to believe. But it's been good, hasn't it? This weekend, I mean. We've had fun, all of us together, just like old times.'

Sharon spun around to look at her friend. Ellie was acting a bit weird. 'Of course it's been good. It's been brilliant.'

'Bloody fantastic.' Lara nodded. 'I've really enjoyed getting away from the life of domesticity for a few days. And it's been great chatting over it all with you girls.'

Ellie put an arm around Lara. 'Aw, you wouldn't be getting all soppy on us now, Lara, would you? I'd hate you to ruin your reputation.'

'Fuck off! My reputation is very much intact, thank you very much! That's not to say I can't appreciate my friends.'

'And we appreciate you too,' said Sharon, joining them.

'Easy now, Sharon.' Lara ducked out of the group hug and flopped down on the sofa. 'I'm not there yet, with the touchy-feely stuff. You girls feel free to hug it out, though.'

Ellie rolled her eyes. 'Come on. It's almost twelve. Let's get these suitcases down to Reception and we can head out for a few hours.'

'Right,' said Lara, standing up. 'Where should we head to first?'

'You're the organiser.' Ellie strained to drag her two cases through the door. 'I thought you'd have it all planned for us.'

'Not today, Ellie. Today you both get to choose. I've done my bit.'

Sharon pushed her case out easily and took a final glance at the room before closing the door behind them. 'I fancy a walk down Canal Street. I wouldn't mind a proper fake designer bag.'

Lara burst into fits of giggles as they rolled their cases into the lift. 'You're hilarious, Sharon. How can you get a "proper" fake bag? Fake is fake!'

'Apparently it's not,' Sharon insisted. 'You'd barely know the difference with these ones.'

Ellie shook her head. 'I bet I would. I've yet to see a fake designer bag that I mistook for the real thing.'

'Well, you're the exception to the rule so.' Sharon was adamant. 'This stuff is meant to be real top quality.'

The concierge took their cases and hand luggage from them and they headed out into the cold, crisp air. 'Right, let's have some fun,' said Lara, quickening her step down Park Avenue. 'My me-time is almost up so I'm going to enjoy every last minute of it.'

Sharon rushed to keep in step with her. Lara might be little but she was like a whirlwind. 'I'm with you there. Dublin is going to seem so drab and boring after this wonderful city.'

Ellie kept up with them but didn't say anything. Sharon couldn't work out what was going on with her. She was full of the joys one minute and quiet the next. That was how it had been over the past few days. She'd definitely need to keep an eye on her in the run-up to the wedding because, despite Lara shrugging it off, Sharon was sure that there was something Ellie wasn't telling them. They'd been friends for so long and had always been there for each other so, no matter how much Ellie shrugged it off, Sharon was going to get to the bottom of what was on her friend's mind.

○

'To Ellie,' said Sharon, holding up her Starbucks cappuccino. 'May she have a wonderful life with her gorgeous fella.'

Lara held up her cup. 'And may she never fall into the domesticity trap that will choke the life out of her.'

'For God's sake, Lara. Do you have to spoil everything? Ellie doesn't need to listen to that sort of crap.'

'It's okay, Sharon,' said Ellie, smiling. 'We know how Lara's been feeling about things at home. She doesn't mean any harm.'

'Jesus, of course I don't. I was only having a bit of a laugh.'

They'd arrived at the airport way too early because Lara had been afraid of getting caught in rush-hour traffic. The check-in desks weren't open so they'd lugged their cases up to the food court to find a Starbucks for their last taste of real American coffee. Although there were plenty of Starbucks in Ireland now, the coffee there never really tasted the same as it did in the States.

'And are you feeling better about things?' said Ellie, watching Lara. 'About Peter, I mean.'

'Actually, I'm feeling much better since our chat the other night. I know I've been letting things get on top of me but I'm definitely going to talk to Peter about it. I think honesty is the best policy.'

'Ah, that's brilliant, Lara.' Sharon couldn't keep the smile off her face. 'I'm so happy you said that. Peter is such a lovely man and loves the bones of you. You two will work it out together.'

Ellie nodded, although the word 'honesty' made her nervous.

'I'm glad the few days have given you the chance to think things through,' Sharon went on. 'It was probably exactly what you needed.'

'It was. I'd been so caught up in feeling sorry for myself that I didn't really stop to think what I could do to change things. That was until …' She seemed to change her mind about continuing.

'Until what?' Sharon urged. 'What were you going to say?'

Lara shifted in her chair.

'Lara O'Toole, it's not like you to be lost for words.' Ellie wasn't going to let it go. 'Come on, spit it out.'

'All right, then. I promised myself I wasn't going to tell anyone yet but I have to tell someone or I'll burst. I've been writing a book and I've finally taken the leap in sending some of it to an agent.'

'Wow!' said Sharon. 'How did we not know about that? That's brilliant. Fair play to you.'

Ellie was surprised too. 'I can't believe you kept that one

quiet, Lara – even during our truth sessions in The Gardens! But I'm delighted for you. What sort of a book is it?'

'It's a fictional story based in the newspaper world. I've wanted to write a book like that for years and decided six months ago I'd have a try. I've been tapping away at it ever since but never thought I'd actually have the courage to send it off.'

Sharon smiled at her friend. 'I'm thrilled that you did. And you're a brilliant writer so I'm sure it's fantastic.'

Lara blushed, which didn't happen very often. 'Thanks, girls. There's a long way to go yet and I only sent it off the other day, but I'm keeping my fingers crossed. I have a good feeling about it.'

'I'm glad you told us,' said Ellie. 'Now we can be excited with you while you wait for the good news.'

'Thanks, Ellie. I don't know why I didn't tell you both before. We never really have secrets from each other, do we?'

'I love that about us.' Sharon beamed. 'I love that we're so honest and open with each other about everything.'

There was that word again. Ellie felt the room spinning.

Sharon noticed straight away. 'Are you okay, Ellie? You've gone very pale.'

'I just felt a bit light-headed there for a second.'

'Here,' said Lara, pouring some water into her glass. 'Drink some more of this. You might be dehydrated. The heat in this airport is shocking.'

'Thanks, I'm fine now.' But she wasn't really.

'And what about you, Ellie?' continued Lara. 'Do you feel the few days away have done you good?'

'Yes, definitely. I badly needed the break. The next few weeks are going to be hectic.'

'And do you think remembering Caroline over here has been a good or bad thing?' asked Sharon. 'I mean, I know you've been upset a few times thinking about her but do you think it's helped you with the healing process?'

Ellie saw Lara fix Sharon with a death stare and couldn't help smiling. 'I'm fine, Sharon. It's been good to remember her and all the good times we had.'

'I'm glad,' said Lara. 'I bet she's looking down on you now and taking in every detail of the wedding arrangements.'

'Yes, and screaming at me to stand up to my mother and not let her take over everything!'

Sharon giggled. 'Well, I'm so glad you're feeling better, Ellie.'

'Thanks,' said Ellie. 'You know, you're so like her.'

'Like who?'

'You're so like Caroline. You really remind me of her.'

'In what way?'

'In a lot of ways. You're so good and kind, always thinking of other people. You're the most selfless person I know – and that's what I used to say about Caroline. I wish I was more like that.'

Sharon blushed. 'That's a lovely thing to say. But you

don't need to be any different. You're brilliant as you are and that's why we love you. That's why Matt loves you.'

'H-he really does, doesn't he?' Ellie's voice wobbled.

'Of course he does,' said Lara. 'You two have an enviable relationship.'

Sharon chimed in: 'I want to be just like you when I grow up.'

Ellie didn't laugh but instead put her head into her hands.

'Jesus, what's wrong, Ellie?' Lara's voice was urgent. 'Are you crying?'

'I don't deserve him,' whispered Ellie, looking at her two friends with tears in her eyes. 'I don't deserve to live happily ever after with him when he doesn't know what I'm *really* like.' She stood up suddenly, shoving her chair back, then grabbed her cases and began to walk away.

'Ellie!' called Sharon, running up behind her. 'What's wrong? What are you talking about?'

Ellie continued to walk as the two girls struggled to keep up.

'For God's sake, Ellie,' said Lara, grasping her shoulder and swinging her around. 'What the fuck is wrong with you? Where are you going? Check-in is the other way.'

Ellie looked her two friends in the eye. 'I'm not checking in. In fact, I'm not going home.'

'Wh-what?' Sharon just stared at her. 'Of course you're going home, Ellie. Our flight is in just a few hours.'

'I'm serious,' said Ellie, trying to inject certainty into her voice. 'I can't go home. I need some time away from everything. Please don't hate me.'

Even Lara was looking upset. 'Ellie, I don't know what's going on with you, but let's just get ourselves onto the flight and we can talk about it on the way home.'

'Lara, you don't understand. I've made up my mind. Being over here has made me realise a lot of things and one of those things is that I'm not the person everyone seems to think I am.'

'Ellie,' said Sharon, putting an arm around her, 'you were feeling like this last week too. It's just wedding jitters. I'm sure it happens to everyone.'

'It's way more than that, Sharon. I don't deserve my happiness. I'm going to stay over here while I figure out a few things.' Even as she said the words, a sense of calm descended on her.

Lara shook her head. 'So you're actually expecting us to get on that flight without you? To leave you over here on your own?'

'That's right. I know it's asking a lot and I promise I'll make it up to you some day, but please, for now, just try to understand that I need to do this.'

'But the wedding,' said Sharon suddenly. 'You'll be home for the wedding, won't you?'

Ellie looked at her friend and hated herself for doing this to her. 'Sharon, that's just it – there's not going to be any wedding. Matt deserves way better than me. He doesn't know the person I really am.'

Sharon's hand shot to her mouth. 'You can't be serious, Ellie.'

Lara was equally shocked. 'But I thought you were happy, Ellie. I thought you were looking forward to the wedding. I don't understand.'

'I was. It's just too hard to explain right now. And I know it's a big ask but can you explain things to Matt and my parents and tell them I'll be in touch soon?'

'You can't spring this on us and not tell us where you're going, when you're coming home.' Sharon was hysterical. 'What about all the wedding arrangements? And work? You can't just walk out on your job.'

'I'll deal with the work thing but can you tell Mam and Dad to go ahead and cancel things for the wedding? The sooner it's dealt with the better. And tell them not to worry. I'll make it up to them soon.'

'But I can't—'

'I'm sorry, Sharon.' Ellie pulled her into a hug. 'It's something I have to do.' She hugged Lara too, then picked up her cases and walked towards the exit. Her head was awash with emotions, but she was doing the right thing. She needed the time to think things through. She needed to deal with her guilt before it consumed her.

THIRTEEN

There was little sound except for the whoosh of wheelie bags gliding over polished floors. Lara just stared ahead into the distance, willing the next hour to be over. She glanced at Sharon, who'd barely spoken during the six-and-a-half-hour flight and now looked as though she might burst into tears at any moment. Lara reached for her friend's hand and squeezed it.

'It'll be all right, Sharon. I know it will.'

Sharon didn't answer. She pulled her hand away and busied herself with rooting in her bag.

'Talk to me, Sharon. You can't keep avoiding it. In ten minutes we'll be walking out into that arrivals hall and we're going to have to explain. Although how we can explain something we don't understand ourselves is beyond me.'

'Got it,' said Sharon, pulling out her passport. 'Let's get into the Passport Control queue quickly. The sooner we're out of here and home the better.'

'Sharon, we really need to —'

'For fuck's sake, Lara! Fuck off talking about it, will you? Just fuck off!'

Lara flinched at her friend's uncharacteristic outburst but was quick to put her arms around her and support her as she crumpled into tears. 'It's okay, Sharon. Just let it out.' She pulled her aside to allow people to pass, trying to ignore the rubbernecking from other passengers.

'I'm sorry,' wept Sharon as she slid to the floor and wrapped her arms around her knees. 'I just can't believe we came home without her. What sort of friends does that make us? We left her there on her own.'

Lara slid to the floor beside her and, ignoring her own tears, spoke with a confidence she didn't really feel. 'Come on, you've got to get it together. If Matt sees you in bits like that, he'll think something really bad has happened.'

'But it has, Lara! Why are you so calm about it?'

'I'm not calm inside. I feel it just as much as you do. I don't know what's going to happen, but we've got to get through the next couple of hours until we've talked to everyone.'

'But – but it's all such a mess. I can't go out there. I just can't face Matt and tell him we left his fiancée behind because she was having a wobbly. We should have *made* her come with us. Whatever she needed to sort out, she could have done it in Ireland.'

'Well, I'm sorry to tell you,' said Lara, standing up and holding out a hand for Sharon, 'first, you *can* and you *will* face Matt. We'll do it together. And second, we couldn't have made Ellie come home. She's her own person and was determined to stay. It's an unfortunate situation but we've just got to deal with it.'

'Do you know what?' said Sharon, standing up and brushing herself down. She wiped her tear-stained, snotty face with her sleeve. 'You're right. I'm still trying to take it in and understand what happened back there, but we've no choice. As you say, we just have to deal with it.'

'Good girl. Now, let's get out there and do it.'

Fifteen minutes later they were pushing a trolley full of suitcases through the sliding doors of the arrivals hall in Dublin Airport. They were met by a sea of faces, all anxious and excited about seeing loved ones.

'There's Peter,' said Sharon, pointing to where Lara's husband sat, with Ethan on his lap. 'Go on and give them a hug. I've got the trolley.'

'Thanks.' Lara dashed over to her husband and son and launched herself at them. 'Oh, I missed you both so much.'

'Steady on,' said Peter, laughing. 'What have you done with my Lara, the one who doesn't go in for public displays of affection?'

'We could both do with a hug,' said Sharon, arriving beside them and embracing Peter as well. 'It's been some trip. Where's Matt?'

Peter looked confused. 'He just texted me to say he's parking. But what do you mean "both"? Where's Ellie?'

'Well, you won't believe this,' said Lara, 'but—'

'Ah, there you are! I couldn't get a bloody spot and I had to go around and around,' said Matt, rushing over to their little group. 'And then this ignorant pig came right out of … Hold on, where's Ellie? Oh, don't tell me she's lost her suitcase. She'll go mad if all her stuff from New York goes missing.'

Lara and Sharon shot a panicked look at each other. 'Listen, Matt,' said Sharon, indicating for Matt to sit down beside her. 'We have some news for you and it's not good. I'm sure it will sort itself out but—'

Matt groaned. 'Oh, God, Customs have her, haven't they? She's been arrested for trying to smuggle the whole contents of Macy's back into Ireland!'

'Matt, just sit down and hear us out.' Lara took over while Sharon bit her lip and Peter looked from one to the other in confusion.

'What is it? Has something happened?' Matt sat down heavily, realising something serious was going on.

Lara took a deep breath. 'Matt, Ellie's not with us. She decided to stay on in New York for now. She wanted us to tell you that she's okay and she'd be in touch.'

Matt laughed nervously. 'She's not with you? What do you mean she stayed over there?'

'We don't know much more than that. Ellie decided just before we got on the flight that she wasn't ready to come home. She also said that she didn't deserve to be happy.' Sharon paused. 'She said she didn't deserve you.'

Silence descended for a few seconds, and Lara's heart broke to see Matt looking towards those sliding doors, as though he was still expecting Ellie to appear.

'Is … is this some sort of a joke?' he asked. 'You're having me on, right?'

'Nobody is having you on,' said Lara. 'I only wish we were. Come on, let's get out of here. We'll go back to ours and have a chat.'

Matt paled. 'Y-you're serious? Jesus, Ellie is *really* still in New York? Is she dumping me? Is that what all this is about?'

'Come on, mate,' said Peter, shooting his wife a quizzical look. 'Lara's right. Let's get out of here and we can find out more back at ours.'

Matt dropped his head into his hands and his body convulsed with sobs. 'Talk about it? *Talk about it?* Jesus, what am I going to do? My beautiful fiancée, the love of my life, the woman I thought I'd be spending the rest of it with, has left me – and no amount of talking is going to bring her back.'

◎

Matt was still in shock when they arrived at Lara and Peter's house. He made a beeline for the bathroom, not sure whether he was going to be sick or cry his eyes out. Either way, he wanted to do it in private. He stared at his reflection in the mirror. He looked as bad as he felt. What the hell was going on? He'd thought that he and Ellie were rock solid. He'd never had any doubts about her love for him. He couldn't believe she hadn't come home. Could she not have spoken to him face to face? Didn't he deserve at least that much?

Lara and Sharon had given him a brief outline in the car of what had happened, but he had a million questions to ask them. They'd said it had been as much a shock to them as it was to him but he doubted it. How could they have been with her for four whole days and not know something was up? Surely Ellie had spoken to them about whatever was going on in her mind. Why were they claiming they knew nothing? It didn't make sense.

Or maybe they really were just as much in the dark as he was. It wasn't fair to blame them. Sure hadn't he seen and spoken to Ellie plenty of times before the weekend. Why hadn't *he* noticed that something was amiss?

He splashed some cold water over his face and grabbed a handful of toilet paper to dry it off. He needed to get himself together. He'd had a moment of doubt in the airport when the girls had delivered the news, but he was positive Ellie loved him. Whatever had caused her to act in this way, he was quite sure it wasn't down to her feelings for him. He had to talk to her and figure out what was going on.

Feeling a little more positive, he glanced at himself again in the mirror and ran his fingers through his unruly dark hair. He took a deep breath before heading back into the kitchen, where the others were waiting.

'Matt, mate, are you okay? I've made you a coffee – black with no sugar, right?'

Matt plonked himself down on one of the wooden chairs and took the steaming cup from Peter. 'Thanks, Peter. And no, I'm not okay, as you can imagine. But I want to hear it all again – every last detail – so I can try to figure out what the hell is going on.'

'Oh, Matt, I don't know what to say,' said Sharon. 'I keep thinking we should have done more. We should have made her come home, or at the very least tell us what exactly was wrong. We should have known something wasn't right.'

'From what you're saying, Ellie didn't give you much choice. And as for realising something wasn't right, I'm just as guilty as you are.'

'I'm probably stating the obvious,' said Peter, 'but I assume you've all tried her mobile?'

Sharon nodded. 'A million times since we landed and it's off. I've sent her an email and Lara has tweeted. I suppose we'll just have to wait for her to get in touch.'

'It just doesn't add up,' said Lara. 'She said she doesn't

deserve you – but she didn't say she doesn't *love* you. Maybe … I wonder …'

'What? What is it?' Matt was desperate for answers.

'It doesn't matter.' She was avoiding his eye.

'Come on, Lara. You can't start saying something like that without finishing. Do you know something?'

'I don't know anything for sure but …' Lara was still reluctant but continued, '… why would she say she doesn't deserve you? Usually people say things like that when they're feeling guilty. Maybe she … do you think she might …?'

'You think she's having an affair!' Peter's heart sank. 'Did she say something? I can't believe she'd do that.'

Sharon spoke up: 'There's no way Ellie is or was having an affair. There's just no way! I would have known about it. I live with her, for God's sake. And she talks about you non-stop, Matt. If she's feeling guilty about something, it definitely isn't *that*!'

Matt was relieved. He hadn't really thought Ellie would cheat on him, but he was having a hard time knowing what to think at the moment. 'Thanks, Sharon. But what could it be, then?'

'I really don't know,' said Sharon. 'She was upset a few times while we were away because of Caroline but I can't see how that would make her want to stay over there.'

'None of this makes any sense.' Matt was sick of trying to work it out. He was tired and his mind was frazzled. 'We need to go away and have a think about it – and let's keep trying to get in touch with her.'

'Eh, I don't want to add to everyone's troubles, but have you thought about Jean and Andy? They're going to have to be told very soon.'

'Jesus, Peter, I'd completely forgotten about them,' said Sharon, her hand shooting up to her mouth.

Lara shook her head. 'Fuck! We should have got everyone together to explain all this. We'll have to go through it again with them. They'll be gutted.'

'I'll do it since I'm the one who's supposed to be marrying their daughter in less than four weeks. Jean is going to have a nervous breakdown when she hears. Poor woman.'

'Ah, Jesus, it'll kill her.' Sharon was close to tears again. 'As if that poor family haven't been through enough.'

'And what about poor Mikey?' said Lara. 'That's both his sisters gone now.'

Matt banged his fist on the table, making everyone jump. 'Ellie's *not* gone – she's just taking some time out. There's a world of difference.'

Lara looked upset. 'I'm sorry, Matt. I didn't mean it like that. I know she's not gone for good. I just mean … I just meant …'

'I'm sorry. I don't know what came over me. It's been such a shock and I want to believe she'll come walking through the door in the next day or two, saying she needed a few days to herself.'

Peter rubbed his friend's shoulder awkwardly. 'I'm sure she will, mate. You've got to think positively about this.'

Matt stood up and took his coat from the back of the chair. 'I'd better head over to the Duggans' and get you home, Sharon. You look shattered.'

Sharon nodded. 'I am. I'll be glad to get home but it will be weird not having Ellie there.'

A cry from upstairs brought Lara to her feet too. 'I guess that's my cue – I thought it was too good to be true that Ethan went straight back to bed when we came in.'

'I'll go,' said Peter, jumping up from the table. 'You go to bed and get some rest.'

'Thanks, but I think I need one of my little man's cuddles.'

'Right,' said Matt, 'I'm off. I'll let you know how I go with Jean and Andy. If any of you thinks of anything else or if she's in touch . . .'

Lara stood on tiptoe to give Matt a hug. 'Good luck with that and take care. Whatever happens, there's no doubt Ellie loves you.'

'Thanks, Lara. That's the one thing I *am* sure of. And because of that, I'm determined that this wedding *will* happen, even though it seems doomed at the moment.'

Matt was happy that Sharon was almost falling asleep on the journey home. It wasn't more than a few minutes away, but he was all talked out. He stuck on the radio for a bit of music. He wished he didn't have to face Ellie's parents now but it had to be done. He wouldn't stay long.

He'd head home afterwards and have a good think. There must be something he could do. Ellie's phone was off now but maybe she'd switch it on later and they'd be able to have a chat. It could be as simple as that. But somehow he didn't think so. Ellie was a complex person and he reckoned whatever was up with her wouldn't be solved with a pleading phone call.

FOURTEEN

Ellie looked out of the window in her little hotel room. She felt numb. What the hell was she doing? She was a sensible, happy young woman with so much to look forward to. She might have made the biggest mistake of her life.

She'd got into a cab after she'd left JFK and asked the driver to bring her back into Manhattan. She'd been lost as to what she was going to do next, but luckily the driver had been friendly, his mind full of information about the city. She'd told him that she was visiting for a few days on a low budget but wanted to stay pretty central so he'd brought her to a basic, but more importantly cheap, hotel just a few blocks away from where they'd stayed at the Waldorf.

Back at the airport, when she'd made her decision to stay, she'd felt empowered. She was taking control of her life and doing something positive. But now, alone in a hotel, thousands of miles from everyone she loved, she just felt stupid.

Bloody hell! What must the girls think of her? She'd behaved like a mad woman in the airport.

She'd kept her phone off all night for fear of an onslaught of calls trying to persuade her to come home. She knew the girls would have been in the air for hours, but if they'd rung home before they'd boarded, it was likely that everyone in Ireland would be trying to get through to her.

The sun was coming up and her stomach was rumbling. She'd spent most of the night either sitting at the window or lying on the bed. She hadn't slept or eaten. She really needed to get herself together and make a plan about what she was going to do. A quick trip to Starbucks for a coffee and a pastry should set her up nicely and then maybe she'd try to get a few hours' sleep. She was still in the clothes she'd worn to the airport so she grabbed her coat and bag and headed out to see if she could find somewhere open.

Ice was glistening on the streets in the glow of the early-morning sun and she was thankful for the Ralph Lauren insulated jacket she'd bought at the outlets. The crisp air was clearing her head and, despite her earlier uncertainties, she was sure she was doing the right thing.

She spotted a diner on the corner of the next block and

made her way across the road. Ten minutes later she was heading back to the hotel, with a steaming cappuccino and a bacon bagel. She imagined what the scene would be like back home. God, they'd all be in an awful state. Her mother would be having a hissy fit – although Ellie wasn't too sure if it would be because her daughter hadn't come home or because her best-laid plans for the wedding had to be cancelled.

No sooner had the thought crossed her mind than she was berating herself. Of course her mother would be concerned about her. It would be a huge blow to her that the wedding was off, but Ellie knew she'd be worried sick about her. And what about Matt? What must he be thinking? Tears sprang immediately to her eyes as she thought of her fiancé. She loved him with all her heart, but she couldn't marry him when she hadn't been fully honest with him about how she was feeling. It was at times like this that she wished her sister was there to tell her what she should do.

Caroline had always been the bigger hearted of the two. She'd been loving and kind and would have done anything for anyone. She had even worked for a charity, such had been her need to make a difference. She'd loved children and Ellie had always laughed when Caroline told her she wanted at least six. More tears welled in her eyes.

At the hotel, Ellie swiped her key card on her door and let herself into the room. Sitting on the edge of the bed, she opened the wrapping on the bagel. Was she completely mad to cancel her wedding? No. If she allowed it to go ahead now, without sorting out stuff in her head, she might find herself running away from her marriage – and, in any case, she couldn't marry Matt without him knowing the truth about what had happened on the day Caroline had died.

God, if only things hadn't become so complicated. Her mind wandered back to when she'd met Matt and how she'd felt that instant connection with him. He'd been hired as a personal trainer in the gym at the hotel where she worked. He'd come to Reception on his first day to ask for the gym manager and Ellie had been there, chatting to Sharon. She hadn't been able to take her eyes off him. Luckily for her, he'd obviously felt something too: over the next couple of weeks, he'd made it his business to bump into her regularly. He'd eventually asked her out and the rest was history. Unfortunately, his contract had been a temporary one but by the time he'd left they were deeply in love. He'd managed to find himself another job at a personal-training gym close to the hotel so they'd still managed to see plenty of each other.

She finished her bagel and drained her coffee. She'd have to stop thinking back to how things were and think instead about what she was going to do. But now she needed sleep. She stood up and slipped out of her jeans, then climbed between the cool sheets.

Although she was exhausted, sleep wouldn't come. Too many things were running around in her head and her brain wouldn't shut down. And that was when she remembered. She grabbed her handbag from beside the bed and propped herself up on the pillows. Pulling out the letter from deep inside the pocket, she unfolded it and spread it in front of her.

She must have read it a hundred times yet it still had the same impact every single time. Tears stung her eyes when she thought of how unfair life was.

'Oh, Caroline, why didn't you tell me? How could I not have known?'

But as she looked at the letter, she suddenly felt a purpose. Maybe Fate had brought her here. Maybe it was her destiny to follow up on the letter. Maybe it would help her deal with her guilt and her pain.

She knew she should switch her phone on and deal with whatever messages were waiting for her but she couldn't bring herself to do that just yet. She didn't want to be swayed and convinced to come home. The letter would keep her strong. That was her motivation now, and after she'd dealt with it, she could think about how to proceed with the rest of her life.

○

'Oh, Andy, I can't believe it. It's like a nightmare.' Jean had just said goodbye to Matt.

'I know, love. But it may not be as bad as it sounds.'

'Not as bad? Jesus, Andy. Ellie is over in New York on her own having – God knows what, but some sort of breakdown, I suspect! How could that not be bad?' She sat down heavily on one of the kitchen chairs, her head in her hands.

Andy put his arms around her. 'I know it seems like the worst thing in the world, Jean, but what I mean is that she might only need some time. She could be home in a few days, saying she'd just had wedding jitters.'

'Do … do you really think so?' Jean sniffed. 'I mean, do you think that's all it is?'

'It could well be. It's hard to know but I'd feel a whole lot better if she answered her phone.'

'You don't think something's happened to her, do you?' Jean began to cry again. 'How do we know she hasn't had an accident? She could have walked out of that airport and been struck by a car or anything.'

'Jean, you'll make yourself sick. You've got to calm down. As Matt said, we'll just keep trying her phone. She's bound to answer our messages at some stage. Let's not panic too much for the moment.'

Jean was grateful for Andy's support. He was a fantastic husband. They'd be celebrating their ruby wedding anniversary this year and even now, forty years on, she loved him as much as the day they'd made their vows. She stood up and brought her cup to the sink. 'You're right, Andy. And it's early still over there, isn't it? She's probably asleep and will get in touch as soon as she wakes up.'

'Exactly,' said Andy. 'Ellie's a good girl. She'll know we're worried about her so she won't leave us hanging.'

Jean busied herself wiping down the already gleaming counter. 'But the wedding, Andy. Can you believe she wants to cancel it? Why would she say that? I know she loves Matt. There has to be something else going on.'

'It's a strange one, all right, love. But I'm sure it won't come to that.' Andy's voice sounded anything but convincing.

'It's less than four weeks away now,' Jean fretted. 'I just wouldn't know where to start if we had to cancel.'

Andy looked pensive. 'We've put a fair whack of money into it too. I'd imagine if we were to cancel things now, we wouldn't get deposits back on most things.'

'Andy! How could you think about the money at a time like this? Jesus, have a bit of sensitivity.'

'I was just saying! The money is the least of our worries, but if it turns out Ellie is fine and has just had second thoughts about the wedding, it's a lot of money to throw away.'

Jean sniffed again. 'I suppose. But, as you said, it may not come to that. Matt seemed pretty sure of her feelings for him, didn't he? He was more upbeat than I would have expected him to be, actually.'

'Ah, he's a good lad, is Matt.' Andy got up from the table, went to his wife and took her hands in his. 'I really thought they were a perfect couple – almost as perfect as you and me.'

'Get off with you!' Jean was unused to her husband showing affection like that. 'You wouldn't say we're perfect when I'm nagging you to put your dirty clothes in the laundry basket instead of leaving them on the floor.'

Andy kept a firm hold of her hands. 'Jean, we *are* perfect. You're perfect.'

Jean blushed and pulled her hands away. 'Andy Duggan, I hope you're not looking for something. You know Tuesday is my beauty night so the only thing touching me in bed other than my nightie will be the face-mask I'll be wearing.'

'Ah, well, it was worth a try.'

'You bloody chancer!' She lifted a tea towel and took a swipe at her grinning husband. 'I know you so well.'

Andy smiled. 'But what I said is true – with or without sex.'

Jean clicked her tongue and pretended to be offended but that was how they were with each other. She loved his banter but her role was to feign shock. Then her mind came back to Ellie. 'Do you think this has anything to do with me?'

Andy stared at her. 'Has what anything to do with you?'

'Ellie not coming home – do you think I've been too overpowering? Maybe she's just had enough of me trying to run her life.'

'Well, you're not exactly trying to run her life, Jean. You just took over the wedding plans – but she seemed happy for you to do that.'

'Maybe I pushed her too much. She was just saying last week that she would have been happy with a meal in The Gardens and a smaller bunch of guests. I thought she was joking but maybe it's all got too much for her.'

Jean was fully aware that she'd been a bit overbearing. For starters, she'd really pushed the wedding list. They'd said originally that they wanted no more than fifty guests but it had escalated to a hundred and twenty and was still growing. Maybe Ellie felt it was out of control.

'You've got to stop second-guessing her,' said Andy, grabbing his jacket and scarf from the back of his chair and putting them on. 'I'm going out to do a bit in the garden. Why don't you join me? It might take your mind off things.'

Jean shrugged. 'I don't think anything will take my mind off Ellie but I'll come out with you anyway.'

'Good girl. You know how therapeutic the garden is – I bet we'll feel a whole lot better afterwards and maybe Ellie will have rung by then.'

'Let's hope so,' said Jean, going to get her own coat from the banisters in the hall. 'Because if I don't hear from her by the end of the day, I'll be tempted to get on a plane and go over to look for her myself.'

She'd said it half jokingly but it had planted a seed in her head. Jean was gutted about the wedding, of course, but the most important thing was that her little girl was okay. It broke her heart to think that she was over there, stressing or worrying about something and no one to talk things through with. They'd never had a very close mother–daughter relationship where they'd go into town together or have lunch regularly. The family didn't go in for displays of affection. But there was no doubt they all loved each other, even if they never said it.

Jean watched her husband kneel down outside to tend his shrubs and felt a rush of love for him. Caroline's death should have made them all realise how important it was to show their feelings. She closed her eyes and said a silent prayer. *Please, God, bring my Ellie home safe and sound. I promise to tell her I love her every single day of her life. I'm so sorry I never told Caroline but I just hope she knew.* She grabbed her gardening gloves from the windowsill and went to follow Andy outside. She paused before opening the door. *Please look after Ellie for us, Caroline. I love you, sweetheart.*

FIFTEEN

Ellie was exhausted. She'd eventually fallen into a fitful sleep but her dreams had woken her several times. She'd dreamed of Caroline getting married to Matt and Ellie had been warned not to show up at the wedding. She'd been at JFK trying to get on a flight but everyone kept telling her they'd been instructed not to let her on a plane. Instead of waking up relieved that it had been a dream, she'd felt overwhelmingly sad. Caroline had seemed so real. She'd seen her face clearly for the first time in ages – it had been like opening an old wound that had never healed properly.

She sighed and sat down on the edge of the bed. She couldn't put it off any longer. She switched on her phone and waited. It took a moment but then there was beep after beep: a variety of texts from Matt, her mother, Mikey, Sharon and Lara, all full of concern about her. She thought for a moment of replying with a group text but she owed them more than that.

One by one, she answered, explaining that she was fine but needed time to work out some stuff. She asked her mam to go ahead and cancel the wedding, and told her she'd talk to her about it when she felt ready. She thanked Lara and Sharon for understanding and leaving her, and said she'd be in touch again soon. Then it came to Matt. She felt a physical pain in her heart when she read his words of love and concern. With a heavy heart she tapped in the words that would leave him in no doubt that it was over.

She switched her phone off again so she'd have no distractions and headed out on her mission. She felt alone and a bit scared and couldn't help thinking of how different things would be if Matt was with her. Fleetingly she wondered if maybe she'd been too impulsive, but pushed aside the thought. She would stick with her decision.

Ten minutes later she was on the bus. She pored over the map and realised how much she'd relied on Matt for directions. He'd always been the navigator because she had absolutely no sense of direction. From what she could gather, the bus would leave her pretty close to the address on the letter. She was nervous about it, but she was determined to go and talk to the lady who'd written it. She wanted to talk to her about Caroline – to tell her what had happened. She needed to describe to her the sort of person Caroline was. And maybe she'd even find out some things about Caroline herself. It was both exciting and daunting, and Ellie's stomach was in knots.

Once off the bus, she found her way to the street and stood a little way back from the house. She tried to imagine the people inside. Were they happy? Were their lives richer because of Caroline? Did they ever think about her?

She walked a little closer to get a better view. The street was quiet except for a couple of old ladies chatting on a corner, laden down with bags of shopping. She did her best to look like she belonged there and, to her relief, the women ignored her as she passed. She admired how clean and well kept the street was. The quaint red-brick houses had white front doors and window shutters. A heavenly scent of freshly cut grass hung in the air and each garden, manicured to perfection, looked as though it belonged in a catalogue. It was a million miles away from the hustle and bustle of Manhattan.

Number thirty-three. Until now, it had only been a picture on Google Earth and a number on a piece of paper. Seeing it up close sent shivers down her spine. Maybe this hadn't been a good idea. She was scared of their reaction if she just knocked on the door and announced who she was. Maybe she needed to think things through a little more instead of making a rash decision. God, if only she had somebody with her to talk to about things. If only she hadn't shut everyone out. Suddenly the front door swung open and a woman came out.

"Bye, sweetie,' she shouted back into the house. 'Be good for Daddy. Mama won't be late.'

A little girl ran to the door and flung her pudgy arms around her mother, who picked her up. The child's black hair fell in tight curls around her neck and she was wearing the prettiest pair of denim dungarees.

"Bye, Mama. I'm gonna make a picture with Daddy for you. So you gotta hurry home and see it.'

The woman kissed her all over her face, then put her down gently. 'I can't wait, honey. I'll see you soon.'

Ellie was frozen to the spot. The little girl had taken her breath away. She hadn't been ready for *that*. It was too soon. She didn't know what she'd been expecting, but now she felt as if she was in a dream. And the way the child looked. Oh, God. There was no denying it. She had to get back and think this whole thing through.

She managed to make it look as though she was adjusting the zip on her boot as the woman went past. When she straightened, she was in time to catch a last glimpse of her as she swept around the corner.

She couldn't get the picture of the little girl out of her head as she headed back to the bus stop. She was so beautiful.

She'd go back to the hotel and think about the best way forward. She didn't want to make them feel uncomfortable but, after all, they had sent the letter.

As she rounded the corner, her heart sank as she saw her bus already at the stop, picking up the few passengers who were waiting. Damn! She ran towards it and jumped on just as the doors were about to close.

'Thanks so much,' Ellie panted as she threw her coins into the slot.

She took a seat halfway down, feeling drained. It was as though she was living in some parallel universe. Life was going on as usual back home in Ireland. She should be there, going through plans for her wedding and getting herself organised for work tomorrow. And that was another thing: she should ring her boss to tell her what was going on. She hadn't thought things through but she reckoned, if she could manage it, she'd stay for another few weeks until at least the wedding date was out of the way.

Another hour and she'd be back at the hotel. She'd pick up a sandwich from the coffee shop on the corner and eat it in the room. She still didn't have much of an appetite but she needed to keep up her strength. She idly glanced around, noticing the diversity of the people on the bus, such a mix of backgrounds in one small space. And that was when she saw her.

She was sitting a few seats closer to the front of the

bus, leaning against the window, with nobody beside her. There was no doubt that she was the woman from the house.

She too was beautiful. Her sleek black hair and dark skin gave her a Hispanic look, and with her red lips, she might have stepped out of an old Hollywood movie. Ellie felt a little twang of jealousy at her long svelte legs and skinny frame. She couldn't take her eyes off the woman as the bus stopped and started, dropping passengers off and filling with new ones. She wondered what was going through the woman's mind, as she checked her phone and smiled to herself. It was strange to think that she and this woman were total strangers yet they had a very close connection. Ellie was fascinated by her and continued to watch her even when she took a book from her bag and became engrossed in it.

With only about ten minutes of Ellie's journey left, the woman looked up from her book. Clearly startled to realise she'd reached her destination, she jumped up. Ellie felt a surge of panic when the bus stopped and she saw her hop off and rush down the street. Without thinking things through, she bolted for the door just before it closed and got off in time to see her a little bit ahead.

Jesus. She was such an eejit. What now? Ellie felt totally stupid as she followed the woman down the street. What on earth did she think she was going to achieve by acting like a mad stalker? Maybe she should cut her losses and get onto another bus. But as the woman turned into a coffee shop, Ellie quickened her step and headed in after her. She was nowhere to be seen. Ellie scanned the seats at the back of the shop but there was no sign of her. Maybe she'd been mistaken and the woman had just disappeared into the crowd.

God, she needed to get herself together and calm down. She wasn't normally one for making hasty decisions like that. It would probably be best if she stayed and had a coffee. Today was turning into a farce. She couldn't believe the twists and turns it was taking. It was one thing checking out the house, but another thing entirely to be chasing a woman down the street. It was probably just as well she'd lost her.

'What can I get you?' came a voice from behind the counter, startling her out of her thoughts.

'Oh, sorry, I was miles away. I'll have …' The words caught in her throat when she saw who was serving. It was her again. She obviously worked there. No wonder Ellie hadn't seen her when she'd followed her in. She must have been in the back getting ready.

'Too much choice, huh?' The woman smiled, showing perfect white teeth, and Ellie suddenly became aware of her own unkempt appearance.

'I'll have a Cinnamon Latte, please.'

'Good choice. And can I get you anything with that?'

'Em … no, thanks.'

Her name was Ann, according to the gold badge on her chest. She didn't look like an 'Ann'. Ellie would have expected her to be 'Jodie' or 'Chantelle'. Ann seemed too ordinary for such an exotic beauty.

'That'll be three dollars and eighty cents when you're ready, ma'am.'

She had a strong New York accent, with a faint Irish brogue. The inflection startled Ellie and made the situation seem more real than ever.

'Ma'am, that'll be three dollars and eighty cents. Are you okay?'

'Yes, yes, I'm fine. Sorry, I'm in a world of my own today!' She paid for the drink and collected it from the end of the counter, then sat at a table at the back of the shop. Jesus, she'd want to get herself together, staring at Ann like a complete gobshite.

She sipped her drink, watching Ann deftly serve customer after customer, all the time smiling and passing a friendly word. She seemed a good person, which made Ellie irrationally happy. What if she hadn't liked her? There'd have been nothing she could do but it would have been very difficult. She also liked the fact that Ann was very pretty and seemed to have good taste in clothes. Even though she'd just come for a shift in a coffee shop, she was wearing a lovely pair of skinny jeans, silver pumps and a black Hilfiger T-shirt embellished with silver lettering.

She was jolted out of her reverie when an oversized

woman knocked against her table, causing her coffee to spill. The shop had filled and there were no free tables. It was probably time for her to go. She zipped up her jacket and headed for the door. Ann was busy behind the counter but waved to her. 'See you next time, hon.'

Ellie left the shop and breathed in the cold fresh air. What a crazy day it had been. Ann seemed a really decent person, which was important to Ellie. It would have been important to Caroline too.

SIXTEEN

'God, am I glad to see you!' Sharon opened the door for Mikey to come inside and pulled him into an embrace. 'Have you heard anything? Has she been in touch since yesterday? How're your mam and dad about it all?'

'Jeez! Give me a chance to answer one question, would you?' grinned Mikey, kissing the top of her head.

Sharon sighed. 'I'm sorry. But I thought work would never end so that I could get home and find out what was happening. I couldn't even get to my phone most of the day because that Pauline was on my back.'

Mikey followed her into the sitting room as she continued to talk. 'And I was in a daze most of the time because I kept thinking back to what we talked about in New York and trying to remember things that might help.'

'Sharon ...'

'I was mortified when a guest asked me if I was okay because I was miles away and—'

'*Sharon!*'

'What?'

'I know you're upset by all this,' he said, sitting down beside her and putting his arm around her, 'but you've got to stop stressing. Ellie is fine – she's said so in her texts, hasn't she?'

'But we don't know that, Mikey.' Sharon was upset. 'She might *say* she's fine but what if she's not? What if she's having some sort of breakdown?'

'Did she sound like she was losing it when you last saw her?'

'Well, no, but—'

'Did she seem happy with her decision to stay on in New York?'

'Yes, but she—'

'Well, then, I think we should all back off a bit.'

Sharon stared at him. 'God, Mikey, I'm surprised you can be so laid-back about it. I thought you'd have been up the walls, especially because of ... you know ...'

'Because of what?' Mikey looked at her blankly.

'Well, because of Caroline. You've already lost one sister. I'd have thought you'd be terrified.'

'Sharon,' said Mikey gently, taking her hand, 'it's *because* of Caroline that I'm so calm. When you've experienced something like we did with Caroline, nothing can faze you. Caroline died tragically. Ellie is alive and well and just having a rethink about things. I know my sister. She'll talk to us when she's ready.'

Sharon couldn't believe the words that were coming out of his mouth. But maybe he was right. They were all completely panicked about the situation but he was looking at it from a totally different perspective.

'Don't get me wrong,' he continued. 'I wish she'd come back. I wish she'd talked to me or to one of us about what she was thinking. I'm not happy about the situation but I'm not sure there's anything we can do about it at the moment.'

Sharon felt overwhelmed with love for this gentle man, who had such a wonderful understanding of life. 'You're probably right, Mikey. I suppose all we can do is to be here for her. But I'd feel better if I could talk to her.'

Mikey pulled her close to him on the sofa. 'Me too. And I'm more than a bit gutted about the wedding. I mean, I want Ellie to be happy, and if that means not marrying Matt, so be it. But Matt's a great guy and he was really good for her. I thought they were for keeps.'

'That's just the thing,' said Sharon, sitting up. 'So did she. She never indicated anything was wrong between them. She was always talking about how lucky she was to have such a fabulous guy. It doesn't really make sense.'

'Hmm.'

Sharon realised she'd got Mikey's attention so she kept talking. 'And even when we were away, she was saying that, only for Matt, things could have been a lot different for her now. She said that he'd come along at just the right time in her life and he'd saved her from herself.'

'It's a bit sudden, all right. But what can we do? If she's not willing to talk to us, our hands are tied unless we go over there and find her.'

'Well, now, that might not be a bad idea,' said Sharon, her mind working overtime. 'Maybe one or some of us should do just that.'

Mikey looked at her as though she was mad. 'I was joking, Sharon. It'd be a bit drastic, don't you think? You're only back since yesterday morning. Shouldn't we give her at least until the weekend and see what happens?'

But Sharon was warming to the idea and wanted to push it a bit more. 'I wonder what Matt's thinking. Have you spoken to him at all?'

'Not yet. I was going to give him a buzz later to see how he was coping.'

Sharon jumped up. 'Why don't I call him now and get him to pop over? We can have a chat about things and see what he thinks.'

'I suppose there's no point in me arguing with you about it.' Mikey looked defeated, and Sharon was sorry she'd railroaded him into something he didn't want to do.

'If you think we should hold off until the weekend, that's fine. I know I'm like a dog with a bone but something doesn't feel right about this and I just want to help.'

Mikey wrapped his arms around her tightly. 'I don't see what harm it can do to ask Matt over for a chat. You're such a good friend. Ellie's damn lucky to have you. I hope she realises that.'

'Aw, thanks,' said Sharon, nestling her head into his chest. Although she wasn't small at five foot nine, she was dwarfed by Mikey's six-foot-five frame. 'Should I give him a call now?'

Mikey laughed and kissed her full on the lips. 'You're incorrigible, Sharon Young! But why don't we take an hour out for ourselves first? After all, I haven't seen you in days.'

'What are you suggesting, Mikey Duggan?'

'Well, maybe a bit of this, a bit of that and a *lot* of the other.' His eyes twinkled and Sharon's heart swelled with happiness.

'Let's not waste any more time.' She took his hand and led him towards the stairs. 'I'll even show you a few of my yoga moves, if you like.'

'Bring it on!' Mikey slapped her bum playfully and Sharon felt completely content. For the first time in her life, she could see her future mapped out in front of her, and Mikey Duggan was a big part of the picture.

◯

Matt quickened his step as the first drops of rain began to fall. Shit! It was typical of his luck at the moment. He'd come out without a rain jacket because the day had been bright and crisp with no black clouds. Still, Sharon's was only down the road so he'd be there in a few minutes.

He'd been surprised to get a call from her, asking him over for a chat. He'd rung in to work sick because he hadn't been able to face anyone and had been sitting at home wallowing all day. His first reaction had been to tell her he wasn't in form for a chat but she'd been insistent. Maybe she'd heard from Ellie and hadn't wanted to tell him over the phone. God, he hoped so.

He crossed the road at Phibsboro Shopping Centre and turned left at Doyle's Corner. He'd walked that route a million times to see Ellie and he felt a rush of sadness that she wouldn't be there this time. He wondered what she was doing in New York. Was she happy or was she regretting her decision? Was she thinking about him at all? He wished she'd get in touch. It had been nice to have the text from her yesterday but it hadn't been enough. She'd indicated that she was fine and that she just needed time away from everything, but she'd been adamant that there'd be no wedding. It had been such a bolt out of the blue that he was having difficulty coming to terms with it.

'God, you're soaked,' said Sharon, opening the door for Matt to step inside. 'Come on in and get yourself dry. I'll put the kettle on.'

Matt shook his head and his hair sent droplets of water shooting all over the place just as Mikey came out of the sitting room.

'Jaysus, Matt. You're worse than a dog, shaking that mane of yours. Next you'll be rolling on the carpet to dry yourself.'

Matt laughed. 'Howareya, Mikey? I didn't expect to see you here. What's the story?'

'Well, em, Sharon rang me earlier to see did I want to come over for a chat about Ellie. She thought a few of us should put our heads together and see if we could come up with a plan.'

Sharon shot him a grateful look. Now wasn't the time for confessions about their relationship. 'Let's go into the kitchen.'

'Have either of you heard any more from Ellie since yesterday?' asked Matt hopefully.

'Unfortunately not.' Sharon busied herself making the tea, trying to avoid Matt's eyes. She didn't want to see the disappointment in them.

'Oh! I thought maybe that's why you'd asked me over. So you haven't heard anything at all?'

'Not a thing, mate,' said Mikey. 'I haven't been overly concerned, to be honest, because I think she only needs some time out. But Sharon here, with her psychoanalytic thinking, reckons we should do something. But what, I just don't know.'

Sharon blushed furiously and glared at him. 'There's no need for that. All I'm doing is trying to understand what might be going through Ellie's head. Only a week ago she was happy, excited and really looking forward to getting married. She was in love with Matt and spoke regularly about having found her soulmate. Then, all of a sudden, she's running away from her life and doesn't even want to get married. That's not normal behaviour.'

Matt sighed. 'I have to agree with you. I haven't stopped thinking about it and trying to figure it out since you came back. I *know* Ellie loves me. Whatever she has in her head, I'm convinced that it's not about me. Tell me again exactly what she said.'

Sharon was still reeling from Mikey's harsh comment but at least Matt seemed to be on her side. 'She said she couldn't go home yet and she couldn't get married. She said you deserved better. She said she needed time to think and that it was just something she had to do.'

'Something must have happened,' Matt mused. 'I can't even begin to imagine what it might be, but something triggered it. It doesn't sound like the Ellie I know.'

'Exactly!' said Sharon.

Mikey, who'd been listening quietly, piped up, 'I'm starting to come around to your thinking, Sharon. And I'm sorry I was harsh with you. I suppose, maybe, I didn't want to think anything was wrong.'

'That's okay, Mikey.' Sharon smiled at him and realised

he was just as worried and upset as they were. 'And the more I think about it, the more I'm coming to the conclusion that it has something to do with Caroline.'

'With Caroline? How?' Matt looked puzzled.

'I'm not sure if I told you yesterday,' continued Sharon, 'but Ellie spoke about her a few times during the weekend. She got really upset one day at the Rockefeller Center because she remembered being there with Caroline.'

'Ah!' Realisation was dawning on Mikey. 'Her last trip to New York was with Caroline. How could we have forgotten that?'

'God, yes, so it was,' Matt recalled. 'I can't believe I didn't think about that. I remember her telling me about their trip. There must have been so many memories for her.'

'That's exactly how it was,' said Sharon. 'While we were there, I was conscious that she was bottling things up. She kept going quiet, and when we'd question her about it, she'd shrug it off, say she was fine and then she'd be in great form again. I even told Lara I was worried about her.'

'And what did she say?' Mikey stood up to get the teapot for a refill.

'You know Lara. She hates me analysing things too much. She just thought Ellie was having moments of nostalgia and that it was perfectly normal.'

Mikey nodded. 'I was guilty of the same thoughts. It's only since you started talking about it this evening that I've wondered if there's more to it.'

Matt rubbed his temples. 'What's puzzling me is that she said she needed to figure some things out. Her irrational behaviour could be put down to emotions running high with the stress of the wedding and memories of Caroline. But what could she need to figure out that she couldn't talk to you about?'

'It's a mystery, all right,' agreed Sharon. 'And that's probably the key to everything.'

'What about her laptop?' Matt stood up suddenly. 'Maybe we'd find some clues on there.'

'Ah, come on, Matt,' said Mikey. 'Don't you think we're getting a bit carried away? What would you expect to find on her laptop? And wouldn't that be an invasion of privacy?'

Sharon stood up too. 'Ellie waived her right to privacy when she decided to disappear and have us all worried sick. If there's something on her laptop that might help us to find her or give us an insight into what she's thinking, I'm all for taking a look.'

'Great!' Matt exclaimed. 'Will you get it, Sharon? I know her password so we should be able to find something that'll help us – if there's anything to find.'

Five minutes later they were huddled around Ellie's laptop, checking back through the Google history. There were sites for cake recipes and she'd been a regular visitor to the WeightWatchers site. Sharon couldn't help smiling to herself. That was so typical of Ellie. As a past member, she still counted the points in food – then had the biggest slice of cake she could find.

'Hold on, here's something,' said Matt, jabbing his finger on the computer screen. 'She was looking up an address in Queens.'

Sharon was puzzled. 'Queens? As far as I'm aware she doesn't know anyone over in New York at all and she's certainly never mentioned Queens.'

They sat in silence, each lost in thought. Sharon couldn't imagine where a house in Queens would fit into all this. She racked her brains but she was sure Ellie had never mentioned anything about it.

'I'm going over!'

Sharon stared at Matt. 'What?'

'I'm going over to try and sort this out.' Matt stood up and grabbed his jacket.

'Hold on, mate,' said Mikey, looking worried. 'You can't just decide to fly to the other side of the world.'

'Yes, I can, Mikey. Ellie is my fiancée, the love of my life. I know she loves me so I need to get over there and find out what the hell is going on with her.'

'I'm coming with you!' Sharon was on her feet too. 'I was already thinking about it but you've made my mind up.'

Mikey stared at her in shock. 'Are you crazy, Sharon? You've just come back. I understand Matt needs to go but there's no need for you to go too.'

'Mikey's right, Sharon. I should do this on my own.'

'No deal,' said Sharon firmly. 'Ellie is my best friend and I feel I've let her down. I need to go back and *this* time I'm bringing her home.'

Mikey looked from one to the other. 'Oh, I give up! I'll check the flights while you two go off and pack.'

'Thanks, love … em … Mikey.' Sharon could have bitten out her tongue for the slip but, thankfully, Matt hadn't been paying attention.

'Right,' said Matt decisively. 'Let's try to fly tomorrow. The sooner we get to Ellie the better. Is that okay with you, Sharon?'

'Yep. I'll just need to sort things with work.'

'Great. I'll head on home and make a few phone calls. Mikey, give me a ring and let me know what flights are available.'

'Will do, Matt. And thanks.'

Matt stepped outside into the cold air. 'What for, Mikey?'

'Looking out for my sister. Just bring her home, will you?'

'That's my intention,' said Matt. 'I'm going to bring her home and, in a few weeks' time, we'll be walking down that aisle.'

Sharon closed the door behind Matt and turned to Mikey. She was shocked to see tears running down his face. 'Oh, Mikey.' She put her arms around him and he clung to her for what seemed like ages. 'We'll find her, love. It's going to be all right.'

SEVENTEEN

Lara held her breath as she tiptoed out of the room. It was almost ten o'clock and Ethan was only dropping off now. She was exhausted and had almost fallen asleep beside him on the bed. It would have been easy to let herself drift off but she'd made a promise to herself that she would never get into that habit. She needed a little time for herself before she went to bed.

Peter had gone to The Gardens to meet a couple of the lads. She'd had a tiring day because Ethan had been tetchy and clingy, and her face had fallen when Peter had come home from work and announced he'd be going out. But what could she say? She was back from a weekend away and he'd been on his own with Ethan for four days. She'd made a feeble attempt to sway him by suggesting a movie and pizza for the two of them, but Peter had clearly felt he needed the time out.

He seemed to have coped well without her. There had been some smudges on the mirrors and dust gathering around the telly but, all in all, he'd done his bit. He'd even managed some ironing. He'd never dream of picking up the iron normally so it just showed what he could do when he needed to.

She headed into the kitchen to put the kettle on for a cup of tea but changed her mind when she noticed the lone bottle of red on the wine rack. Why shouldn't she treat herself, since Peter was in the pub? And there was a big bag of Tayto cheese and onion too. She'd take a bowl of them with her glass of wine into the sitting room and catch up on the last few episodes of *Coronation Street*. Maybe tonight wasn't going to be a write-off, after all.

It was hard to believe they'd only arrived home from New York the previous morning. It seemed like ages ago. What a drama. She wondered what Ellie was doing. Was she enjoying being in her favourite city or was she sitting alone, mourning what could have been? And why on earth had she called off the wedding? Lara just couldn't figure it out. Part of her felt sorry for her friend, because she was obviously going through some stuff, but the other part of her felt a bit jealous. Imagine having the freedom to decide to take some time out just like that. Imagine being able to put your life on hold for a while until you'd worked out what you wanted.

She sighed as she settled herself on the sofa and flicked on the telly. She had two episodes of *Masterchef* to watch also, a couple of hours of escapism. She took her first sip of wine just as the opening credits came on the screen and almost jumped out of her skin when the phone rang.

'Fuckit, fuckit, fuckit!' Red wine dripped onto her T-shirt as she rushed to grab the phone before it woke Ethan.

'Hello,' she whispered, ready to give someone an earful for ringing so late when they knew there was a small child in the house.

'Hi, Lara, it's Sharon.'

'Oh, Sharon, hi. I wasn't expecting to hear from you. Is there some news about Ellie?'

'Are you okay? Why are you whispering?'

Lara could have strangled her. 'Oh, no reason. I just like talking in a low voice.'

There was a pause before Sharon spoke. 'Why are you acting weird, Lara? What's wrong?'

'My sarcasm was wasted on you. I've just put Ethan down and I don't want him to wake up.'

'Oh, God, sorry. I didn't think. But I have news and I knew you'd want to know.'

Lara perked up. 'What is it? Has she been in touch again?'

'Nobody's heard anything,' said Sharon. 'Matt and I are heading over there in the morning.'

'Wh-what? To New York? How come? You and Matt?'

Sharon laughed. 'I know it sounds weird, me going with Matt, but we had a chat today and it just happened. Matt decided he wanted to go over and bring Ellie home for the wedding. He says he knows it's what she wants and that she loves him so he's not letting her get away. How romantic is that?'

'Very.' Lara was at a loss for words. She felt inexplicably jealous of Sharon swanning off to New York while she was back to the drudgery of the house. 'But why are you going with him? Is it not a bit over the top, both of you going over there?'

'No, I don't think so. I think it's good that two of us are going. And, besides, I still can't help feeling we let her down by coming home and leaving her there. We should have dug a bit deeper and found out what was really going on.'

'But we've been through that, Sharon. Even you had to admit there was no way we could have convinced her to get on that flight.' Lara took a big slug of her wine and felt it go straight to her head.

'That may be so, but I'd like the opportunity to make things right and bring her home this time.'

'Fair enough.' Lara sighed. 'But if she doesn't get in touch again, how will you find her?'

Sharon filled her in on the events of the evening and Lara listened, feeling that pang of jealousy again. Why hadn't they rung her to join them? She'd been there as much as

Sharon had all weekend. Did they not think her opinions were valid?

'Lara, are you there?'

'Yes, but I've just heard Ethan stirring so I'd better head up to him. Peter is out so it's just me. Listen, have a safe flight over tomorrow and keep in touch. I hope you manage to find her and talk her into coming home.'

'Thanks, Lara. I'll keep you up to date. Night.'

Lara hung up and threw the phone to the end of the sofa. 'Fuckin' lucky bitch,' she mumbled.

She knew she was being unreasonable – Sharon and Matt were going on a mission of mercy, but she'd have loved to be the one heading over there. And Ellie would think Sharon was the better friend because she'd done that for her. Life was so unfair. She was sick of always feeling second best.

She drained her glass of wine and headed into the kitchen for a refill. Maybe she should start looking on the bright side. Things weren't so bad, really. She didn't have to be up at the crack of dawn to get herself ready to go out to work. She could stay in her pyjamas and plant Ethan in front of the telly while she relaxed over her breakfast. There were definitely advantages to being a stay-at-home mam.

Feeling a little more upbeat, she took her full glass back into the sitting room and was about to put the telly back on when a noise disturbed her again. She closed her eyes and wanted to cry. So much for seeing the bright side.

'*Maaaammy!*'

She sighed and switched off the telly. Tomorrow was another day.

○

'So, let me get this straight,' said Jean, trying to keep up with what Mikey had told her. 'Matt and Sharon are going to New York first thing in the morning. They've no idea how they're going to find Ellie but are hoping that an address you found on her computer is going to lead them to her?'

Mikey opened the fridge and took a slug of orange juice straight out of the carton. 'That's about it. I thought they were mad initially, but it's probably for the best.'

Jean glared at him and tutted. 'But do you really think it will do any good?'

'What harm can it do?' Andy piped up. 'The worst that can happen is they don't manage to find her, but if they do, they could have her home in the next few days.'

Jean stood up and took a cloth to clean down the already spotless counter. 'I suppose it just makes the situation seem so much more urgent. I've been telling myself that Ellie had a dose of the jitters and would walk back in that door any minute.'

'But that could still be the case, Mam. Sharon and Matt are only trying to hurry the process along. And, to be honest, if that was my fiancée over there, I'd probably do the same.'

'Chance would be a fine thing,' sniffed Jean.

Mikey glared at her. 'And what's *that* supposed to mean?'

'Well, look at you, son. You're twenty-four and you've never brought a girl back to this house. I think you have it too good here, with your mammy doing everything for you.'

'Ah, leave the lad alone.' Andy patted his son on the back. 'He's got loads of years ahead of him yet. Let him live a bit before he settles down.'

'And maybe there *is* a woman, Mam.' Mikey had a glint in his eye. 'Maybe I'm just waiting for the right time to introduce her to the family.'

Jean's eyes lit up. 'Is there, Mikey? Why wouldn't you tell us? God, this family could do with a bit of good news. What's she like? Where did you meet her?'

'Whoa, Mam! I didn't say there *was* a woman – I just don't want you to assume there isn't!'

Jean sniffed again. 'Well, I'll believe it when I see it. But back to Ellie. What's this address that you found on her computer?'

'It's in Queens. Ellie had been looking at it on Google Earth. It's a bit of a mystery. As far as we're concerned, Ellie doesn't know anyone over there so we can't make out who the address might belong to. But Matt said that if she doesn't answer their texts when they're over there, they'll go to the address and see what they can find out.'

'Seems like a good plan,' said Andy, turning the pages of his newspaper. 'And I'm sure once she knows they're over there she'll agree to meet them. She's not a bad girl, our Ellie. She just seems to have lost her way a bit.'

Jean had to close her eyes to stop the tears coming. She was still blaming herself for all her interfering. Even though Andy had assured her that Ellie wouldn't be thinking that way, she wasn't convinced. She imagined Ellie in New York all by herself, just because she didn't want to come home and face her interfering mother. God, imagine if she was solely responsible for ruining her daughter's life!

'Jean, are you okay?' Andy was rubbing her arm. She opened her eyes and he was looking at her, concern filling his kind eyes.

'I ... I'm fine. I was just thinking about Ellie on her own. It probably *is* a good idea that Matt and Sharon are going over.'

Andy nodded. 'It is, love. And don't you be worrying yourself. Matt is a good man and he adores the ground our Ellie walks on. He'll bring her back, I know he will. As soon as she sees him, she'll remember why she fell in love with him.'

'You're such a hopeless romantic, Dad,' laughed Mikey. 'It's not exactly a fairytale, you know.'

Jean wiped her eyes. 'But it could be, Mikey. If we think

positively, there could be a fairytale ending to all this. You know I believe in the power of positive thinking so let's just put it out there to the universe that things will work out.'

She shut her eyes again but instead of putting the positive vibes out there to the universe, she had a quiet word with Caroline. *Please watch out for your sister, love. Keep her safe and bring her home to us soon.*

EIGHTEEN

Matt gazed at the opulent Waldorf Astoria as he and Sharon stepped out of the cab. It was his second visit to New York but things were a lot different this time around. Previously he'd been with two of his friends and they'd had a blast, doing all the touristy things during the day and checking out various comedy clubs at night. This time he was here with his fiancée's friend and a heavy heart. Had he been mad to think this was going to be easy? Ellie still wasn't answering any of his calls or texts so he hadn't a clue where to find her. At least he'd managed to get two fairly cheap rooms in the Waldorf when he'd explained his dilemma to a lovely manager on the phone.

'Are you okay?' asked Sharon as the cab driver lifted their suitcases onto the kerb.

'I'm fine. Well, actually, no, I'm not. But I will be. I'll be fine when we find Ellie and talk some sense into her.' He paid the cab driver and tipped him generously.

Sharon nodded. 'I know what you mean. And we *will* find her, Matt. Once she knows we cared enough to come all the way over here for her, she'll come to her senses. I'm sure of it.'

'I hope you're right. Let's get ourselves checked in and we can start looking for her.' The inside of the hotel took Matt's breath away. He'd seen it in the past in movies but being there was something else entirely. He felt as though he'd stepped into a vat of gold. Everything from the rugs on the floor to the ornate golden clock in the centre of the lobby was beautifully over the top. He'd usually ridicule places that were too fancy but somehow he felt that it was right for the Waldorf. Thankfully there was no queue at Reception so they were able to check in quickly and get the keys to their rooms on the twenty-eighth floor.

'Right,' said Matt, when they got to the rooms, which were next door to each other. 'Will we take half an hour to get freshened up and I'll see you down in Reception? If I get sorted sooner, I might take a stroll around and get my bearings.'

'Perfect. I'm going to have a quick shower and I'll be ready by then.'

The room was exactly what he'd expected. The deep-burgundy curtains against the striped yellow wallpaper gave the room a regal air, and the fresh white linen on the bed looked inviting. He felt physically and emotionally drained, and there was nothing he'd have liked better than to put his head down and sleep for a few hours, but he couldn't afford the time.

They hadn't told Ellie they were coming. They'd toyed with the idea of texting her with the details but decided against it. If she knew they were coming, she'd either try to put them off or go deeper into hiding. But if they were actually in New York when they made contact with her, she was bound to give in. He'd wait until Sharon was ready before deciding how they were going to make contact.

He opened his suitcase and left it propped against the wardrobe. He hoped they'd be there for just a few days so he wouldn't bother to unpack. He pulled out a fresh tracksuit and underwear and threw them onto the bed, then took off the clothes he'd travelled in. He welcomed the warm, powerful spray of water as he stepped under the shower and felt immediately better. A little later, refreshed and energized, he headed down to meet Sharon.

'I don't know about you,' she said as he joined her at the ornate golden clock in the centre of the lobby, 'but I'm starving. How about we grab something to eat quickly in the restaurant? We can discuss what we're going to do first.'

Matt nodded. 'Good idea. I'm pretty hungry myself.

And Ellie was raving on the phone last weekend about the Waldorf salad here.'

'It's delicious – probably one of the nicest things I've ever tasted.'

'Right, you have me sold. Let's go and grab a table, and we can send Ellie a text while we order.'

They headed towards the restaurant in silence. Matt thought about the phone call he'd had with Ellie less than a week ago. The hotel had blown her mind when she'd seen it and they'd just had their first meal in the restaurant. She'd been full of enthusiasm and excitement. It was hard to believe it had come to this.

Sharon was the first to speak. 'It'll be all right, Matt. I know it will. We'll find her and get her talking. In just a few days' time we'll be bringing her home and life can get back to normal.'

Matt had to blink away tears. 'I hope you're right, Sharon. I really hope you're right.'

○

Ellie picked up her Starbucks coffee and looked around for a place to sit in the lobby at the Waldorf. The hotel she was staying in at the moment was only a few blocks away and she'd been lucky to find somewhere so cheap in such a central area. But it didn't have a Starbucks in the lobby. She'd loved that about the Waldorf when she'd stayed there so when she'd found herself passing the hotel she hadn't been able to resist popping in for a coffee.

Ellie loved the atmosphere in the hotel. All the staff were pleasant and welcoming, and she felt really comfortable there. She noticed an elderly lady getting up from one of the lovely high-backed armchairs and Ellie made a beeline for it before anyone else sat there.

She switched on her phone and waited for the usual ping indicating the incoming emails and texts. She'd been keeping it mostly off because she knew that any contact from home would make her feel guilty about what she was doing. She hadn't contacted anyone since the texts she'd sent on the first day, but she knew she'd have to be in touch with them soon. She was torn. On the one hand, she just wanted to shut out her usual life and everyone in it so that she could think about things and continue with her plans here. But on the other hand, she knew she owed it to the people who loved her to make sure they knew she was okay.

There were only two emails today – one from Lara and one from Mikey. Her heart melted when she read her brother's. She really hadn't given him proper consideration in all this. They'd grown very close these last few years and she adored him. Both she and Caroline had always looked on him as an annoying little pest – the one who always told on them when they were up to mischief and got away with murder himself. It was only when Caroline had died that she'd noticed he'd grown into a lovely, considerate young man and she was very proud of him.

She typed a few words to him. Despite her vow of silence, she wanted Mikey to know she was okay. She didn't say anything of where she was or what she was up to, just that she was fine and would be home when she felt ready.

Lara's email was a repeat of the other few she'd sent. In typical Lara style, she wasn't mollycoddling Ellie or getting too emotional. She simply said that they were all completely confused and in shock about her not coming back. She was sorry she hadn't realised anything was wrong but surely whatever it was could be fixed in Ireland. She hoped she'd get in touch and get her arse back over there so they could help her through whatever was going on. Ellie couldn't help being amused at her friend's straightforwardness. She knew Lara meant well – she just had such a different approach from everyone else.

She took a gulp of her coffee and refreshed her emails. It was kind of strange that there'd been nothing from Sharon or Matt since yesterday. Was it a case that out of sight was out of mind? If she stayed here long enough, would all the emails and texts become fewer and fewer until they stopped altogether? Would everyone forget about her and get on with their own lives?

Her heart quickened when she thought about what she'd done but she knew it had been right. Matt would move on with his life and begin to accept that they were no longer together and she'd … Well, she wasn't sure what she'd do. But Matt would be happier than he would have been if he'd married a woman like her.

She was contemplating ordering something to eat. Her appetite wasn't quite back to normal but she'd kill for a Waldorf salad. She'd had it as a starter when she and the girls had eaten there last week and she'd never had anything like it. The apple and celery were shredded and mixed with the most divine lemon mayonnaise, and the walnuts were the nicest she'd ever tasted. Maybe she'd treat herself.

As she was heading to the restaurant to see if they had a free table, her phone pinged. Damn! She'd meant to turn it off. But she couldn't help having a little peep to see who was texting her. Her heart jumped when she saw Matt's name. She couldn't help feeling relieved that he hadn't given up on her yet.

Hi Ellie. I know you said you're fine and you need time to yourself, but I can't accept that right now. We're due to be getting married and I know you want that. I believe in us. Sharon and I are here in New York and we're not leaving until you at least agree to meet us. All my love, Matt xx

Her mind was in a whirl. Jesus! She couldn't believe they'd come all the way over just to speak to her. She felt a pang of guilt for the upset she'd caused. It must have cost them both a fortune to get flights at this late stage and accommodation too. They must both really love her to do that. A little bubble of excitement rose in her chest but she tried to suppress it. Nothing had changed. She was sorry that Sharon and Matt had made the journey because it was going to be a wasted one. Much as she'd love to see them, her mission now was to follow up on that letter, and it was between her, Caroline and the people in that house.

She plonked herself on a nearby chair and read the text again. God, it would be so easy to reply and say she'd meet them. She was trying so hard to be strong and independent but she was also very lonely. No, she wasn't even going to answer it. If she kept her phone off for a couple of days, they'd get the message. She was about to slide her finger along the screen to shut her phone off when another text pinged in:

I meant to say in my last text that we've got rooms in the Waldorf. I hope you'll get in touch as soon as possible. We're heading down to the restaurant now for a bite to eat and we'll be there for at least an hour. Hopefully see you soon. Love Matt xx

Oh, fuck, fuck, fuckity-fuck! What were the chances? She couldn't believe it. She needed to get out of there – and fast. She jammed her phone into her pocket and made a dash for the nearest exit, eyeing everyone she passed on the way. Oh, God, she didn't know what she'd do if they saw her and called her name. She could hardly run away from them – that would be way too childish. She managed to get out onto the street in seconds and continued down Park Avenue until she was well out of sight of the hotel.

She stopped at American Girl to catch her breath and leaned against the window. She watched for a few minutes as excited little girls wandered in and out of the shop with their prized dolls. She wished she was ten again. If only Caroline was with her and their mother was bringing them for a treat to get a special doll. God, if only she could zap back to her childhood when everything was fun and she hadn't a worry in the world. There were so many if-onlys …

As soon as she felt normal again, she continued to walk. She wanted to put as much distance as she could between her and the Waldorf Astoria. She decided to cut over to Seventh Avenue and head down towards Times Square.

It was like a physical ache in her heart to know that Matt was so close by and yet she couldn't see him. Part of her brain was screaming, 'Yes, you can,' but she was trying to shut it down. And then there was Sharon. She'd always been able to confide in her. They'd been lifelong friends and there was nothing they hadn't shared.

She quickened her pace and, with every step, her resolve grew. Her time in New York wasn't about Sharon or Matt or her mother – it wasn't even about her. This was about

Caroline and making things right. Her sister could no longer do things for herself so Ellie wanted to do this for her. She'd just have to trust in God that everything would work out and she'd be able to go home to her family and friends, a stronger, more fulfilled and happier Ellie.

NINETEEN

'So, what do you think?' asked Sharon, watching Matt from across the table of the little diner. They'd come in for a late breakfast and to talk about their plan of action. 'Should we just head out to that address and see what we can find out?'

'It's all we have, really, isn't it?' Matt looked deflated and Sharon felt sorry for him.

'It's definitely worth a try. Who knows? Maybe Ellie's staying there. Maybe she *does* know someone here and that's why she was looking up their address.'

Matt sighed. 'It seems unlikely but we have to try something. I was so sure she'd respond to our texts. I'm beginning to wonder if maybe … if …'

'Don't say you're regretting coming over, Matt. I still think we've done the right thing. It's early days yet.'

'Actually, I was going to say I'm beginning to wonder if maybe Ellie was speaking the truth and if in fact this *is* all about me. Maybe she's just decided that I'm not the right guy for her and that's why she's staying away.'

Sharon shook her head. 'Matt, we've established that there's something bigger going on here. Please don't lose faith. Ellie loves you – I know it. And you know it too.'

Matt sighed. 'But it's hard to keep the faith when she hasn't even bothered to reply to our texts. It's been almost twenty-four hours since we sent her the first, saying we were here. I really can't believe she'd be so cold-hearted as to ignore that we've come all this way to find her.'

Sharon reached across and patted his hand. 'Let's not forget that Ellie seems to be going through some sort of crisis. She's probably not thinking straight.'

'You're right. I need to cop on to myself.'

'Well, that's not exactly what I —'

'No, really. I need to stop wallowing and do what I came here to do. You're right. Ellie loves me. I'm dead sure of that. So whatever she's going through or whatever she thinks she has to do over here, she can damn well do it with me on her tail.'

'That's the spirit.' Sharon smiled to herself. Matt was such a fabulous guy. Ellie was dead lucky to have him and she hoped that she'd realise it before it was too late.

He was willing to chase her halfway around the world at the moment, but if she kept pushing him away, he might eventually back off.

'So where do you think Caroline comes into all this, Sharon? Do you still think Ellie's disappearance has something to do with her?'

'Yes, I do. I could be completely wrong, but I think that Ellie had suppressed a lot of memories about Caroline and coming back here last week brought them all to the forefront of her mind. While we were here, I felt she was experiencing real grief for Caroline for the first time.'

Matt gave a low whistle. 'That's pretty heavy stuff. Are you saying she's never dealt with Caroline's death?'

Sharon thought about it. 'Not exactly. I think she dealt with it as much as she had to when it happened but I'm not sure she allowed herself *enough* time to grieve. She may have put certain thoughts and memories to the back of her mind because they were too painful for her to cope with at the time.'

'Jesus, Sharon. You sound like a grief counsellor. You're wasted in that hotel. You should be doing this for a living.'

Sharon blushed. 'Feck off, will you? I get enough slagging about that from Lara.'

'No, seriously. You're brilliant at this stuff. And it makes sense. If Ellie hasn't dealt properly with Caroline's death, maybe the memories of their holiday together over here were just too overwhelming.'

'Exactly!' said Sharon triumphantly, pushing her empty plate away. 'That's more or less what I was trying to say to Lara but she wasn't having any of it. She said I psychoanalysed things too much. Thank God somebody sees things the way I do.'

'Ellie's lucky to have you as a friend.'

Sharon blushed again. 'It works both ways. She'd do the same for me if the roles were reversed.'

'She probably would. She's a good one.'

'And you're not bad yourself, Matt. When Ellie comes to her senses, she'll realise that.'

Matt chuckled. 'We're a mutual admiration society! But, seriously, you really *are* a great friend to her. She told me how brilliant you were after Caroline died. You were the one who helped her through it the most.'

'We all did what we could. It was a terrible time. But thank God she met you soon after. You came along at exactly the right moment in her life.'

'We're good for each other, I think. And what about you, Sharon? Is there no love on the horizon for you?'

Sharon paused just long enough for Matt to become suspicious.

'Sharon Young! Come on, spill the beans.' He leaned across the table in anticipation.

'I – I don't know what you mean, Matt.' Maybe she should tell him about Mikey. She'd planned on telling Ellie anyway so what harm could it do?

'I, too, am a good judge of people, Sharon, and I can tell when you're holding back. Who is he? Do I know him?'

Sharon laughed. 'Well, actually, yes, you do. You know him pretty well.'

'Aha! It's Mikey, isn't it? Mikey Duggan!'

'How did you know?' Sharon was shocked that he'd guessed so easily. Maybe she hadn't been as discreet as she'd thought.

'The other night in your place – I could have cut the tension between you with a knife!'

'No way! I thought we were being very aloof with each other. I can't believe you sussed us out.'

Matt laughed. 'The fact you both looked a bit dishevelled when I came into the house was a bit of a giveaway. I meant to ask you about it but, with everything else going on, it went clean out of my mind.'

Sharon was mortified. 'Jesus, were we that obvious?'

'Yep! Totally. But why is it a secret? Does Ellie know?'

'Of course not. She's the reason we're keeping it to ourselves for now. You know how protective she is about Mikey – we were just afraid that she'd take it badly since I'm six years older than him.'

'Sharon, she'd be delighted. Her best friend and her brother – she couldn't wish for a better pairing.'

'Well, I'd planned on telling her while we were over here but I didn't find the right time. But I will. When we find her and sort her out, I'm not going to hide it any more.'

'That's good. And how long has it been going on?'

'Four and a half months.' Sharon's heart soared when she thought of her boyfriend. 'We're like soulmates, Matt. We just get each other and it feels right. Do you know what I mean?'

Matt sighed. 'Of course. That's how it is with me and Ellie. I'm just praying she still feels it because I certainly do.'

'She does, Matt. Come on, let's get going. If we catch a bus soon we can be at that house in Queens in half an hour. Let's start trying to put this puzzle together and get Ellie back where she belongs.'

○

'Well, here we are,' said Matt, pointing to number thirty-three but not going too close. 'What now?'

'Knock on the door and ask if they know Ellie?' Sharon looked unsure.

Matt sucked in his breath. 'It seemed like a good idea in theory, didn't it? But I can't imagine walking up to the house now and asking.'

Sharon sighed. 'Me neither. So what *are* we going to do?'

'Well, since we've come all this way, why don't we just hang around for a bit and see if there's any sign of Ellie?' It was a long shot and he knew it. Ellie could have been looking up that address for any amount of reasons. It didn't mean she would come here. But something told him that this house held the key to Ellie's behaviour.

'If we're going to hang around,' said Sharon, 'at least let's take out a map and try not to look so suspicious.'

Matt leaned against the wall of the house opposite and took a map from his pocket. He pretended to study it but instead he stared across the road at the house. It was strange to see it in real life after Google Earth. He wasn't sure what he'd expected but he felt a little disappointed. A little part of him had hoped it would lead him straight to Ellie, yet it seemed he'd have to do a bit more work to find her.

'This is hopeless, Sharon. We really didn't think it through, did we?'

Sharon looked thoughtful. 'No. But maybe our first instincts were right. Why don't we just go across there and knock on the door? What do we have to lose?'

'Do you think so?' Matt felt rattled. He wasn't sure why, maybe he was afraid he was going to hear something he wouldn't like.

'Yes, definitely.' Sharon was decisive. She grabbed the map from him and marched across the road.

That was when the side gate swung open and a little girl raced out, squealing with delight, as a man ran after her and swept her up in his arms. She laughed as he tickled her and begged him to put her down.

'Shit,' whispered Matt. 'Let's just walk past.'

'Come on, Matt. There's no turning back now.' Sharon pushed him forward.

Just then, the child turned in their direction as she ran from her father, laughing her little head off.

Matt looked at her face and froze. He turned to Sharon. It was obvious she was thinking the same.

'Hey, can I help you with anything?'

Matt was startled, not only because the guy had obviously seen them watching the house but because he spoke with a thick Cork accent. It somehow seemed out of place in this very American neighbourhood.

He spoke again: 'Are you okay? Are you looking for someone?'

Matt quickly composed himself and whipped the map out of Sharon's hand. 'Sorry, I think we're in the wrong place altogether. We were looking for number thirty-three but I think we have the wrong street.'

'Ah! A fellow Irishman. Are you on holidays?'

'I, em, yes. We're over here for a few days and were just looking up a friend.'

'What street are you looking for?' he asked, walking over to peer at the map with Matt. 'These streets can be like a maze if you don't know them.'

Sharon eventually spoke: 'It's … em … it's this one here … Topaz Street.' She pointed at the map and tried to sound convincing.

'Oh, you're not too far away. Just go to the end of this

road and take a left, keep going for a few hundred metres and swing a right. That should get you there.'

'Thanks very much,' said Sharon. 'We appreciate your help.'

'Not at all,' said the guy, swinging his daughter over his shoulders, much to her delight. 'I hope you enjoy your stay.'

The two walked in silence until they rounded the corner and were well out of sight of the house.

Sharon looked at Matt. 'What was that?'

'I … I'm not sure. What did you think?'

'The child?' She watched him carefully.

Matt leaned against a wall to steady himself. He didn't want to say the words. 'Did you think that she … that she was …'

Sharon nodded. 'The image! But it doesn't make sense.'

'Let's get out of here,' said Matt, beginning to walk quickly down the street. 'She was about three, do you think?'

'I'd say so. But, Matt, it couldn't be … there's no way …'

Matt was close to tears. 'We can't deny what we saw, Sharon. I'd love to think it's a coincidence but there's no denying that the little girl we just saw is the spitting image of Ellie.'

○

Ellie ducked into a garden and hid behind the wall as Matt and Sharon passed by. Jesus! What the hell were they doing here and how had they found this address? She'd taken the letter with her and hadn't told anyone about it.

Ellie had come out to the house today with the intention once again of knocking on the door and introducing herself, but when she'd rounded the corner, Matt and Sharon had been standing outside, talking to the dad. The sight of her fiancé and her best friend had sent her into a spin. She'd been shocked to see them, scared of them seeing her, but most of all she'd felt a pain in her heart to see two of the people who were closest to her within touching distance.

She shivered as the cold wind whipped across her face. She watched them walking back towards the bus stop. She pulled the collar of her coat up tightly around her neck and began to walk in the opposite direction.

Everything was getting muddled in her head as she wandered aimlessly through the streets. She didn't even notice the rain beginning to fall and her hair getting soaked. She didn't care. It was all too complicated and she wasn't sure she had the drive or the energy to follow things through. Maybe she should just go home and forget the whole thing. But that wasn't really an option. She'd come with a mission in mind and she wasn't going to leave until it was sorted. Matt and Sharon being there made things a bit more difficult but she would simply have to find a way of getting around it.

All of a sudden she realised she was wet through. Luckily her walk had led her down a busy street where there were plenty of coffee shops. She'd go into one and get warm before heading back to the hotel. She had to think logically because she was in danger of letting her emotions take over and that was when things would start to unravel.

TWENTY

Tears stung Lara's eyes as she wheeled the pram through the gates of the Botanic Gardens. She hated arguing with Peter but sometimes he made her so mad. Was he really so blind as to think that everything was fine? Couldn't he see she was crumbling before his very eyes? *Can you bring my two good suits to the dry-cleaner's?* he'd said. *Can you pop into the bank and lodge that cheque I left out on the counter? Can you make sure my blue shirt is ironed for tomorrow night?* She was just sick of it! While he was out making a career for himself, being respected and looked up to, she was at home in her mangy tracksuit, cleaning toilets and making herself available to run his errands. Well, he might be happy with that traditional domestic set-up but she absolutely hated it.

The park was filled with mothers and young children. Women walked side by side while their children ran ahead, squealing with delight at being allowed some freedom and others, like herself, wheeled their youngsters in buggies. But there was one big difference – everyone *else* looked happy.

She peeped over the top of the buggy to see if Ethan was enjoying his stroll and was delighted to see he'd almost dropped off to sleep. Thank God for that. She wasn't in the humour for running around with him, and she knew that as soon as she stopped walking, he'd want out of the buggy. She began to relax a little. The park was beautiful at this time of year and the spectacular array of colours from the emerging pansies and crocuses, as well as the many other early spring blooms, made her heart feel a little lighter.

She was so lucky to have such a beautiful park on her doorstep and had spent many happy hours there as a child. *She* was once the child running ahead, squealing with delight, and had then become the teenager, who'd felt grown-up to be allowed go to the park with her friends. It was hard for her to believe that she was now the mother, creating the next generation of park-goers.

When she was sure Ethan was sound asleep, she headed for one of the benches so that she could take the weight off her feet. She sat down and swung the buggy around to look

at her son. He was adorable. The fringe of blond hair was stuck to his head with sweat from his anorak and his head was tilted to the side. Little bubbles formed on his lips as he breathed and his pudgy cheeks were glowing from the fresh air.

Lara sighed. She wished she could be content as a mother. It was painful to admit it but being with Ethan wasn't enough. She felt like a real failure even thinking that way but it didn't mean she didn't love him. She loved him with a love she'd never thought she would be capable of. But she knew she'd be a better mother for having something else in her life. If she was fulfilling her own career ambitions, she'd be more content to spend time with him. As things stood, she was beginning to resent the endless hours of nothing but him.

She'd tried to broach the subject with Peter on a number of occasions. She'd gently hinted at him cutting back his hours in work so that she'd have more time to pursue her own career. 'But haven't you got your freelance stuff?' he'd replied. 'Isn't it great the way you can fit it in around being at home with Ethan?' It wasn't that he was being mean or selfish – he just didn't understand.

Ethan shifted a little in his buggy and opened his eyes a slit. 'Shush, baby, go back to sleep,' Lara whispered into his ear while rocking the buggy. She couldn't let her peace be interrupted just yet. Ellie probably had the right idea, disappearing in New York and dodging a life of being shackled to the kitchen sink.

She immediately felt guilty. God, she was becoming unbearably cynical. Ellie was hardly living it up. She must be going through hell. Imagine having your perfect life torn to shreds like that. She might have made the decision to cancel the wedding but she'd be upset about it. Well, at least Sharon and Matt were over there now. Hopefully they'd find her and bring her home.

How romantic it was that Matt had travelled thousands of miles to bring his love home for their wedding. He hadn't doubted Ellie's love for him. Lara wasn't usually into the soppy stuff but perhaps that was exactly what she and Peter needed – a bit of romance. It suddenly dawned on her that maybe she should take more control of her situation at home. She was waiting for Peter to make some sort of gesture but why did it have to be him? Why couldn't *she* be the one to make changes? Why couldn't *she* inject a bit of excitement into their relationship? She'd been well able to take charge of a roomful of men when she was working for the paper, so why not take charge now at home and spice things up a little? Maybe if she got the spark back into their relationship, Peter would be more willing to listen to her gripes.

There was no time like the present. The seed of an idea was growing in her mind and she was going to take action. She'd pop into Eurospar on the way home and pick up a few bits for dinner. She'd dust off the candles that hadn't seen much use lately and set the table nicely for the two of them to have a romantic meal. She'd make sure Ethan was in bed early so that they could have a bit of time on their own. God, it felt good to have a purpose. It was just a simple thing but it meant she was taking steps to get her life back within her control.

She loved Peter. That had never been in doubt. They had settled into a mundane rut that she hated but it hadn't changed how she felt about him. And tonight she was going to show it. She'd make him remember what it had been like when it was just the two of them. She might even disconnect the Sky box so he couldn't watch his beloved sport. She was really warming to the plan.

'Come on, Ethan,' she whispered to her son. 'We've got to get home and organise things. Mammy and Daddy are going to have some grown-up time and you're going to be the best little boy and stay asleep all night.'

Ethan stirred again and turned his head to the other side. God, was that a smile on his lips? If Ellie was here, she'd say it was a sign. Usually Lara ridiculed Ellie and her theories about signs but on this occasion she was going to embrace it. It was a sign that things were looking up. Things were going to get better – she just knew it. As she left the park, she felt like a different person. Her mother had always said that the Botanic Gardens had magic about them, and for the first time in her life, Lara was thinking she might have been right.

◎

'You really do make the best bolognese, love,' said Andy, pushing his chair out from the table and stretching. 'I'm fit to burst after that.'

Jean smiled at her husband as she began to clear away the plates. 'I'm glad you liked it. I wasn't too hungry myself, to be honest.'

'Jean, love, you've got to eat. We're all worried about Ellie but we'll be no good to her when she comes home if we make ourselves sick.'

'I know, Andy. But I can't help worrying. I wonder if Matt and Sharon have seen her yet.'

'I'm sure they'll let us know as soon as they have.' Andy stood up and took the plates from his wife. 'Why don't you go out for a walk and blow away the cobwebs? I'll clean up here. The fresh air will do you good.'

'That's not a bad idea,' said Jean. 'I'll just pop upstairs, get myself ready and head out for half an hour.'

Upstairs in the little bathroom, she looked at herself in the mirror. It seemed she'd aged in this last week. Well, if she was honest with herself, she'd aged a lot since Caroline's death. The happenings of the last few years had taken their toll on her. She'd always prided herself on being quite a good-looking woman, despite her advancing years, but she hadn't been caring for herself as she should. She hadn't had her greys done in about three months and her hair was wiry and dull. She hadn't even been bothering to put on any makeup.

She'd promised herself that Ellie's wedding would mark a change in her own life. She'd bought a whole lot of new makeup for the big day and she'd planned on getting Ellie to give her a few lessons on how to put it on properly. Her body was in pretty good shape for a sixty-three-year-old, but she needed someone to tell her how to make the most of her figure. Luckily her friend Josephine was a personal shopper in Debenhams and was brilliant at her job. She'd promised to take her in hand before the wedding and find her something drop-dead gorgeous that would make her feel a million dollars.

Jean blinked away the tears. She probably wouldn't be bothered with any of that if the wedding didn't go ahead. What would be the point? But she wasn't one to wallow so she threw some cold water over her face in an effort to perk herself up. She hated negativity and liked to think positive thoughts. She believed that you get back what you put out so she was going to put out some positive vibes and hope for the best. She pulled the scraggy ends of her hair into a ponytail and was ready to go.

"Bye, love. I won't be long.' Andy was already snoozing in his armchair and didn't even wake when she called into him. She'd been thinking of paying Caroline a visit all week and hadn't been able to bring herself to do it but now seemed the perfect time.

Glasnevin Cemetery was just ten minutes' walk from the house. She'd found that very comforting in the early days after Caroline's death. She'd found herself wandering down to the grave almost every day. It had made her feel close to her daughter and had given her time to think about things and come to terms with what had happened.

She pulled the cream mohair scarf that Ellie had bought her for her birthday last year up around her neck to fend off the cool breeze. Tears sprang to her eyes at the thought of her daughter alone in New York. She hoped to God she was okay and that Matt and Sharon would bring her home soon.

She'd forgotten her gloves and her hands were going numb with the cold. Thank God she was already at the gates of the cemetery. She'd pick up a few yellow freesias in the shop just inside the gates. They'd been Caroline's favourites. She'd developed a love of gardening when she was very young and had spent many happy hours helping her father to plant and nurture the flowers he prided himself on. Caroline had got such a kick from people saying the Duggans had the prettiest garden on the estate.

Glasnevin Cemetery was enormous and it took her a further ten minutes to get to Caroline's grave. In comparison with the others around, it was fresh and cared for. It always troubled Jean to see the neglected ones. She'd often walk around reading the headstones and wonder why their loved ones didn't visit. Had too much time elapsed and they'd forgotten or had everyone belonging to that person passed on? Either way, it was a depressing thought.

Placing a plastic bag she'd brought with her on the ground, she knelt beside Caroline's grave. She neatly arranged the freesias just under the headstone and tidied away the fading flowers and plants that had been left there recently by other visitors. When she was happy with how it looked, she blessed herself, closed her eyes and said a silent prayer. Then she glanced around to see if there were any other visitors nearby. Satisfied she was alone, she began her usual chat with her daughter.

'Caroline love, you'll never guess what's happened now. Honestly, just when I thought things were looking up, everything has come crashing down around me again. That bloody inconsiderate sister of yours has only gone and disappeared in New York. She says she doesn't want to get married any more and has left us to cancel everything. Can you imagine it? Just a few weeks to go and she hits us with this. One part of me wants to get it all cancelled and be done with it but the other part wants to believe it will still work out. And Matt, God love him, he's gone off to New York with Sharon to try to find her. He's determined to bring her home for the wedding. He says he knows she loves him and he's not coming home without her. But me – I'm afraid to allow myself to hope.'

A couple walking hand in hand passed by and Jean bowed her head as if in prayer. It seemed perfectly logical to her that she'd talk to her daughter, but others might think she was mad. As soon as they were out of earshot, she continued: 'You see, Caroline, hope scares me. If I don't have hope, I don't get my dreams dashed. I know that sounds awful and depressing but it's how I feel. Hope didn't do me any good the day you died, did it? No amount of hope saved you. I'm so scared that if I hope Ellie will come home and that the wedding will go ahead, I'll be let down again. Please, sweetheart, you've got to help us. I know you're up there watching over us. Can you please look after Ellie, the way she looked after all of us after you died? Whatever she decides to do, please just let her be okay.'

She was interrupted again by another passer-by. The man obviously worked there as he was pushing a wheelbarrow and had on those green wellies that go up to your thighs. He wore a soft cap on his head that he tipped when he saw Jean. 'Cold one today, isn't it?'

Jean nodded politely. 'It certainly is. At least it's not raining.'

'Let's hope it stays that way.' He stopped briefly to rebalance the load of wood he had in his barrow. He gave her a toothy grin before heading off. 'And sure we have to have hope, haven't we?'

We have to have hope. Jean was rooted to the spot. Like Ellie, she believed in signs and they didn't come much clearer than that. She felt buoyed up all of a sudden. She needed to stay positive and believe things would work out. She'd had some serious knocks in her life but Ellie's disappearance was just a temporary thing and would be resolved very soon. She needed to believe it.

She pulled herself up from her knees and put the dead plants and flowers into the plastic bag. She'd drop them in the bin at the entrance. She brushed down her coat and had one last look at her daughter's grave. 'Thanks, love. I knew you'd listen.'

TWENTY-ONE

'Matt, talk to me. Are you okay?' Sharon was concerned about him. He hadn't said a word since they'd left the house. They'd been silent on the bus journey into Manhattan, and when she'd seen how pale he was, she'd dragged him into the nearest coffee shop as soon as they'd got off.

'Come on, Matt. You're going to have to talk about it at some stage. And it may not be what we think.'

He looked at her with defeated eyes. 'Did you see her, Sharon? Did you see that child? Do you honestly think there's nothing in it?'

Sharon shoved the double-shot espresso towards him and watched him carefully. 'She's the image of Ellie, all right, but let's just look at the facts. Do you actually think she might be Ellie's child? How on earth could Ellie have gone through a pregnancy without any of us knowing? The child looked to be between three and four and I can't remember a time back then when I didn't see Ellie almost every day.'

'But the address, seeing the child, Ellie's erratic behaviour – when I add everything up, I can come up with only one answer.'

Sharon wished she could say something to allay Matt's fears but she couldn't think of a single thing. Maybe they were jumping to a very big conclusion here yet everything seemed to be pointing to that child being Ellie's.

Matt continued: 'The guy even had a Cork accent. I'm trying very hard to find something to contradict my theory but the pieces keep clicking into place.'

'So what are we going to do?' Sharon took a big gulp of her coffee. 'Do we text Ellie, tell her we know about the child and see how she reacts, or should we go back to the house again?'

Matt shook his head. 'I definitely won't be going back to the house – well, not without Ellie. I mean, what would we say? We could hardly bulldoze our way in and ask if the child is theirs or if Ellie is the mother! Even if we're right, we just don't know enough about the circumstances.'

'We really need Ellie to talk to us.' Even the thought of Ellie having gone through something so huge without her knowing was upsetting Sharon. 'But maybe we should go to the house again and see if we notice anything. Maybe Ellie *is* staying there – or she might be going to visit.'

'No!' Matt was adamant. 'Let's do this properly. If this is what we think it is, there've been too many lies already. We should try to ring Ellie or text her and tell her she needs to get in touch with us. I want to hear her side of the story.'

Sharon looked at Matt's anxious face. 'But would it make a difference?'

'Would what make a difference?'

'If Ellie had a child, would it make a difference to how you feel about her?' She bit her lip as she watched Matt thinking.

'It would be a shock, Sharon, I can't deny that. It would mean she hasn't been honest with me about stuff, that she didn't trust me enough to share something so important with me.'

'But?' Sharon could tell Matt had more to say.

'But I love her, Sharon. I'm in love with Ellie, and no child, no past secret, can change that. If the child *is* hers, it's something that happened before I met her. I can't say I'm not upset that she didn't trust me enough to tell me, but to answer your question simply, no, it wouldn't make a difference.'

Sharon was relieved. 'You have no idea how happy I am to hear you say that. But let's not get ahead of ourselves. We could be still wrong.'

'We could, but I doubt it. Well, there's no time like the present. Will I send her a text now? With a bit of luck, we could be arranging to meet her later today. If she realises we know, she's bound to want to talk.'

'Yes, go on, send it,' said Sharon, excited at the prospect of finally getting to the bottom of what had been going on. 'Tell her we're still here and still waiting to see her. Tell her that we know about the child and we want to be there for her. That should be enough to get her to reply.'

'Right, here goes.' Sharon watched as Matt typed words that were probably some of the most important he'd ever say to Ellie. They were letting her know he understood. They were letting her know he'd support her. They were letting her know he cared.

'Now let's go and get some fresh air.' Matt was on his feet. 'We'll drive ourselves mad if we sit around waiting for her to answer.'

'Brooklyn Bridge?' suggested Sharon. 'We didn't go there last weekend and I believe it's a lovely walk.'

'Brooklyn Bridge it is. As far as I can remember, it's just a quick subway ride there, and then we can walk the whole way across. Maybe we'll have something to eat in Brooklyn. There are some gorgeous little restaurants with delicious, locally sourced food.'

'Perfect.' Sharon followed him outside. 'And if Ellie rings and wants to meet, we can just hop in a taxi and get back quickly.'

Twenty minutes later they were enjoying the scenery from the famous bridge as they made their way across it. There was an air of excitement as children squealed and pointed out the landmarks, and the tinkling of bells as cyclists passed created a lovely, happy atmosphere. Sharon loved the cut and thrust of the city, but this was exactly what they needed now – a long, straight walk, without negotiating maps, allowing them time to get their thoughts together. They were good friends and were comfortable enough in each other's company not to feel the need to fill the silence with inane chatter.

She was glad of the wonderful views to take her mind off Ellie for a bit. The iconic Statue of Liberty could be seen in the distance over to the right, and Sharon felt in awe. She'd seen it on the telly so many times but to see it in reality was something special. They were still a distance away from it and Sharon was in no doubt that it would be even more amazing close up. That was another thing the girls hadn't fitted into their few days: their planned boat cruise to Ellis Island, taking in the statue. Maybe if things worked out in the next few days, she could do the trip herself, giving Matt and Ellie time to sort things out on their own.

She glanced at Matt and felt a huge rush of affection for him. She admired how he'd handled everything, right from the moment he'd realised Ellie hadn't come home. He'd never faltered in his belief that Ellie loved him and even now, with the new turn of events, he still remained strong and focused with one thing in mind – to get her back.

'Bloody cold, isn't it?' said Matt, pulling his collar up tighter around his neck. 'I can't believe I didn't bring gloves. My hands are like blocks of ice!'

'It's very exposed out here.'

Matt blew on his fingers. 'Gorgeous view, though, isn't it?'

'It's supposed to be even better at night,' said Sharon.

They went quiet again.

'Are you hungry?' Matt was first to break the silence.

'Not really. You?'

Matt stopped dead and leaned on the railings. 'Bloody hell, Sharon. What are we like? Why are we trying to take our minds off Ellie? I don't know about you but I can't think of anything else.'

Sharon grinned. 'Me neither. I'm so glad you said that.'

Matt checked his phone again. 'Still nothing. Do you think she's ignoring us or just not checking her messages?'

'I honestly don't know, Matt. Ellie isn't the type to ignore us, though. I'm sure she'd get in touch if she knew we were here. Come on. I don't think either of us really wants to go to Brooklyn for dinner, do we?'

'I was thinking exactly the same,' said Matt, smiling. 'Let's head back to the hotel in case she gets in touch. I wouldn't say no to another Waldorf salad.'

'That's the best plan I've heard all day.' Sharon was glad that Matt seemed more upbeat. He'd been so determined to find Ellie that she'd hate to see him waning now. She hoped Ellie would be in touch soon. Sharon was dying to get some answers. Nothing made sense to her. Everything was pointing at Ellie having had a baby but Sharon couldn't think how she would have hidden it from her. And they were best friends. *Why* would she have hidden it? No, they must be missing something. Well, whatever it was, hopefully they'd find out soon and they could all get their lives back on track.

○

Ellie sat on a park bench lost in thought. Things were spiralling out of control and she wasn't sure how to pull them back. A few days ago, everything had seemed so straightforward and simple. She'd decided to stay in New York because she wasn't getting married any more and didn't want to go home. And then she'd remembered the letter and realised it was the perfect opportunity to follow up on it. It had come into her hands at that particular time for a reason – she was sure of it. It was her destiny to do something about it.

She'd known everyone at home would be worried about her, but she hadn't banked on Matt and Sharon coming over. That had thrown her. She felt a pang of excitement at the thought that her fiancé and best friend were so close by, but she'd promised herself she would complete her mission alone, and that was exactly what she was going to do.

She'd almost died when she'd seen them at the house earlier. How had they got that address? And what did they know about it? None of it made any sense.

Her thoughts were interrupted by a woman sitting down beside her on the bench. She had with her a shopping trolley that was piled high with a variety of items which Ellie suspected were her worldly possessions.

'Wanna share?' said the woman, holding out half a sandwich to Ellie.

Ellie balked at the sight of the fingerless gloves and dirty hands. 'Eh, no, thank you. I've just eaten.'

'Sure.' The woman began to eat slowly and methodically. 'Don't like to eat too fast cos it'll be gone. Can't say when I'll get another.'

Ellie wanted to get up and leave – the woman gave off a powerful stench – but was afraid it would look rude.

She continued: 'Not from around these parts, are ya?'

'I, em, no. I'm from Ireland.'

'Ah, an Irish *cailín*. My mother's grandmother was Irish. So what brings you here? On holidays, are ya?'

'Yes,' said Ellie. 'Sort of.'

'But you're sittin' here all on your lonesome. Just like me!'

'Oh, I've just come out for a bit of fresh air. I'm meeting my friends in a minute.'

The woman finished her sandwich and stood up. 'Well, just you make sure you keep your friends close and don't end up a lonely old soul like me.'

Ellie couldn't find the words to answer. She'd certainly make sure it didn't happen to her but, right now, she had other priorities. She watched the old woman's crooked frame as she slowly made her way across the park.

Maybe it was a sign that she should stop procrastinating. Her life back home wouldn't wait indefinitely for her to get her act together. A chill ran down Ellie's spine. She needed to get moving. She knew what she had to do.

TWENTY-TWO

'Hi there. Let me guess – a Cinnamon Latte?'

Ellie was thrown by Ann's memory. She hadn't expected her to remember her face, let alone her order.

'And still you're in a world of your own.'

'Oh, em, yes, sorry. How can you … I mean, how did you remember?'

'I have a good head for this sort of thing, honey. And, besides, my husband is Irish so I never forget an Irish accent. Do you live around here or are you on holidays?'

'I'm just here for, em … I'm on business. I won't be around for much longer. I have meetings – yes, lots of meetings.' Oh, God, she needed to shut up. Every word that came out of her mouth made her sound more stupid. She needed to talk to this woman and she wanted to make a good impression.

'So, you're a busy lady,' said Ann, handing over her change. 'Well, enjoy your drink – nice to see you again.'

'Thanks, and you too.' Ellie took her cup from the end of the counter and skulked off to the back of the shop where she managed to get the same table as last time. She hung her jacket on the back of the chair and gratefully wrapped her cold hands around the steaming cup.

As Ann was busy with customers, Ellie took the letter out of her pocket and smoothed it on the table. A ball of excitement rose in her stomach when she realised that this could be the last time she'd read the letter before showing it to Ann and maybe finding out some things about her sister that she'd never known.

'Would you like another of those?'

Ellie almost jumped out of her skin when she saw Ann hovering over her, wiping down the empty tables. Ellie quickly refolded the letter and stuck it into her jacket, praying she hadn't noticed it. 'I'm still nursing this one, thanks. It's delicious.'

'So where in Ireland are you from? My husband is from Cork – I actually lived over there with him for a while.'

Ellie felt a bubble of excitement. This could be an opener for the conversation she needed to have. 'I was born and bred in Dublin, but Cork is gorgeous. I used to visit there a lot with my family when I was little. Why did you leave? Did you not like it?'

Ann checked over her shoulder to make sure there were no customers in the queue. 'West Cork is one of the most beautiful places on earth, especially in the fall. I really loved it, but all my family are over here and I guess I was feeling homesick.'

'Ah, I can imagine. I've never lived anywhere except Ireland and I'm always glad to get home after a holiday.' Ellie was surprised to feel a pang as she said the words. She really was missing home. It had only been a week but the longest week of her life. She missed her family and friends. She missed the security of her routine. She missed Matt.

'Me too,' said Ann, smiling. 'I settled into life in Cork pretty well and began to look on it as home, but when the little one came along, I missed having my own family around.'

Ellie could hardly breathe. She wanted to probe a bit more. 'You have a child?'

'Yes, a little girl. She's three and a half now, but we moved back here when she was just a few months old.'

'She was born in Ireland?'

'Yep. She sure was. She's our little princess. We waited so long to have her, we can barely believe we've been so lucky.'

This was it. It was the perfect time for Ellie to speak up. She felt inside her jacket and rested her hand on the letter. 'Ann, I have something to . . .'

'Uh-oh! I'd better get back to work.' Ann pointed to

the counter where a queue was building. 'I'm due a break shortly, though, so if you're still here, we can continue our chat, if you like. I didn't catch your name?'

'El— Eleanora. Eleanora is my name.' For fuck's sake. Bloody Eleanora! She'd almost said 'Ellie' but panicked and stopped herself. She was such an eejit.

When she saw the queue of customers and realised Ann would be busy for a while, she decided to check her messages. It was funny – at home, she'd be lost without her mobile. It was like her third hand. It was always on and never more than a few feet away from her. But here she'd got used to not using it. She was keeping it off most of the time, switching it on briefly for messages from home.

The screen pinged to life and the familiar beeps indicated more messages. She scrolled through them to find one from Matt. She was curious to see if he'd mention the house. Ah, there it was:

Ellie, I really need you to get in touch. You'll know by now we're here and we just want to talk to you. We want to help you. We know about the child. Ring me please. Love, Matt xx

Holy fuck! He knows about the child! What does he know? She rubbed her eyes and read the text again. It seemed pretty clear. She'd definitely have to get in touch with them now because she didn't want them wading in and saying something to Ann and her family before she'd had the chance herself. God, what a bloody mess!

'Here you go, hon.' Ellie jumped as Ann sat down opposite her and pushed another coffee towards her. 'I reckon yours is pretty cold by now.'

'Sorry, Ann. I …I've had a phone call and have to run.'

'Aw, that's a pity, hon. But no problem. It was nice talking to you. Pop in again if you're around.'

Ellie thought she'd never get out of the place. Shit, shit, shit! She hurried down the road until her legs were like jelly and she couldn't catch her breath. She leaned against a wall and gulped in lungfuls of air.

What was it that the woman in the park had said? Keep your friends close. Now her friends were a little too close and it was quite possible that her carefully laid plans would come undone before her eyes. She needed to get the situation under control. It was time to talk to Sharon and Matt.

○

Matt turned the dial to ice cold and winced as the water sluiced over his body. He loved to do that at the end of a shower. It was supposed to be good for mind, body and soul. It was certainly good for waking him up, that was for sure. He lasted about ten seconds before switching it off and grabbing a fluffy bath towel from the heated rail. He dried himself and wrapped the towel around his waist before padding into the bedroom.

He glanced at his mobile for about the hundredth time, then threw himself onto the bed. It looked like another day was going to pass without any contact from Ellie. It was soul-destroying. He wasn't sure what their next move should be. It was hard to believe they'd arrived only yesterday afternoon. Time was dragging and Matt wished he had a magic wand to sort everything out.

He was glad now that he hadn't come alone. It was great having Sharon with him. They'd always got on well and had grown even closer in the last couple of days. But they also needed a bit of time apart. Sharon wanted to ring Mikey and Matt wanted to be alone with his thoughts. They'd had a bite to eat in the restaurant and had then gone to their own rooms. They were going to meet a bit later in the bar for a nightcap before an early night. They were mentally exhausted and badly in need of a decent night's sleep.

He'd rung Jean before his shower to update her on things but hadn't said anything about the child. That wasn't his story to tell. He'd sensed she was very down and he'd tried to lift her spirits, to assure her they'd find Ellie. But it had fallen on deaf ears. She'd been devastated to hear that Ellie wasn't answering their texts. She hadn't been answering the ones from home either, but Jean had been sure that once she knew Matt and Sharon were over there, she'd arrange to meet them.

He hated not being able to send any good news home. He felt he'd failed somehow. He really liked Jean and Andy and he wanted them to see him as the heroic son-in-law who'd go to any lengths to ensure the well-being of their daughter. But as time ticked away, he feared that the title 'son-in-law' was slipping through his fingers.

He was drifting into sleep when the shrill ringtone of his phone woke him with a jolt. Shit! He'd lost track of time. Sharon was probably waiting in the bar.

'Hiya, Sharon. Sorry – I'll be down in –'

'Hello, Matt.'

He jumped off the bed at the sound of her voice. 'Ellie! Oh, Ellie! Thank God. Are you okay? Where are you? We've all been so worried.'

'I'm fine, Matt. And I'm really sorry about everything. You must hate me but –'

'Hate you? God, Ellie. Why do you think I came over here? I love you. Everything's going to be all right. I promise. We'll work it out.' Matt slumped down on the bed, cradling the phone to his ear. He was so happy just to hear her voice.

'Matt,' she said gently. 'I love you too but nothing's changed. I still don't want to get married.'

His heart sank, but he quickly recovered. 'It's okay, Ellie. I know you've had a lot to cope with and I'm sorry I haven't been there for you. I know you've been dealing with memories of Caroline and I should have been more sensitive. And now this …'

'It's not your fault, Matt. Believe me, none of this is down to you. Look, I'm really touched that you and Sharon came all the way over here, and I want to meet you and fill you in on everything, but you need to back off for a day or two until I'm ready. There's something I have to do first.'

'The child?'

There was silence for a few seconds, then Ellie spoke: 'Yes, the child. I don't know how you know, and I want to talk to you properly about it but let's leave it until we meet.'

Matt felt excited. He knew that if he could just see Ellie, if he could hold her in his arms and let her feel the love they shared, she'd realise she didn't need to run away. 'Whatever you want, Ellie. I'm here for you and so is Sharon. She'll be thrilled you rang.'

'Thanks, Matt. Tell her I'll see her in a day or two. I'll keep in touch.'

Matt blinked away the tears. 'And … and I know you don't really want to talk to me about it yet, Ellie, but I'm here if you need support. You don't have to go through this on your own.'

'I'm not on my own, Matt. Caroline's with me. I hadn't a clue about all this until a few weeks ago so I can't help thinking she's up there, feeding me bits of information and egging me on. Now I know about it, I can't leave it at that. I have to follow things up.'

Matt was really confused now. How could Ellie only

have found out about it a few weeks ago? What was she talking about?

Ellie was still talking. 'And I look forward to telling you all if it goes well. Keep your fingers crossed for me.'

'I will, but—'

'Night, Matt. We'll talk again soon.'

Jesus! So *that* was what it was! The child was Caroline's. Why on earth hadn't they thought of it? By all accounts, Caroline had been the image of Ellie – certainly it was difficult to tell them apart in all the family pictures dotted around the Duggan house. Wait until he told Sharon.

Ellie had said she still didn't want to get married but he was refusing to believe it. He knew her inside out. And she'd just said she loved him, for God's sake! She'd had a lot to deal with lately, God love her. And he should have been more attentive. She'd just found out she had a niece that she hadn't known about. That must have been the thing that tipped her over the edge, after the stress of the wedding plans and the memories of Caroline haunting her.

He felt elated as he slipped on his jeans and pulled a lemon Hollister T-shirt from his case. He couldn't wait to get down to the bar to tell Sharon. She'd be over the moon. And maybe, if things worked out, he and Ellie might even be able to grab a romantic day or two before heading home. He was sure Sharon would be delighted to give them a bit of space. He could scarcely believe that the day he'd written off not half an hour ago was turning out to be one of the best ever.

TWENTY-THREE

Jean felt exhausted as she trudged back from the shops weighed down with bags of groceries. Thank God she was almost home because the sweat was dripping off her. She'd hoped Andy would bring her for a proper grocery shopping at Tesco but he'd stayed in bed, claiming he was sick. Bloody men! As if she didn't have enough to contend with. But she had to concede that it was unlike him to make a fuss. *She* was the one more likely to look for sympathy if she was ill. Still, it was Saturday and there were lots of things to be done around the house so she could have managed without having to look after him as well.

She rounded the corner and was glad she was only minutes away from the house. The plastic bags of groceries were stretched to the limit and she feared one would break if she didn't get home soon. Once she was in, she'd make herself a nice cup of tea after she'd unpacked the shopping. She had last night's double episode of *Coronation Street* to catch up on and it would be the perfect thing to take her mind off Ellie.

'Howareya, Jean? Are you all set for the big day? Not long to go now.'

'Not too long at all, Frannie. It's busy busy busy.' Jean continued walking, hoping Frances O'Malley would see she hadn't time for a chat. The woman meant well but she lived on her own and thrived on a bit of gossip. If she got wind that Ellie wanted to cancel the wedding, everyone would know about it by the end of the day. But the nosy neighbour wasn't going to let her off that easily.

'Here, let me take some of those bags. More wedding shopping, is it?'

Bloody cheek! 'No, Frannie. Just a few groceries. Now, if you don't mind ...'

'And how's Ellie doing? Is she getting excited? Are the nerves kicking in yet?'

Holy Mother of God! She had to get rid of this woman. 'She ... she hasn't had much time to get excited or nervous because she's been working so hard.'

'Ah, but I bet you can't wait for the big day. Why

don't you stick the kettle on and you can tell me about the plans?'

'Frannie, I'd love to but I have so much to do. Maybe another time.' She got to her front gate and rooted in her pocket for her key.

Frannie sniffed, clearly put out. 'No bother, Jean. I'll leave you to it so. And thanks for the *evening* invitation. I'll be there with one of the girls. Do you have many going to the *full* affair?'

'Mostly just family and a few close friends,' said Jean, lying through her teeth. 'And I'm glad you can make it to the reception. I'll tell Ellie – she'll be delighted.'

'Ah, she's a lovely girl, that Ellie. Well, let me know when you have time for that cup of tea and chat.'

Jean breathed a sigh of relief as Frannie turned to leave. She hadn't wanted to be rude but she just needed a bit of time to herself. But her relief was short-lived when, suddenly, she heard a snap. She heard herself give a low scream as her shopping spilled onto the driveway. Feck!

'Ah, Jean, you poor thing. Here, let me help you with that.'

'It's – it's fine, Frannie. I can manage.'

'Don't be silly,' said Frannie, running around gathering up the rolling apples and oranges. 'Those plastic bags are completely useless. I always carry a canvas one in my handbag for when I'm shopping.'

Jean sighed. 'Thanks, Frannie. I have a heap of those

bags at home but keep forgetting to bring them with me.'

'Are you going to stand there all day or open the door?' Frannie's arms were laden with fruit and tins.

'Oh, of course. Sorry about that.' Jean had no option but to open the door and let Frannie inside with the groceries. 'You can just leave them on the kitchen table and I'll take it from there. I really appreciate it.'

'Ah, it's no bother. Sure that's what neighbours are for.'

As soon as they'd everything inside, Jean wanted Frannie gone so she ushered her out to the hall. 'Thanks again for that. I won't forget my own bags next time.'

'Ah, would you look at that,' said Frannie, pointing to the floor. 'You must have a burst milk carton.'

Sure enough there was a trail of milk all down the hall from the front door into the kitchen.

'Feck it!' said Jean, rushing back into the kitchen to find the offending carton. 'Oh, no!' It was on the table, milk oozing out of the bottom. The bread was sitting in a pool of it.

Frannie picked it up quickly and threw it into the sink but it was too late to save some of the groceries. 'You'll be days getting that smell out of the house too. Milk is one of the worst things you can spill.'

Jean couldn't take any more. She plonked herself on a kitchen chair and began to cry. It started with a sniffle and, within seconds, had built up into heaving sobs.

'Jesus, Jean. It's not that bad. It's only a bit of spilled milk. Don't be crying over it. I'll help you clean up.'

'It's not the feckin' milk! It's just … it's just …'

Frannie grabbed a roll of kitchen towel from the counter and pulled up a chair beside her. Her voice was gentle. 'Jean, what's wrong? Surely things aren't that bad.'

'No … I mean yes … I mean …'

'Look, you just sit there and relax. Where are your mugs? Looks like we're going to have that cuppa after all.'

Frannie took over and Jean didn't object. She even let her take a mop to the trail of milk to clean it up. Although she usually tried to avoid Frannie and her probing questions, she was a good sort. She was nosy but she had a big heart, and at that moment, Jean needed to offload.

'So, go on, tell me about the wedding. Judging by the state of you, I gather it's been a stressful time.' Frannie placed two mugs of tea on the table and sat down beside Jean.

'Frannie, it's not the wedding I'm stressing about. Well, it's one of the things but not the biggest.'

'What is it, then? I presumed all the organising was getting to you.'

'It's Ellie. There's something going on. She went to New York last week and didn't come home. She says she wants us to cancel the wedding but it seems so out of character for her.' It was a relief to say the words – to share the burden.

'What? Oh, my God, Jean. That's awful. You must be in

bits. No wonder you're all over the place. So did something happen? Is she over there on her own?'

Jean felt the tension in her head ease with every mouthful of tea and every word she uttered. She didn't have a lot of friends and, at that moment, Frannie seemed like the best one she'd ever had. She was listening intently, nodding at everything, and Jean was sorry she'd shunned her in the past.

'And then to add to it all,' she continued, 'Andy isn't well – or so he says! So I've got a wedding to either organise or cancel, a missing daughter to find and a husband who's taken to the bed. It's no wonder I'm frazzled.'

Frannie patted her hand. 'You poor thing. Well, for starters, let me make you dinner and I'll drop it over. I've bought too much steak for just myself so I'll make a nice big stew.'

'I can't let you do that, Frannie, but thank you so much for offering.'

'It's not negotiable so you can take that off your list for today. Now I'm going to leave you in peace, unless you want help with anything else.'

'No, you've done enough already. Thank you so much.'

'It's not a bother,' said Frannie, standing up and hugging Jean briefly. 'Now go and check on that husband of yours and I'll be over with the stew later. Why don't you give yourself a break today? I know you feel there's a lot to be done but one day won't make a difference.'

Jean went to the door with her neighbour. 'You've been so good, Frannie. I guess I really needed to offload and I feel so much better for it. And thanks for doing dinner. I honestly don't think I could have faced cooking today.'

As she walked back into the kitchen, Jean had a spring in her step. Whatever else was going on, she'd made an unexpected but welcome new friend. She brought the mugs over to the sink and gazed out of the window to the back garden. Just like the front, it was looking fabulous. Andy had been working on them for months to get them just right for the visitors coming to the wedding. Oh, God, the wedding! Panic rose in her again, merely thinking about the weeks ahead.

She'd spoken to Matt the previous day and he hadn't had much news. Her heart had sunk when she'd heard that Ellie hadn't even bothered answering their texts. Jean had been sure she'd be delighted they'd gone over to find her. But, still, it was early days and Matt had assured her that they weren't giving up yet.

Then there was the dilemma about whether or not to cancel the wedding. Andy had pointed out that the longer they left it, the less likely it would be that they'd get their money back. She'd initially snapped at him for thinking about money when their daughter was having some sort of crisis but, in truth, they could scarcely afford to throw so much money away. He'd also pointed out that Ellie had been insistent in her texts. She'd said that she didn't want to get married and that they should go ahead and cancel the wedding.

Matt, on the other hand, was insisting they do no such thing. God love him, he really adored Ellie. Jean was very fond of him and would be devastated if he wasn't going to be her son-in-law, but she couldn't help wondering if he was being blinded by his love. He said he knew Ellie still loved him and this was just a temporary glitch, but Jean thought there was a lot more to it. What a bloody, bloody mess.

She glanced at the old black and white clock on the wall. Two o'clock. They'd be waking up in New York now. With a bit of luck, there'd be some better news today. Right: she wasn't going to let herself wallow any longer. What was it the old man in the cemetery had said? *And sure we have to have hope, haven't we?* Ellie was a sensible girl. She was going to be fine. And, regardless of any wedding, the most important thing was that her little girl came home safely soon.

○

'You too, Mikey. Talk to you later.' Sharon lay back on the bed and threw her phone onto the pillow beside her. God, she wished she could say, 'I love you,' to Mikey. She so badly wanted to tell him how she felt. Because she *did* love him. She'd known that from very early on in their relationship and she was pretty sure he felt the same, but it just wasn't something they said.

He'd often say things like 'Sure you know I'm mad about ya' or 'You're the only one for me' or, in his more romantic moments, 'You make me so happy'. But she really craved those three little words and, she knew she was being old-fashioned, she wanted *him* to be the first to say them. She was a hopeless romantic and Mikey was the complete opposite, yet they were the perfect fit for each other.

She'd spoken to him regularly since they'd arrived but she hadn't said anything to him about the child. She'd agreed with Matt that they'd keep it to themselves until they knew more and until Ellie was willing to talk about it. It was just as well they hadn't told anyone at home what they'd been thinking because, according to Matt, they'd got it wrong. The child was Caroline's. It hadn't even crossed her mind. But it seemed like a reasonable explanation, although Sharon still didn't know how Caroline would have hidden something like that from everyone. At least now Ellie was talking and hopefully they'd be meeting up with her in a day or two. The sooner they got her on that plane home, the better.

Matt had said that Ellie still wanted to cancel the wedding but that he wasn't going to allow her to. Sharon was all on for the big romantic gestures but she worried that Matt might be taking things a step too far. He couldn't *make* Ellie marry him if she didn't want to. He was sure that the only thing on Ellie's mind was the child, and once she'd sorted that out, she'd be ready to marry him. Sharon didn't think it was that simple.

But why would Caroline's baby affect Ellie's wedding plans? Where was the connection? Sharon knew Ellie better than anyone else on earth, Matt included, and she was sure that something else was going on. Yes, it must have been traumatic finding out about the child and, yes, the memories of Caroline throughout their weekend must have been difficult to deal with but it still didn't add up.

She glanced at the clock and knew she should get up. Matt had texted an hour earlier to say he'd gone for a run. She'd been tempted to join him but she hadn't been able to unglue herself from the bed. This was her second trip to New York in just a week and she was really feeling the effects of the jetlag. Still, they probably didn't have much time left in New York so she was going to make the most of it. Since they were going to back off Ellie for a day or two, she wanted to fit in a few of the touristy things that Lara hadn't managed to squeeze into their jam-packed schedule.

As she headed into the bathroom to take a shower, Sharon wondered what Ellie was doing. She couldn't wait to hear the whole story about the child. It was like something you'd see on the telly. But she was determined to get to the real reason for Ellie's withdrawal from everyone. Although Matt thought he'd solved the mystery, Sharon knew better.

TWENTY-FOUR

Ellie sat in the coffee shop sipping her tea. She'd been there almost an hour now and was on her second cup yet there was no sign of Ann. She'd give it another ten minutes and then she'd have to admit defeat and leave things until later on.

It had been lovely to hear Matt's voice last night, but she'd kept up her barriers. She'd wanted nothing more than to go to him and have him wrap his arms around her even though she'd remained aloof. She knew she'd probably sounded cold but it was better that way.

The little coffee shop had gone quiet after the lunch rush and Ellie was beginning to feel conspicuous, sitting there for so long. She'd just have to come back later. But what if Ann wasn't working? She didn't want to go back to the house, now that Sharon and Matt knew about it. And, besides, it would be easier to talk to Ann alone without her husband and child being there.

She drained the last of her now cold tea and wrapped her scarf around her neck. She might take a walk to clear her head. Maybe she'd even consider ringing Sharon. She knew Matt would have told her about their chat but it would be nice to talk to Sharon herself.

She pulled her coat tightly around her and searched in her bag for her wallet to leave a tip. Laying a five-dollar bill on a saucer, she stood up, ready to face the cold February air.

'Thanks.' She nodded to the bored-looking girl behind the counter.

''Bye, ma'am, and thank you.'

Just as Ellie was about to pull the door open, bracing herself for the blast of cold air that would hit her, somebody pushed it and sent her flying onto the floor.

'Oh, my God, I'm so sorry,' said the woman, rushing to where Ellie sat dazed beside the counter.

Ellie was mortified, but she composed herself quickly and stood up, brushing herself down. 'Don't worry – it was an accident.'

'Eleanora, I didn't realise it was you.'

Ellie didn't answer and headed towards the door.

'Eleanora. Are you okay? I really am sorry!'

Shit! Eleanora! How could she have forgotten? She swung around and there was Ann, concern all over her face. 'I – I'm sorry, Ann. I didn't recognise you there. Yes, yes, I'm fine. No harm done.'

'Oh, come back in and sit down for a minute. I'll get you something to drink.'

Ellie was torn. Here was the perfect chance for her to talk to Ann but she was feeling silly and a bit dazed from the fall. 'I'm okay, really.'

'Humour me, honey. I'm not due to start here for another ten minutes so I'll join you for a drink and a chat.'

'Em, okay so.'

'Great. You go and grab a table and I'll be over in a second.'

Ellie made for her usual table at the back of the shop, the bubble of excitement returning. She was finally going to talk to Ann.

'Here you go,' said Ann, placing a Cinnamon Latte in front of her. Her stomach lurched at the sight of it – she'd already had two cups of tea, but she just smiled politely and took a sip.

Ann watched her carefully. 'Are you sure you're okay, honey? You've gone awfully quiet.'

'Honestly, I'm fine. I … I just can't stay too long because I have stuff to do.'

'Don't worry. I've got to start work myself in a few

minutes. I just wanted to make sure you were okay before you left or I'd be worried about you all day.' She emptied a sachet of sugar into her own coffee and stirred. 'So what's going on with you? Are you going to be over here for much longer?'

Ellie stared at the woman in front of her and had an overwhelming urge to tell her everything – not just about the letter but everything about her life. She felt so alone and here was someone offering a friendly ear – someone who wasn't involved, someone who could be impartial.

'Well, it sort of depends ...'

'What does it depend on? I bet you're on the cusp of a very big deal and you're awaiting the outcome of a meeting to let you know whether you've been successful and will be Ireland's next millionaire. Am I right?'

Ellie stared at her.

'I'm only yanking your chain, honey.' She giggled. 'Tell me.'

'I'm not really over here for meetings, Ann. I know I said I was but that's because I ... because I wasn't ready to talk yet.'

Ann leaned her two arms on the table and shuffled her chair in closer. 'Go on, then. I'm all ears, as you Irish would say.'

Oh, God, this was harder than she'd thought. Maybe Ann and her husband had changed their minds since they'd written that letter. Silence hung heavily in the air as she tapped her fingers rhythmically on the table, a habit she'd picked up from her dad.

'I understand if you don't want to talk, Eleanora, but a problem shared and all that.'

'I'm supposed to be getting married back in Ireland in three weeks,' she blurted out. She couldn't bring herself to discuss the letter yet. 'I came over here for my hen weekend and decided I didn't want to go back.'

Ellie watched Ann's mouth open in shock as the enormity of what she'd said sank in.

'Holy crap! Golly, honey, that sure is a big one. What happened? Did you discover your fiancé was playing around or something?'

Jesus, these Americans didn't beat around the bush. 'No, nothing like that. Matt is a good man.' She could feel a big sob forming in her gut but tried valiantly to suppress it before she made a total fool of herself.

'Oh, you poor thing,' said Ann, jumping up to grab a handful of napkins from the counter. 'Here you go. No wonder you're in such a state. I can't imagine what you're feeling. Do you want to tell me what happened?'

Ellie blew her nose loudly on a napkin and tried to compose herself. 'Sorry, I don't know where that came from. It's just a build-up of emotions, I suppose. I can't say it was one thing in particular – more a combination.'

'Hold on a sec.' Ann jumped up from her seat and went to talk to the other girl behind the counter. She was back in seconds. 'Now I have all the time in the world. Ieesha is happy to manage on her own because it's so quiet. Why don't you start at the beginning?'

Ellie couldn't believe the words that spilled out of her mouth. She talked about Caroline first. She told Ann about her untimely death, how it had affected them all and how she'd lost her way for a while as a result. She told her about meeting Matt, how that had turned things around for her and how happy they'd been. She told her about the cancelled wedding plans, about sending the girls home without her and about Sharon and Matt coming after her. But she said nothing about the guilt.

'Gosh,' said Ann, when Ellie finally stopped to take a breath. 'That's some story. But I don't get it – why don't you want to get married?'

Ellie sighed, exhausted from pouring out her heart. 'I can't explain it, Ann. There are other things – private things. And it just doesn't feel right any more.'

'And is there any hope of you two sorting it out? I can't think of a better declaration of love than a man flying thousands of miles to get his woman.'

'He *is* pretty special,' admitted Ellie. 'But there's no going back now. Even if I felt differently, which I don't, it's too late because I've already told my parents to cancel the wedding.'

'Well, do me a favour, hon. Just sort out your feelings and think about what you want. Because the one lesson I've learned in life is it's *never* too late!'

Ellie nodded with tears in her eyes. She reached into her pocket. 'Ann, I—'

Ann jumped up suddenly, looking at the front of the shop. 'Where did that queue come from? Poor Ieesha looks frantic. Sorry, hon, I have to fly.'

Ellie sighed. It was the second time that had happened so maybe it was a sign. Talking to Ann about something so important in her place of work probably wasn't a good idea. She'd have to rethink and maybe visit the house again. There was no point in hanging around any longer so she buttoned up her coat for a second time and headed towards the door.

'Here,' said Ann, reaching over the counter and putting something into Ellie's hand as she passed. 'My phone number. Don't think I'm being weird, only just having met you and all that, but I want to know how the story ends.'

Ellie nodded and went outside. She blinked away the tears. How had her life become so complicated? She, too, wanted to know how the story would end.

TWENTY-FIVE

'Oh, my God!' said Lara, shocked at the turn of events. She'd been in the middle of writing an article that had to be with the newspaper by Monday when Sharon had rung. She was due a break anyway so she balanced the phone between her head and shoulder while she saved the document and closed her laptop.

'It's mad, isn't it, Lara? I kind of feel like I'm in the middle of a TV drama and I'm biting my nails waiting for the conclusion.'

'Ha-ha! At least you're seeing it as it unfolds. We Irish always get the American dramas well after they've aired in the US.' She went into the sitting room and curled her legs under her on the sofa. She was enjoying catching up on all the news and was dying to tell Sharon about how things had changed for her.

Sharon continued: 'And Matt and I agreed we weren't going to tell anyone about the child so you can't say anything. I'm sure Ellie will tell her parents and Mikey when she's ready.'

'I won't say a word, Sharon. And I'm glad you filled me in. I've been so worried about Ellie. Thank God we know why she's been acting strange. It must have been such a shock to find that out about Caroline.'

'Well, I think there's more to it.'

'Like what?' Lara groaned inwardly. She hoped Sharon wasn't going to go all deep and meaningful again.

'I think she's still bottling things up about Caroline's death. She always puts on a brave face and shrugs it off but she needs to talk about it more and tell us how she's really feeling.'

'We'll make her talk when she's home. We'll drag her down to The Gardens and put her in the spotlight. She'll be sick of talking once we get our hands on her!'

'I'm not sure that's the way to —'

'And I know you'd probably prefer a more touchy-feely approach, Sharon, but if we get a few drinks into her and have her laughing again, she might be more inclined to talk to us.'

Sharon hesitated. 'I'm not sure getting her tipsy is the answer but I'm willing to give anything a go.'

'Great. So that's sorted. We'll arrange something as soon as you both get home. And how are you getting on with Matt? I hope you two are behaving yourselves.'

'Jesus, Lara. Your mind is permanently in the gutter. I can't believe you even said that.'

'The gutter? I just meant I hope you two aren't indulging in any super-sized portions over there!'

'Oh, sorry. I thought—'

'Ha-ha! Gotcha! You're so gullible, Sharon. I'm only having you on.'

'Bitch! So what has you in such good form anyway? Last we spoke you were down in the dumps.'

'Oh, things are looking up here. I sat Peter down yesterday and we had a really good heart-to-heart. He hadn't realised I was feeling so bad. I'd spoken to him about it before but he'd thought it was just because I was tired or having a bad day. When he grasped it was more serious than that, he promised he'd do all he could to support me.'

'Ah, that's brilliant, Lara. I knew Peter would understand. He's one of the good guys.'

'You were right – and he is. And what about you? Are you pining for your secret love over there?'

'Feck off! It's only been a couple of days!'

'I know. And they say absence makes the heart grow fonder.'

'I have to admit,' said Sharon slowly, 'he's one of the

good ones too. He's such a fabulous bloke, Lara. I've never felt like this about anyone and I know he feels the same.'

'Well, I'm delighted for you. You'll have to tell Ellie soon. I bet she'll be over the moon.'

'I've told Matt. He'd already guessed!'

Lara laughed. 'I'm not surprised, considering how you two are with each other. I'm surprised Ellie hasn't sussed it herself – although I suppose she's been too caught up with other things lately.'

'I'm going to tell her as soon as possible – for all our sakes. I can't stand this sneaking around any longer. How come it's so quiet there, by the way? Is Ethan in bed?'

'Peter took him out for a walk so that I could get some work done.' Lara hugged herself as she said the words. She hadn't even had to ask Peter this morning but he'd got Ethan his breakfast and taken him off to watch a DVD. He'd told Lara she could take the day to write and he'd keep everything afloat. She was kicking herself for not having said anything sooner but it was better late than never.

Sharon gave a low whistle. 'Wow! It looks like Peter's a new man. I'm glad you're getting things sorted. Next you'll be telling me he's cooking the dinner.'

'I'm home, love.' Peter pushed Ethan's pram in the front door and popped his head into the sitting room. 'I picked up some mince in the butcher's so I'll go and make a start on some chilli con carne while Ethan is asleep.'

'Did you hear that, Sharon?' asked Lara, giggling. 'You're definitely right about the new-man stuff!'

Sharon was laughing too. 'Good on him. But listen, I'm going to have to go. Matt and I are heading out for a few hours. We thought if we kept busy, we wouldn't keep checking our phones for a call from Ellie. She said a day or two so it will probably be tomorrow before she rings.'

'Right, Sharon. I'd better see if I can lend a hand in the kitchen – although it sounds like my man has it all under control.'

'Give him my love and give that little darling Ethan a big kiss from his auntie Sharon.'

'Will do. Let me know as soon as you hear anything more.' Lara ended the call and threw the phone down on the sofa beside her. She took the remote control and switched on the telly. The article could wait until later. God, she could get used to this. She couldn't remember when Peter had last cooked dinner – other than a microwave meal. They were going to sit down over the next few weeks and look at possible options for Peter to reduce his hours in work and for Lara to increase her workload. Lara felt a million times better because he'd listened to her. She'd realised last night that it wasn't so much the stay-at-home job she hated but the lack of acknowledgement for how difficult it was. She'd probably never worked so hard in her life. It would be good for Peter to have a taste of it, even if it was just for a short while.

'Lara, do we have some yoke for making the vegetables into small pieces – like a machine or something?'

'Yes, we have a *yoke* – and it's called a knife!' She sighed and got up off the sofa. Maybe he wasn't as in control as she'd thought. Still, Rome wasn't built in a day. And it would be worth it in the end.

○

Jean took her cup of hot chocolate into the sitting room and switched on the telly. She was just in time for Brendan O'Connor's Saturday night show. She could do with the bit of distraction after the day she'd had.

After Frannie had left, she'd brought Andy up a cup of tea and she'd been shocked at his pallor. He'd refused anything to eat, saying he felt full, and had asked for a couple of Rennies. She'd suggested bringing him to the doctor but he hadn't felt like getting up, and when she'd mentioned maybe getting the doctor out, he'd snapped at her, telling her she was being way over the top as usual.

She'd left him for a while but it hadn't stopped her worrying. It seemed it was all she did at the moment. Everything in their lives was upside down and she was sick of it. Was it too much to ask that, for once, things would run smoothly for them? Hadn't they had enough heartache to last them a lifetime?

But Andy had come down a bit later, saying he was feeling a lot better and apologising for his harsh words. She'd sniffed and said, 'And so you should be sorry, speaking to me like that,' but she'd been delighted to see a bit of colour back in his cheeks. He'd even eaten a sandwich and watched a bit of football before deciding to go back to bed. He'd claimed he was probably just exhausted and a bit of extra sleep would sort him out.

She made herself comfortable on the sofa and cupped her hands around her mug. Mikey was out and Andy was fast asleep so she was going to enjoy a rare night on her own. Just as Brendan was introducing his first guest, the phone rang. Sighing, she dragged herself up off the sofa and grabbed the phone off the mantelpiece.

'Hello, who's speaking, please?' She knew her usual greeting sounded less than welcoming but she could have done without any interruptions to her night of peace.

'Hiya, Mam.'

'Ellie! Oh, love, it's you! Are you okay? I've been so worried.' She burst into tears at the sound of her daughter's voice. 'Please say you're coming home, love.'

'Ah, Mam, don't cry. I'm fine, honestly. And I'm really sorry I've been acting so weird.'

Jean took a cotton hanky from inside her sleeve and blew her nose. 'But why? What's wrong? Why won't you come home? I don't understand.'

'Mam, you've got to stop getting yourself all worked up.

Maybe I'll start by saying I'm hoping to come home in the next few days. How about that?'

'Oh, love, that's the best news I could ever have heard. But you didn't tell me what happened. Why did you stay over there?'

'I'm not going into it all now, Mam. I have loads to tell you but I'll wait until we're sitting down together in the kitchen, drinking tea and having some of those Tunnock's Teacakes you always have stashed away.'

'How did you know about …? Listen, forget the teacakes. Can't you tell me anything about what's going on? You know Matt and Sharon are over there, right?'

'Yes.' Ellie sighed. 'I've spoken to them and told them I'd meet them. It'll probably be tomorrow.'

'That's brilliant news, love. That boy loves the bones of you, you know. He never lost faith in you two, not for one minute. I'm so glad you're going to sort things out.'

There was silence at the other end of the phone. Jean continued: 'You *are* going to sort things out with him, aren't you?'

'Mam, I'm still not marrying him. Nothing has changed. I've told him that.'

'I don't understand, Ellie. I thought you loved him.'

'I did … I do. But it's complicated.'

Jean sniffed. 'Evidently.'

'Ah, Mam, don't be like that. I'll explain everything when I'm home. But please go ahead and cancel everything if you haven't already done it. I don't want you and Dad losing money because we've left it too late.'

'But, Ellie, would you not just talk—'

'Mam! I'm *not* getting married to Matt. I've done a lot of thinking over here and I know I'm doing the right thing. Matt is wonderful and he deserves better than me.'

'What the bloody hell are you talking about now?' Jean couldn't keep up with her daughter. 'What do you mean he deserves better? What have you done? Jesus! You haven't... don't tell me you've ...'

'What?' Ellie was obviously becoming agitated.

'Have you done the dirty on him? Oh, God, Ellie. Is that what this is all about?'

'Oh, for God's sake, Mam! No, I have *not*! Just what do you take me for?'

'I'm sorry, love. But why on earth would you say he deserves better? As far as I can see, you're a great catch and he's very lucky to have you.'

'I've got to go, Mam. Just please cancel everything. I'll tidy up all the loose ends when I'm home, but for now make sure you cancel the hotel at the very least.'

Jean sighed. 'Right, if you're sure. And when did you say you'd be home?'

'I didn't. I'll let you know though, maybe the middle of next week. Say hi to Dad and Mikey for me and tell them I'll see them soon.'

'Okay, love. And, Ellie ... I love you, you know. Please look after yourself.'

'You too, Mam. Talk to you soon.'

Jean put the phone down. What a relief it had been to speak to Ellie. Thank God she was okay. She felt the weight of the world lift off her shoulders as tears sprang to her eyes. But this time they were happy tears. She had so many questions to ask her daughter, but nothing in the world really mattered except that her Ellie was coming home.

TWENTY-SIX

Ellie could feel the veins at the side of her head pulsating as sweat dripped off her temples. God, she was in a right state. As she began to regain her composure, she became aware of the stares of passers-by so headed into her hotel on wobbly legs.

'Morning, ma'am,' said the jolly concierge. 'Cold one out there today, isn't it?'

'Yep!' Ellie didn't want to be rude but she could barely breathe, never mind stop to have a chat. And she wasn't sure whether or not he was teasing her, saying it was cold when quite clearly she was burning up. She hit the button for the lift and was glad when the doors closed, cutting her off from any more conversation.

Going for a run probably hadn't been one of her better ideas. She'd done a bit of running in the past and had been walking a lot over the last few months, but she was still a long way off being as fit as Sharon.

The lift pinged at her floor and she emerged to head for her room. She swiped the key card with shaky hands and launched herself at a bottle of water as soon as she got inside. Slowly her breathing evened out and she began to feel almost human again.

She hadn't been able to sleep the previous night so had got up and begun sorting out her clothes. She'd been living from her two suitcases and everything had been in complete disarray. That was when she'd found her barely worn running shoes. Sharon had said she wanted to go running in Central Park because it was something she'd seen so often in movies and she'd made Ellie promise to go with her. They'd both taken their jogging kit, but a run in Central Park hadn't been on Lara's list.

Eventually she went into the bathroom and switched on the shower. She stepped out of her sweaty clothes, stood into the cubicle and closed the door. The water was warm and Ellie began to relax.

She hadn't quite made it to Central Park but instead had run around the streets close to her hotel. She hadn't wanted to go too far because she knew how unfit she was, yet she'd pushed herself to the limit, alternating between walking and running for almost an hour.

She lathered herself with the gorgeous Aveda rosemary mint shower gel provided by the hotel and breathed in the fresh scent. She felt strangely at peace for the first time in ages. It was as though her run had cleared her head of all negative thoughts, leaving her ready to face the next few days with a renewed energy and faith that it would all work out. The first thing she'd decided while she was out was that she would meet Matt and Sharon today. She was fed up dealing with everything on her own and she was going to tell them about the letter and see what they thought the best approach would be. She was excited at the prospect of seeing them and a little nervous too. They had every reason to hate her for what she'd put them through, but she knew they were good friends and would be happy that she wasn't shutting them out any more.

She'd never grieved like the rest of her family had when Caroline had died. Seeing the utter grief and shock on the faces of her parents and Mikey, she'd gone onto autopilot, organising everything and helping everyone through it. She'd done it all – from picking out the coffin to choosing the hymns that would be sung at the church. She'd spoken to the priest, the undertaker and had even organised food at a local hotel for afterwards. She'd co-ordinated the neighbours' offerings of freshly cooked meals and had kept things afloat at home while everyone else was falling to pieces. Anything but face the guilt.

It was months later before her parents began to enter the

real world again and that was when Ellie had decided to have some fun. She hadn't wanted to have any time on her hands to think so she'd tried to drag her friends to parties and night-clubs – anywhere she could dance the night away and forget her troubles. But Sharon had never been the party type and Lara had just had Ethan so she'd ended up doing a lot of the partying alone. Alcohol had become her best friend, which had led to some very dodgy encounters of the male kind.

After months of drinking herself into oblivion, she'd eventually listened to Sharon when she'd sat her down one day and pointed out the obvious. She was either going to drink herself to death or one of the men she so willingly went with would turn out to be a bad one. God only knew what would happen then. It had been a wake-up call and had frightened her enough to turn things around. It was lucky she had because soon after that she'd met Matt.

The thought of not marrying Matt scared her. The thought of them not living the rest of their lives together was almost too much to bear. But sacrificing her life with Matt was the least she could do. Why should she be allowed to live happily ever after when her sister was cold in her grave?

She switched off the shower and stepped out. Wrapping a towel around her hair and one around her body, she padded into the bedroom. The morning was flying by and she wanted to meet up with Matt and Sharon soon. She looked forward to getting some support and advice from them before talking to Ann and her family.

Sitting at the little dressing-table, she unwrapped the towel from her head and gave her hair a quick rub. She struggled to get her brush through it before squirting some serum into her hands and rubbing it into the wiry curls. Although she often craved smooth, sleek locks, she knew she was lucky to have hair that needed very little attention.

She applied some moisturiser to her face and picked out a pair of Guess jeans from her case. She teamed them with her favourite Zoe Karssen long-sleeved T-shirt and was ready in minutes.

Right, it was time to start making amends. Her heart quickened as she took her phone from the locker and dialled Matt's number. Oh, God, what if he'd changed his mind? What if they'd both decided she was a lost cause and had gone home? That was when she realised how much she needed them both.

○

'Sharon, open up. Come on, you've got to get ready.' Matt pounded on Sharon's door as an elderly couple passed and gave him a disapproving look. He didn't care. He continued banging on the door.

'Jesus, Matt,' said Sharon, swinging it open. 'Where's the fire? What's up with you?'

Matt pushed inside the room. 'It's Ellie. She wants to meet us. I knew she would. Come on, we've to meet her in an hour at Grand Central.'

'Really? That's brilliant. Did she ring?'

'Yes, just now. We only spoke for a minute. She just asked if we could meet her and of course I said yes. You're not even dressed yet. Come on, Sharon, we can't be late.'

Sharon pulled her robe tightly around her. 'Calm down, Matt. We'll be at Grand Central in five minutes. I'll be showered and ready in twenty minutes and I'll see you downstairs.'

'Right, right. Sorry, I'm just excited and nervous and —'

'Don't worry, Matt. It'll be fine. This is Ellie we're meeting – our Ellie. We need to remember that. She's not some stranger we've never met before.'

Matt sighed. 'That's how it feels at the moment, though. She feels like a stranger. I still don't understand what's happened.'

Sharon shoved him towards the door. 'Well, we're going to talk to her and find out. And then we're going to bring her home to where she belongs.'

'Right,' said Matt, feeling less confident than Sharon. 'Let's hope it all works out that way.'

Matt went back to his room. He was ready to go and the thought of waiting for an hour was killing him. He walked into the bathroom and checked his face in the mirror. Maybe he'd give himself another shave. He'd only shaved yesterday but his face felt rough and Ellie hated the scratchiness of stubble. He filled the sink with water and began the ritual of lathering his face with foam and carefully running the blade over it. He wondered if he'd get to hold Ellie close. Would she let him rub his smooth face against hers?

As the first seeds of doubt entered his head, he tried desperately to push them away. He'd been so positive until now. It was in his nature to look on the bright side – his mother always said he was a 'cup half full' kind of guy. And it was true. He hadn't for one moment entertained the idea that Ellie might not want to marry him. He'd held fast in his belief that this was just a bump in the road and they'd be back on course soon. But hearing her say the words yesterday had rattled him. Maybe he really was part of the problem.

He splashed water over his face to wash off the remaining foam and grabbed one of the hotel's lovely soft towels to dry it. Looking in the mirror again, he noticed that his eyes were dull and sad. They were reflecting everything he was feeling – worry, doubt, fear. He couldn't let Ellie see him like that. He needed to be strong for her, show her that he believed in them and wasn't giving up. He had to fill his head with positive thoughts and make sure they were reflected in his face.

He ran his fingers through his thick black hair and he was ready. Grabbing his brown leather jacket from the end of the bed, he took one final look in the full-length mirror before heading out of the door.

It was quiet downstairs in Reception and he found a seat easily enough. He loved it in the hotel lobby. There was such a friendly air about the place and the soft furnishings and beautiful carpets created a lovely sense of calm. As the minutes ticked by, his worries lifted. He was going to make sure Ellie knew today how much he loved her and that he wasn't giving up, no matter how much she tried pushing him away. If she said she didn't love him, that would be a different story, but he knew she did.

He whipped out his phone. He was going to get this meeting off to a good start. He quickly found Ellie's number and tapped in a message:

Ellie, I love you. Now and forever – I love you.

If he had to tell her a million times a day he would. It seemed like she needed reassurance at the moment and that was what he was going to give her. After all, very soon she would be his wife.

TWENTY-SEVEN

Ellie paused before she went into the Oyster Bar. A million emotions were rushing through her head and she was finding it difficult to sort them out. She wished things were different. On the one hand she was dying to see Matt and Sharon but on the other she was scared.

Should she rush over and hug them? Would they even want her to? She knew that there were things she still had to deal with herself, but she was hoping they could help her make the right decisions and handle the letter in an appropriate way.

She drank some water from the bottle she'd brought with her. Her mouth was dry and she was going to have to do a hell of a lot of talking. Her attention was drawn to a young couple with a child who were testing out the magic of the Whispering Gallery. It was a little-known treasure of Grand Central Station – Ellie and the girls had discovered it by accident the previous week. Voices carry along the curved walls so a whisper can be heard at the other side of the room. She laughed at the squeals of the child, who couldn't have been more than six or seven. She was running from one end to the other, ordering her parents to whisper so she could hear. Ellie wondered idly if Ann would bring her little girl here to experience the magic.

Right. She shook herself. She needed to go in and talk to them. It was just Matt and Sharon, after all, not some random strangers. There was no need for her to feel intimidated or fearful of what they'd say. They were her friends and they were here to support her. She took a deep breath and pushed the door.

'Ellie,' exclaimed Sharon, jumping up to greet her friend. 'Thank God you're okay.' She flung her arms around her, and Ellie wondered why she'd worried about this moment.

'Hi, Sharon. It's so good to see you.' She hugged her friend tightly while blinking back tears. 'I know it's only been a few days but it feels like a lifetime.'

Sharon released her grip and looked at her. 'I know what you mean, Ellie. What a week, eh?'

'Is either of you going to let me in for a hug too?' Matt

smiled, and Ellie's heart melted. He wrapped his arms around her and buried his head in her hair. 'God, you smell so good.'

'Matt, I—'

'I know, Ellie. It's just so good to see you.' He stood back and indicated a seat for her to sit down.

'You too,' she said, taking off her jacket and throwing it on the back of her chair. 'And you, Sharon. I can't believe you two came all the way over here for me. It's … it's too much.' To her shock, big fat tears appeared in the corners of her eyes and threatened to spill. She tried to blink them away but it was too late.

'Oh, Ellie, you poor pet.' Sharon reached into her bag for a tissue and handed it to her. 'It seems like you've had an awful time of it lately.'

'And why wouldn't we come over for you, Ellie?' said Matt. 'There was no way we were going to just leave you here. I hope you know how many people love you and are worried about you.'

Ellie sniffed. 'That's just it. I feel like such a fool. I've upset so many people and that wasn't my intention. I … I just didn't think things through. That's me all over.'

'I blame myself.' Both Matt and Ellie stared at Sharon.

'What are you talking about?' said Ellie, dumbfounded. 'This has nothing to do with you.'

'But I *knew* there was something up with you last weekend. I should have tried harder to get you to talk about it. Maybe if you'd confided in me and Lara, none of this would have happened.'

Ellie shook her head adamantly. 'Don't you see, Sharon? None of that would have made any difference.'

'So tell us everything from the beginning,' urged Matt gently. 'It must have come as a real shock to you to find out Caroline had a baby. How on earth did she manage to hide it? Did you have no idea at all?'

Ellie stared at him and tried to compute what he was saying.

'Ellie, what's wrong?' Sharon looked concerned.

'Oh, my God! Do you guys think Caroline got pregnant and had a baby? And none of us knew about it?'

Matt looked confused. 'Well, yes. Isn't that what this is all about? We found the address on your laptop and then we went there and saw the child.'

It suddenly made sense to Ellie. 'God, I can see where you got that now. The child is the image of Caroline. You just assumed she was hers.'

'And is she not?' asked Sharon. 'I don't understand.'

'Well she's not exactly … but kind of …'

Matt reached across and took Ellie's hand. 'You're talking in riddles now, Ellie. She either is or isn't Caroline's child. Or are you just not sure?'

Ellie sighed and reached into her pocket. 'I suppose the best way for you to understand is to read this. I found it in Caroline's stuff when I was clearing out the dresser in our old room a few weeks ago.' She unfolded the letter and turned it around to Sharon and Matt, who immediately began to read it.

Hello there,

It seems so cold to address you with no name, considering what you've done for us but, as you know, we don't have that detail about each other. Hopefully, some day we will. If you're reading this, the clinic must have decided to forward the letter to you and I'm very grateful they did.

It's hard to know where to begin so I'm just going to tell you a little about me and my husband. We're in our early thirties and have been together for twelve years. I'm a New Yorker and he's a native of County Cork and we met in Ireland when I was backpacking around Europe with my friend. We fell in love, had the fairytale wedding and thought we'd live happily ever after. We both come from large families and wanted more than anything else in the world to start a family of our own. But it soon became apparent that there were problems. After a few years of trying to conceive naturally, we decided to get checked out and subsequently had two failed IVF attempts. To cut a long story short, we were told that our best option for having a baby would be an egg donor.

And that's where you came in. Fast forward another few years and because of your wonderful generosity in donating your eggs, we have the most beautiful baby girl. She means everything to us, and although she's only a few months old, we can't imagine not ever having her.

I'm writing to you now because, for a number of reasons, we're going back over to New York to live. We've talked a lot about you, and although the donation was done on an anonymous basis, we'd love for you to get in touch some day – only if you wanted to, of course. We'd love for you to see first hand the wonderful gift you've given us and, if you were willing, maybe even be involved in her life on some level. We understand you may never want to follow up on this but we've included our forwarding address in New York in case you ever do.

Please know how eternally grateful we are to you. I never thought it would be possible to have so much love for a complete stranger, but that's how my husband and I feel about you.

I hope you have the happy life you deserve. Take care and hopefully we'll meet some day.

With love

Ellie watched for their reaction. She wanted them to feel the enormity of the situation. She wanted them to understand how those words had made her feel – *I hope you have the happy life you deserve.* They were the words that had been going around in her head since she had found the letter.

Sharon was the first to look up. 'Oh, Ellie! That's amazing. I … I don't know what to say.'

'Jesus,' said Matt, indicating to a hovering waiter that they weren't ready to order yet. 'That's huge. No wonder you've been all over the place.'

Ellie blinked back the tears. 'Life can be so bloody unfair, can't it?'

Matt reached across and took her two hands in his. 'It's awful, Ellie. Caroline was such a good person. But you ought to be very proud of her.'

'Oh, I am,' said Ellie, pulling her hands away. 'I'm so proud of what she's done – not just this but everything else in her life. I only wish I could be like her.'

'But you don't need to be like anyone else, Ellie.' Sharon's face was full of concern. 'You're you and that's why we love you.'

'Thanks, Sharon. But you don't know the half of it.'

'Well, tell us,' urged Sharon. 'You'd feel a whole lot better if you just talked to us.'

'I – I can't, Sharon. Not yet. I'm still trying to deal with it myself. Maybe some day.' She wasn't ready to talk about the guilt she was feeling about that day. She didn't know if she ever would be. 'Right now, my main priority is following up on this letter. I could do with some advice on how to go about it.'

Matt nodded. 'You haven't introduced yourself to the parents yet?'

'Well, not exactly … but kind of …'

'Oh, Jesus, there you go with the riddles again!' Sharon threw her hands up into the air.

Ellie couldn't help laughing. 'I do make things very complicated, don't I? Well the thing is, I've been speaking to the mother but she doesn't know who I am.' She began to tell the story. Matt and Sharon hung on her every word as she described how she'd gone to the house, followed Ann and subsequently befriended her. She said that she'd gone back on a few occasions to the coffee shop and had found Ann really easy to talk to. She'd even told her about Caroline's death but hadn't mentioned who she was.

'Jesus!' said Matt, sitting back into his chair. 'That's one hell of a story. I honestly am not sure what to suggest you do. Maybe you should just go back to the shop and make sure you tell her this time.'

Ellie shook her head. 'No, that was my intention initially but I really don't think it's a good idea. She's busy when she's in there and doesn't have much time to talk. It wouldn't be fair to land that on her and then for her to have to work for hours afterwards.'

'Well, then,' said Sharon, propping her elbows on the

table. 'The only thing you *can* do is go to the house – that is, if you're sure you want to talk to them.'

'Oh, I'm sure, all right. I didn't go through all of this to chicken out at the final hurdle. I owe it to Caroline to follow it up.'

The waiter came back to see if they were ready. Matt ordered the clam chowder, while Ellie and Sharon went for the seafood salad. They handed back the menus and Ellie waited until he was out of earshot before she continued.

'I'm not sure whether to ring first, though. Ann gave me her number the last time I was in the coffee shop. Maybe I could ease them in with a phone call rather than just appearing at their door.'

Matt nodded. 'Probably best to ring. Tell Ann you need to talk to her about something and you don't want to say it over the phone. Ask her outright if it would be okay if you dropped by the house.'

'They might think she's a weirdo or something.' Sharon looked concerned.

'No, Matt's right. I'll do exactly that. I told Ann about me cancelling the wedding and you two coming over and she said she'd be dying to hear what happens.' Ellie glanced at Matt to see how he'd react to that.

But he still seemed upbeat. 'Well, that seems like a good plan. And would you like us to come with you?'

'No, but thanks anyway. This is something I need to do alone.' She bowed her head and felt a lump in her throat at the willingness of her friends to forgive her so easily for causing such upset. 'But I'm so glad you two are here. It really means a lot, considering everything I've put you through. Especially you, Matt.'

Matt reached across and took her hand again, this time holding on to it tightly in case she pulled away. 'Ellie, you've got to stop worrying about what's happened. You've had a lot to deal with and everything just got on top of you. Once you've done what you have to do over here, I'm taking you home and we can look forward to the rest of our lives together.'

Ellie paled. She knew Matt had been taking it all far too well. For feck's sake. How was she going to make him understand? She sighed. She didn't know what to say.

'Ellie,' said Sharon gently, 'is there something else?'

'Sharon, would you mind giving us a minute, please?'

'Of course, no problem.' Sharon grabbed her bag and scurried off to the Ladies.

Ellie looked at Matt. She could see from his eyes that he knew what was coming but he was desperately trying to avoid it.

'I know what you said, Ellie, but I thought that once you sorted things out with those people that you'd be able to get on with things.'

'I'm sorry, Matt. It's just …'

'Come on, Ellie. This is me – your fiancé. The man you loved up until last week. How can things have changed so much?'

'Matt, I *do* still love you but I'm not going to marry you.'

'I really don't understand what's happened but we can wait. We can move into the flat and we don't have to get married until you feel you're ready. I knew it was all too much with your mother pushing for—'

'Matt!'

'What?'

'It's nothing to do with the actual wedding or my mother. I don't want us to move in together or continue going out together. It's over, Matt. I'm really sorry but it's over. I want you to know it's nothing to do with you – it's me. I'm pretty messed up at the moment.'

Matt stared at her. 'You can't seriously be giving me the it's-not-you-it's-me speech after all this time?'

'I'm sorry,' whispered Ellie. 'Maybe one day I'll be able to explain it to you – when I figure it out myself.'

'Ellie, I know in my heart of hearts we're meant to be together. I'll accept what you're saying for now because there are other things to be dealt with. But I'm telling you here and now, I'm not giving up.'

'Matt, I—'

'Look into my eyes and tell me you don't love me, Ellie. Tell me you don't want to spend the rest of your life with me. If you tell me that I'll back away. But you have to be honest.'

'I – I can't. But it can't always be about what I want.'

'It can if you want it to be.'

Silence hung heavily between them until Ellie eventually spoke: 'Look, Matt, I know I must seem like a selfish bitch. You've come all this way and I'm still telling you I don't want to be with you. I'm really sorry – you'll never know quite how sorry.'

'Ellie, just have a think —'

Ellie wasn't letting him continue. 'And I understand if you don't want to hang around. I know you said you wanted to support me and you've done that already. Just being able to talk to both of you today has been a great help. It would be stupid of me to expect anything more from you.'

Matt looked close to tears. Maybe it was beginning to sink in with him after all.

'And maybe when we're back in Ireland we can talk,' continued Ellie. 'But only if you want to.'

'I don't know what to do or think, Ellie. I can't get past the fact that you still love me. It would be easier if you didn't.'

Ellie let those words sink in and felt a huge emptiness. Because without Matt that was how she felt – empty. She didn't have time to think any further because Sharon appeared beside them.

'Have you two had your little chat or do you need me to disappear again?'

'Don't be silly,' said Ellie, watching Matt carefully. 'And I'm sorry for asking you to leave.'

'No problem. I was glad to give you a bit of space to talk things through. Now let's tuck into this. I'm starving.'

Ellie took her fork and began picking at the salad. She really didn't have much of an appetite and it looked as though Matt was the same.

'God, this is gorgeous,' said Sharon, stuffing a forkful into her mouth. 'How's your chowder, Matt?'

'Delicious.' Matt didn't even try to sound convincing as he dipped his spoon in and barely let his lips touch it.

The tension between herself and Matt must be obvious to Sharon, Ellie thought, although her friend didn't comment. She felt her resolve faltering slightly. Was she mad to cut off her own happiness like that? Who was going to benefit from it? She'd been so caught up in wanting to punish herself that she hadn't given much consideration to how it would affect others. But maybe it was too late for her and Matt anyway. Could they ever recover from all the drama?

Well, she wasn't going to think about that at the moment. She had to put all her energy into handling things properly with Ann. She and her family had never met Caroline but they would be devastated by the news of her death. And then there was her mother. She would be shocked to hear when Ellie told her the whole saga. The few days ahead were set to be very emotional and Ellie was sure that they would play a big part in deciding the rest of her life.

TWENTY-EIGHT

'Lara, love, come on in.' Jean opened the door wide for Lara to push the buggy through. 'Ah, the little pet, he's fast asleep. You can put him in the sitting room where it's quiet, then come on into the kitchen and we'll have a nice cup of tea.'

'Thanks, Jean. I'm parched after walking for about an hour to get him to sleep. He still wakes at night no matter what so I usually try to get him to have a good nap during the day.'

'Well, the fresh air will do him the world of good,' said Jean, leading the way into the kitchen. 'Now sit yourself down. Tea or coffee?'

'A coffee would be lovely, thanks. What's the latest from New York?'

'Well, you knew that they'd made contact with Ellie and

were hoping to meet up with her, didn't you?'

'Yes, Sharon told me on Saturday when she rang. I texted her last night to get an update but I haven't had a reply yet. Has something else happened?'

'Yes, thank God. They met up with her yesterday. Ellie rang to tell me yesterday afternoon and then Matt rang last night. It's funny, though – they were both pretty vague about things.'

Lara took a cup from Jean and sipped gratefully. 'What do you mean? Vague about coming back or about what's been going on?'

'Well, the good news is they're planning on catching a flight tomorrow evening so they'll be home on Wednesday.'

Lara's eyes widened. 'Really? All three of them?'

'It seems so, Lara love. I can't believe they're actually going to be bringing my Ellie home.'

'That's brilliant,' said Lara, beaming. 'The best news I could have hoped for. I honestly wasn't sure how all this was going to turn out.'

'But I'm not sure they're telling me everything, Lara. There's more – I just know it.'

Lara nodded. 'I know what you mean. I keep thinking the same. You know, I was worried at first that maybe she'd taken all the stuff I was saying about marriage to heart.'

'Why? What were you saying?' Jean was curious. As far as she knew, Lara had the perfect marriage – a lovely, considerate husband and a gorgeous little boy.

'Well, it was nothing, really – just bits and pieces.'

Jean didn't want to let a bit of gossip escape her. 'Come on, love. You know you can tell me anything and it won't go outside these walls.'

'It's not a big deal, really. It's just that me and Peter were having a few problems and I sort of indicated to Ellie that marriage wasn't all it was cracked up to be.'

'Ah, love, I didn't realise yours was in trouble. What happened?' She shoved the plate of chocolate biscuits she'd produced closer to Lara in the hope she'd feel comfortable to continue.

'Nothing *happened*, Jean. And my marriage isn't in trouble. It's a long story, but I was getting a bit fed up being in the house all the time. We've sorted things out and we're absolutely fine.'

Jean plastered a smile on her face. She wouldn't wish anything bad on Lara, but she'd have loved a bit of idle gossip to distract her from everything else that was going on.

Lara continued: 'And I just thought that maybe all my negative comments had affected Ellie and were part of the reason she'd stayed away.'

'Well, you've nothing to worry about there, love. Sure hasn't Ellie been listening to myself and Andy sniping at each other all her life? If that didn't put her off marriage, nothing will.'

'I suppose,' said Lara. 'And have you any idea why she's been behaving so strangely?'

Jean looked at Lara. 'Well, I was a bit worried about something but Andy said I shouldn't get myself worked up over it.'

'What was that?' Lara took a chocolate biscuit and nibbled at it.

'It's all this wedding stuff. I think I went over the top. All Ellie and Matt ever wanted was something very small. They never wanted the big palaver that I organised. I thought maybe that was what drove her away and led her to cancel the whole thing.' Despite Andy's reassurances and even after she'd spoken to Ellie, Jean still worried that everything was her fault.

'No, Jean. Ellie wasn't thinking that way at all. I know she appreciated your help. The big "palaver", as you put it, may not be what she wanted originally but she was really grateful to you and Andy for everything you've done for her.'

Jean felt a lump in her throat. 'Thanks, love, for saying that. It really means a lot to know that she doesn't hate me for all my interfering.'

'Of course she doesn't, Jean. Ellie loves you – you and Andy and little Mikey. I would have included Matt in that too but I'm really not sure what the story is there.'

'That makes two of us, love. She got me completely confused the other night – she loves Matt but can't marry him. What sort of a thing is that to say? What on earth would be stopping her?'

'It's a mystery, all right. But now that they've met and they're talking, maybe the wedding will go ahead after all.'

Jean looked down at the table and didn't reply. She'd gone over and over things with Andy last night and they'd made a decision. She still wasn't sure whether or not it was the right one but only time would tell.

'Jean, what's wrong? Do you not think there's any hope that it will go ahead?'

'It's not that, Lara. It's just … Ellie was insisting we cancel the wedding. I tried to talk her around on the phone on Saturday but she wasn't having any of it. And Andy was worried about the money. I know that sounds cold but Ellie was worried about it too and that we could lose a lot if we didn't cancel and—'

'So you've cancelled,' said Lara matter-of-factly.

'We have, love. Andy rang the hotel first thing this morning and notified them. It seemed like the right thing to do at the time but now I'm not so sure, hearing you talk about a possible reconciliation.'

'Well, not to harp on about it, but marriage really *isn't* the be-all and end-all, Jean. I think you were right to go along with Ellie's wishes. It still doesn't mean they can't get married in the future or maybe just live together in their new place.'

Jean stiffened. Even though it was the done thing, these days, she wasn't too keen on the idea of her children living 'in sin'. 'Well, I don't think Ellie would be into that, to be honest. If she wanted to be with Matt, she'd just go ahead and marry him. What would be the point in cancelling the wedding, then still going to live with him?'

'I suppose.' Lara didn't sound convinced. 'So you have no other ideas on what might be wrong?'

'Not a clue, Lara. I've barely slept for thinking about it. It doesn't make sense.'

Lara groaned as Ethan gave a screech from where he'd been sleeping in the sitting room. 'Shite! I'd better head off with him. If I let him out of the buggy, he'll never get back into it and I'll have to walk home wheeling it with one hand and holding him with the other.'

'Well, thanks for coming over,' said Jean, standing up and following Lara out into the hall. 'It's always lovely to have Ellie's friends round, whether she's here herself or not.'

'No problem, Jean. You know I'll always pop in if I'm passing. And listen, don't be worrying that this has anything to do with you. I have a feeling that whatever was bothering Ellie has nothing to do with either of us.'

Jean had taken one of the chocolate biscuits off the plate and handed it to Ethan, stopping his wails immediately. 'Thanks, Lara. And no doubt we'll see you over the coming days when Ellie's home.'

Jean waited at the door until Lara disappeared around the corner. Then she went back into the kitchen, her head spinning again. Now she was even more convinced that something was going on. First Ellie had been vague, then Matt. Lara had definitely been fishing to see how much she knew. She'd thought she was being subtle about it, but Jean was a pro at fishing for information and had spotted immediately what Lara was up to. And then she'd been adamant that Ellie's behaviour had nothing to do with them. Yes, there was definitely something going on. At least she had only to wait until the day after tomorrow to find out what it was.

○

Ethan continued whimpering as Lara wheeled the buggy in the direction of home. There was no chance he'd go back to sleep now and he was going to be tetchy for the rest of the day. She'd picked up a few lollies in the shop yesterday so she might just take out the Peppa Pig DVD and let him have one. She had some work to do this afternoon and the lolly would keep him quiet for a while.

She was still reeling from what Sharon had told her the other night. Fancy Caroline having a child. She was dying to find out more but she guessed she'd have to wait until they were home. Still, it would only be a couple of days if everything worked out this time and they managed to get Ellie on the plane.

She'd been trying to suss Jean out without her getting suspicious. If she really didn't know about Caroline having had a baby, she was going to get a right shock. And imagine her thinking she was to blame for Ellie's disappearance. The poor woman. She'd already been through enough heartache to last her a lifetime.

And it looked like they wouldn't be having any more dress-fittings with Monique. Lara felt inexplicably sad about that. It was the first time since this had started that she'd realised the wedding wasn't going to happen. She'd been sure, up until about ten minutes ago, that Ellie would change her mind and everything would still be in place.

She turned her key in the door and pushed the buggy inside.

'Out, Mammy!' Ethan wriggled and twisted in the buggy until Lara opened his straps and released him.

'Come on, cheeky monkey. Let's go and get Peppa Pig set up and I might even have a treat for you.'

'Yay!' squealed Ethan, running towards the kitchen.

Ten minutes later, Ethan was happily sucking a lolly and engrossed in his DVD while Lara waited for her computer to spring to life. She really needed a new one but she couldn't be bothered with having to set it up and transfer stuff. Eventually it came on and she hit her email icon. And there it was. The email she'd been waiting for. She opened and read it. Thank God! She felt like dancing around the kitchen. She hadn't dared to hope she'd get a response like that – and so quick too. Things were changing very rapidly in her world and this email could be the start of something huge, something she'd always dreamed of.

TWENTY-NINE

Ellie's heart was pounding as she walked up to the front door. She'd rung Ann first thing and asked if she could talk to her. She'd told her she had some news. At first Ann had suggested she come in to see her in work later but Ellie had lied and said that she was going home that evening. The conversation had ended exactly as Ellie had hoped – with an invitation to the house. She rang the doorbell and waited anxiously.

'Hey there, Eleanora. Come on in. It's good to see you.'

'Thanks, Ann. It's miserable out there today.' She stepped inside and wiped her feet before following Ann into a beautifully decorated sitting room.

'Have a seat,' said Ann, pointing to the oversized sofa. 'I don't have any Cinnamon Lattes here but would an ordinary coffee or tea do?'

'Ha! Believe it or not, I don't do those fancy coffees in my own house either! A tea would be great, thanks.' Ellie felt herself begin to relax. Ann was lovely. Surely she'd understand why Ellie hadn't introduced herself properly from the start. It wasn't as though she'd tried to trick her. It hadn't been calculated – it had just happened that way.

She looked around the room and felt a pang of envy. It was such a gorgeous house and they certainly knew how to decorate. The sitting room looked like it had been done by an interior designer. The style was eclectic yet everything blended really well. The sofa was purple suede and the armchairs mustard and green stripes. Ellie would never have dreamed of putting such colours together but they worked. She'd always been a bit conservative about decorating, feeling that neutrals were the way to go, but this had opened her eyes to a whole new world of colour.

Her mind wandered to the apartment she and Matt had bought. That was another thing to be sorted. God, she'd really created a mess. They'd got the mortgage jointly so they'd probably need to talk to the bank about it. Maybe they'd even have to sell. Her heart felt heavy. They'd had such wonderful plans for the future. They were going to start off in a small apartment as it was only the two of them, and maybe move somewhere with a garden if they were ever lucky enough to have children. The thought of children brought her back to where she was and the reason she was there. She needed to concentrate on what she needed to say to Ann.

'Right, here we go.' Ann came back with a tray of tea and biscuits and placed it on the big rosewood coffee-table in the centre of the room. 'Help yourself, Eleanora. Actually, do you ever shorten your name? Don't get me wrong, "Eleanora" is beautiful – I was just wondering.'

Ellie couldn't help smiling. Matt and Sharon would get a good laugh out of this. 'They call me Ellie.'

'Ah, that's lovely. Ellie it is. So come on, don't keep me in suspense. What's happening? Are you back with your guy? Are you going to get married?'

'I've met up with him and Sharon,' said Ellie carefully. 'We've chatted and everything is fine, but I'm still not getting married.'

'Oh, no!' Ann looked as though she was going to cry. 'I *so* wanted you to have a happy ending. I know I'm an old romantic but I loved that he came all the way over here to find you and bring you home.'

'As I said, Ann, he's a good guy. But there are other factors and I really don't want to go into them now. Actually, I don't want to talk about me or the wedding. That's not why I'm here.'

Ann looked confused. 'It's not? But I thought that *was* the reason you came. I thought you needed someone to talk to about it all.'

'Ann, are your husband and little girl here?'

'No, but they'll be back shortly. Gracie hasn't been sleeping well lately so Conor thought some fresh air in the park would do her good.'

Gracie! Her name was Gracie. Caroline would have loved it. She'd been a huge fan of the golden age of films and Grace Kelly had been one of her favourite actresses.

'Ellie, are you okay?' Ann was looking a bit uncertain. She was probably wondering why the hell she'd asked a stranger into her house. Ellie knew she'd have to say something.

'I'm fine, Ann. But there's something I have to tell you – something huge.'

Just before Ellie could launch into her story, the sitting-room door opened and a man stuck his head inside. 'We're home, honey. Gracie is asleep in the buggy so I'm just going to wheel her into the back room and let her sleep for a bit.'

'Aw, she's probably worn out, poor pet. Come in and say hi to Ellie. Remember I was telling you about her?'

'Hi, Ellie,' said Conor, holding out his hand to shake Ellie's. 'Nice to meet you. The Irish are always welcome around here.'

'Nice to meet you too, Conor.'

'Well, I'll leave you two girls to your chat. I have a few emails to do.'

'No, wait!' The words were out of Ellie's mouth before she could stop them. Both Ann and Conor looked at her.

'I mean … I want to talk to both of you. There's something you need to know.'

Conor glanced at Ann and raised an eyebrow. 'Just give me a sec and I'll put Gracie in the other room.'

'Ellie, what is it?' asked Ann, watching her intently. 'Why do you need Conor here too?'

Conor came back into the room and sat down. 'Now, what's all this about, Ellie?'

Ellie took a deep breath. 'I really don't know how to say this so I'm going to start by showing you this.' She reached into her pocket, as she'd done so many times over the last few days. She pulled out the letter and unfolded it. She handed it to Ann.

It took Ann only seconds to react. Her hand shot up to her mouth and Conor jumped up from his chair and rushed to her side. He looked at the letter in her hand, then back at Ellie. Ellie held her breath.

'I … I don't understand,' said Ann, looking from Ellie to the letter and back again. 'How did you … I mean … it's you?'

Conor put his arm around his wife. 'Sssh, love. Let her explain. Ellie?'

'I'm really sorry, Ann. I just couldn't bring myself to come out and say it. And I didn't mean to trick you or deceive you but it's how things happened, and every time I tried to talk to you in the coffee shop, it got busy and you had to go and ...' Oh, fuck! She was babbling, like she always did when she was nervous.

Tears streamed down Ann's face as she looked at Ellie. 'I can't take it in. But none of that really matters – what matters is you. You're our donor – I can't believe you're here.'

Shit! She was just going to have to come out and say it. 'Ann, I'm not your donor. I wish I was but it wasn't me.'

'Then what brings you here?' Conor's face scrunched up in confusion. 'How have you got the letter?'

'Oh, my God,' screeched Ann, staring at Ellie. 'It's *her*, isn't it? It's Caroline.'

'Who? What are you talking about?' Conor looked from one to the other.

Ellie nodded, tears stinging her own eyes. 'Caroline was your donor. I only found the letter in her things a few weeks ago.'

'But I don't understand,' said Conor. 'Who is she? Why are you here instead of her?'

Ann took her husband's hand and tried to talk through her sobs. 'Caroline was Ellie's sister, sweetie. She died a few years ago. Ellie was telling me about her.'

Conor paled. 'Oh, my God. That's awful. I don't know what to say.'

Silence hung in the air for a few moments. Ellie felt relieved to have told them but was conscious of how desperately sad they must be feeling. It made her confront her memories too – made her think about Caroline and how fabulous she was. How generous and kind, how selfless and giving.

Ellie was first to break the silence. 'Caroline was an amazing person. I didn't know about the egg donation until a few weeks ago, but that was Caroline all over. She was constantly doing good things and would never really talk about them. She wasn't one of those people who'd donate money to charity and tell everyone about it – she just did things in her own quiet way. She had the biggest heart of anyone I ever knew.'

'People are always saying that about our Gracie,' said Ann. 'Even at this age, she's aware of the world around her and always tries to make people feel better. Just the other day, there was a little girl crying in her playgroup and she went over to her and offered her Pinkie. Pinkie is her little pig that goes everywhere with her. Her teacher said she couldn't get over how kind she was.'

Ellie's tears fell. 'That was exactly how Caroline was. When we were kids, she was always looking after me and making sure I was okay, even though she was just two years older than me.'

'It must have been awful for you,' said Conor, who was visibly shaken by the whole thing. 'I mean, losing a sister so young. It must have been such a blow for you and for all the family. What happened?'

The door suddenly opened and there was Gracie, her eyes still red with sleep, sucking her thumb and clutching what Ellie assumed was Pinkie to her chest. 'Mommy, where was you?'

'Come on over, sweetie. We were just having a chat.' Gracie ran to Ann and jumped onto her lap. 'Say hello to our guest. This is Ellie.'

'Hello, Lellie,' whispered the little girl, her thumb still stuck firmly in her mouth.

'Hello, Gracie.' Ellie tried to control her tears. She was beautiful. She had Caroline's eyes and the same-shaped face. It was really uncanny.

Conor nodded towards Gracie. 'This is what your sister did for us, Ellie. You should be really proud of her. She gave us our little girl.'

'She ... she's beautiful,' said Ellie, her voice quivering. 'I have a picture of Caroline here somewhere.' She rooted for her wallet to find the photo she always carried with her. 'Here, look how much like her Gracie is.'

Ann gasped when she took the photograph from Ellie. 'Oh, my God! That's unbelievable. She's the spitting image of her.'

Conor shook his head. 'She really is.'

'And now that I think of it,' said Ann, 'Gracie looks like you too, Ellie. I don't know how I didn't see it before.'

'Well, it's not exactly something you'd think of unless you were looking for it. I was just a stranger to you.'

'Did you bwing sweeties?' Gracie suddenly found her voice and was looking at Ellie.

'Don't be rude, Gracie,' said Conor, wagging his finger at his daughter.

'No, no, it's fine.' Ellie rooted in her bag again. 'As a matter of fact, I did, Gracie. Now will we ask your mommy if you're allowed to have some?'

The little girl's eyes lit up as Ellie produced a big bag of the colourful jellies she'd bought in Dylan's Candy Bar when she'd been in the city with Sharon and Lara. 'Can I, Mommy, can I, *pleeeeease*?'

'Well, maybe one or two,' laughed Ann as Gracie bolted out of her arms and headed straight for Ellie.

'Thank you,' the little girl said, hugging her.

Ellie couldn't stop the tears this time. 'You're welcome, Gracie.'

'Why are you crying? Are you sad?' Gracie was fixed to the spot, watching as tears streamed down Ellie's face.

'Well,' said Ellie, 'I'm a little bit sad but I'm a big bit happy to see you.'

'Oh, okay. Here, you can mind Pinkie. She makes people better.'

'Thank you, Gracie. That's very kind.' Ellie watched as she brought the sweets over to Ann to get them opened. She was adorable. All of a sudden, Ellie felt a weight lift off her shoulders. Her sister was gone but one thing was for sure: her spirit would live on in little Gracie.

THIRTY

'It's really weird,' said Ann, pulling her scarf tighter around her neck. 'I didn't even know Caroline but I feel like I've just lost a friend.'

Ellie shivered. 'That's a nice thing to say, Ann. Caroline was everyone's friend. Everyone loved her.'

'I can imagine. She sounds wonderful.'

The two walked in silence for a bit. Conor had taken Gracie into the kitchen for lunch and Ann had suggested that she and Ellie go out for a walk, since the rain had stopped. Ellie had been glad to get out of the house and breathe in the cold, crisp air.

'So, anyway, tell me how you found me in the coffee shop. I can't figure it out.'

'You'll think I'm a mad crazy stalker.'

'Ha! How do you know I don't think that anyway?'

Ellie laughed. 'Well, you have a point there. I actually came out to the house last week with the intention of knocking on the door to introduce myself. But before I had the chance, you came out with Gracie running after you. When I saw her I was really taken aback.'

'I can understand that,' said Ann, nodding. 'She sure is the image of Caroline.'

'Anyway, I skulked off without saying a word, and when I was on the bus back to the hotel, I noticed you sitting there. I suppose I was intrigued by you. You have to remember that I knew nothing about Caroline's egg donation until I found the letter a few weeks ago. It was like I was being carried on a journey that I wasn't sure I was ready for.'

'So you followed me?' Ann spoke slowly. 'So in actual fact, I really *did* have a stalker.'

Ellie turned to look at her and saw a smile on her lips. 'Yes, I followed you. So I suppose technically I *was* your stalker.'

'Good. I'm glad we cleared that up.'

It seemed weird to be joking about it, but for the first time in ages, Ellie felt relaxed and comfortable. Ann had no expectations of her. She didn't know her and didn't expect her to be a certain way. She wasn't being careful what she said to Ellie or watching to see if she'd cry at the mention of Caroline's name. Ellie could just be herself.

'It wasn't easy to tell you, Ann. Every time I saw you in the shop, I planned to do it, but it just never worked out.'

'It's probably as well that you didn't tell me at work, Ellie. Can you imagine? I'd have been a wreck serving customers afterwards. No, I'm glad you came to the house.' She stopped suddenly and looked at Ellie. 'And I'm *so* glad you decided to find us and tell us about Caroline. We're so lucky that such a wonderful girl is a part of Gracie and we'll make sure Gracie knows about her as she gets older.'

Ellie swallowed a lump in her throat. 'Thank you. I still have so many questions, though. I wish Caroline was here to answer them because I may never find out the full story.'

'Well, is there anything I can help with? What did you want to know?'

'Well,' said Ellie slowly, 'did Caroline ever answer your letter?'

'I'm afraid not, sweetie. And from what you said, she would have died about six months after we wrote it.'

Ellie shook her head. 'I'll probably never know why she did it, then. And why she didn't tell anyone. I just wish she'd told me. I could have been there for her – given her support.'

'And you would have been fantastic, Ellie. But from what you told me about Caroline, it was probably something she wanted to do by herself. The really worthwhile acts of charity are those we don't talk about. It sounds like Caroline was simply doing it to help someone out. And weren't we lucky it was us?'

Ellie was bowled over yet again by her sister's generosity and selflessness. 'I've looked up what's involved in egg donation, and if it had been me, I'd have been looking for everyone's sympathy. She would have had to go through hormone medication, injections, scans – I'd want to be pampered for months.'

Ann laughed. 'You're a better person than you think, Ellie.'

Ellie shook her head. 'No, I'm not. I'm not at all.'

Drops of rain began to fall and Ann indicated a little coffee shop across the road. 'Come on, let's go in there and we can chat without getting wet or freezing to death.'

Inside, they ordered two hot chocolates and sat at a private table at the back of the shop. Ellie could feel Ann's eyes on her as she spooned cream from the top of the cup into her mouth.

'Come on,' said Ann. 'Why did you say that? Why do you think you're not a good person?'

'I'm just not. Caroline was the good person in our family. It should have been me who died, not her.'

Ann sucked in her breath. 'Whoa! That's a very big statement, Ellie. Of course it shouldn't have been you. You deserve to be here and to be happy.'

'But that's just it – I don't deserve it at all.' Ellie began to cry softly.

'Aw, you poor girl.' Ann took a packet of tissues from her bag and handed Ellie one. 'I can't imagine how hard it must have been for you. And now this is probably bringing it all back. I'm so sorry.'

'Thanks.' Ellie sniffed. 'But don't be sorry for me. You should be sorry for Caroline. I don't deserve to be here at all, let alone be happy.'

'I don't understand. Why don't you deserve happiness?' Ann suddenly put her cup down hard on the table and stared at Ellie. 'Hang on, is *that* why you're not getting married? Because you think you don't deserve to be happy?'

Ellie cupped her hands around her drink and kept her head bowed as she sipped it.

'Ellie!' Ann reached across and lifted Ellie's chin.

'Yes, Ann. I don't deserve Matt and I don't deserve to have a happy-ever-after.'

'But I'm sure a lot of people feel like that after a bereavement. I'm sure it's natural to wonder why that particular person was taken. Don't let it consume your own life and happiness.'

Ellie shook her head. 'You don't understand. Nobody does.'

'Well, *make* me understand!' Ann's eyes bored into Ellie's, and for the first time since it had happened, Ellie wanted to talk about it.

She took a deep breath to gather herself. She told Ann how she and Caroline had gone to the beach that scorching day in June – how they'd enjoyed basking in the sun until the sky had grown dark and the sea had become angry and threatening. They'd realised most people had already left so had begun packing their stuff. Then they'd noticed a girl in the water. The waves had become vicious and were threatening to swallow her. Ellie had frozen for a moment before whipping out her phone to dial the emergency services. But Caroline, without a second thought, had run to the water and dived straight in, swimming strongly towards the distressed girl.

'Oh, my God,' gasped Ann. 'What a brave thing for her to do.'

Ellie nodded. 'I know, but at that moment, I thought she was the most stupid person alive. I kept shouting at her to come back, that she should wait until help came. But she swam on until she reached the girl and somehow managed to push her out of the grasp of the rip tide so that she could swim to shore.'

Ann bowed her head. 'But it got Caroline.'

'Yes. I could see she had no control and the waves were taking her. I was at the edge of the water at that stage and tried to make myself go in but I ... I just couldn't. The waves were vicious and I was soaked but my feet were like lead in the sand. I froze.' Ellie looked at Ann. 'I was the stronger swimmer, Ann, but I just froze.'

Ann patted her hand. 'Most people would have in that situation. So what happened next?'

'Some guy came running over and dived straight in. He made sure the young girl was safe, then headed out to Caroline but it was too late. He tried to revive her but she was gone. If I'd swum out to her instead of freezing, I could have saved her.'

Ann began to cry too. 'I'm so sorry, Ellie, I really am. I don't know what to say. Poor Caroline. Poor you.'

'And that's not all,' continued Ellie. 'In the confusion, everyone just assumed I'd been in the water too. I was soaked from the waves and was very distressed. I never corrected them. I led everyone to believe that I'd gone in too and had managed to get out again.'

'But you were there playing your part, Ellie. You did the sensible thing – you rang for help and you waited.'

But Ellie wasn't listening. 'I shouldn't have even let her go out there in the first place. *I* should have been the one to try to save that girl. Why couldn't I, just for once, have done something good?'

'Ellie, you can't think that way. If you'd gone out there first, the chances are that Caroline would have followed you and you'd probably both have drowned.'

Ellie had never thought of it like that. 'But she didn't even stop to think of her own safety, Ann. That was the sort of person she was. She put everyone else first. It should have been me instead of her. She was way too good a person to die like that.' What had started as a soft cry turned into heaving sobs and Ellie could barely breathe.

'Have you ever spoken to anyone about this, Ellie? A grief counsellor or a psychotherapist? There are lots of people out there who could help you.'

'I've never spoken to anyone about how I feel – not my family, not my friends, not even Matt. Mam made me go to a grief counsellor with the rest of the family in the beginning, but I didn't tell her anything.'

'But it's been three years. I can't believe you've bottled it up for so long. Ellie, you can't carry the burden of your sister's death. It *wasn't* your fault.'

Ellie blew her nose and sighed. 'I don't know, Ann. It's like the guilt is part of me now. I can't see how I'll ever get rid of it.'

'Well, you can start by realising that denying yourself happiness won't bring Caroline back. I know that sounds harsh but it's true. Who's going to benefit from you making yourself miserable?'

Ellie knew Ann was talking sense, but she didn't feel quite ready to let go of the guilt yet. 'But if I allow myself to move on, to be happy, it's like saying I don't care that Caroline died. It's as though I'm not honouring her memory.'

Ann banged her hand on the table, making Ellie jump. 'Now that's where you're completely wrong. It's just the opposite. By allowing yourself to be happy, you *are* honouring Caroline's memory. Do you think she'd want you to be miserable? Do you think she'd want you to throw away the chance of happiness? I bet she's looking down on you right now and screaming at you to get your act together.'

'That sounds like her, all right,' said Ellie, smiling faintly.

Ann continued: 'And besides, by denying your own happiness, you're also hurting other people – Matt, your mother, your friends. In fact, I think you owe it to Caroline to be as happy as you can be and live life for the both of you.'

Ellie looked at Ann with admiration. How was she so wise? Only a few days ago she had been a stranger, and now she was helping her make sense of things that had never made sense before.

'Am I getting through to you yet, Ellie?'

Ellie smiled again, properly this time. 'You just might be. It's like a fog is lifting and I'm seeing things a lot more clearly. I can't say I feel completely guilt-free, and that's something I'll have to work on, but you're right about a lot of things. I've been such a fool.'

Ann reached over and grabbed her hands. 'No, you have *not*, Ellie. You've been human. You lost one of the people closest to you in the world and you just haven't dealt with it properly. My advice would be to get home, go and see a counsellor, talk to your family, bloody well get that man of yours and *run* to the altar with him. You deserve it, Ellie. You deserve to be happy.'

Ellie's heart soared. She felt lighter than she had in years and, all of a sudden, her future seemed bright. 'Do you know what, Ann? I came here to do what I thought Caroline would have done if she was alive. I believe she would have followed up on the letter. She loved children and she would have loved to see little Gracie. She'd have been so proud. But the truth is, I think she sent me to you for another reason. I think she knew how much I'd benefit from meeting you. Her generosity is still working from the grave. No one else could have made me see things as clearly as you have. I don't know how I'll ever be able to thank you.'

'No, Ellie. It's us who have to thank *you* – you and your family. I'm guessing that being part of a lovely, supportive family such as yours made Caroline the type of girl she was. So it's down to all of you, in a way, that we have our Gracie.'

'She's a credit to you and Conor, you know. You're bringing her up to be a gorgeous, kind little girl. God, I'm just thinking what my mother will say about all this. She's going to be bowled over by everything.'

'Well, if she wants to meet Gracie, she'll have the chance this summer. We've booked to go and stay in Cork for a couple of weeks in July so we can all get together then, if you like.'

Ellie couldn't believe it. She'd somehow thought that she wouldn't see Ann or Gracie again. 'That would be wonderful, Ann. I'd really love that.'

'Me too. And I want your family to see the difference

Caroline has made to our lives. You should all be very proud.'

'Thanks, Ann. I can't wait to get back to Matt and Sharon now and tell them everything. It's been an emotional but fantastic few hours.'

They stood up and Ann hesitated for a moment. 'I don't want to bring it up again, Ellie, but I'm really curious. What happened to the girl? The one in the sea?'

Ellie smiled. 'She survived. Her parents even nominated Caroline for a water safety award. All the family went to the ceremony and my dad accepted the award on Caroline's behalf. It was an emotional night, but we were very proud.'

'And you were bottling up your feelings all that time.'

'I suppose I was but I just didn't realise it at the time. Not any more. Thanks to you, I'm going to be an open book from now on.'

Ann left a tip on the table and they headed outside.

'Do you want to come back to the house and say goodbye?' asked Ann, pulling her scarf up tightly around her neck.

Ellie shook her head. 'I won't, if you don't mind, especially now that I know I'll be seeing you all again in the summer. I'm feeling so emotional right now that if I saw Gracie again I might never want to say goodbye. She really is so like Caroline.'

'So it seems,' smiled Ann. 'And we're so lucky for that. Lucky and grateful.'

Ellie hugged her. 'Say 'bye to Conor for me and give Gracie a hug. It's time I went and sorted my own problems out. As you said, I need to go and nab that man of mine, make sure he doesn't get away.'

'Good for you,' said Ann, hugging Ellie back tightly. 'I'm so glad I met you, Ellie. You're a really good person and never forget it. Go off and live the happy life you deserve.'

'Thanks, Ann. Thanks for everything.' Ellie walked away, a huge smile on her face. The final words of the letter resounded in her head: *I hope you have the happy life you deserve.* She knew now that she needed to take those words and apply them to her own life. It was as though they had been meant for her all along.

She quickened her step as she thought about Matt. She couldn't believe she'd almost let him get away. He meant everything to her and she was going to let him know. The future was looking bright and it was all thanks to finding that letter.

THIRTY-ONE

'I miss you too, hon.' Sharon cupped her hands around the phone so that nobody could overhear. 'And I'll show you just how much on Wednesday.'

'You big tease,' said Mikey. 'That's two whole days away. I may have to find someone else to amuse me until then.'

'Mikey Duggan! If you're threatening me with other women, I may have to withdraw your privileges.'

'Ah, g'wan, then – I'll wait until Wednesday. But the moment you're off that plane, I'll be collecting what I'm owed!'

Sharon laughed. 'I suppose that might be acceptable.

Although it would probably be best to wait until we're alone.'

'You see? There you go again, teasing me. There's only so much a man can take.'

'But I'm worth it,' giggled Sharon, enjoying the banter. 'Listen, it's getting really noisy in here so I'll let you go. Ellie should be back any minute and I want to grab us a couple of teas.'

'Right, Shaz. Keep me up to date and let me know how Ellie is. I still feel you're not telling me the complete story.'

'Look, we'll talk when I get home. But there's nothing for you to worry about.' Sharon sighed. She hated keeping things from Mikey but this was something huge and it wasn't her business to tell.

'Okay.' Sharon could hear the sulk in his voice. 'But once you're home, no secrets, okay? I want to hear everything that's happened.'

'Deal,' said Sharon, wishing he was beside her. 'I'll see you Wednesday.'

She slipped her phone back into her pocket and looked around the lobby at the Waldorf. She checked her watch. She was supposed to be meeting Ellie at six and it was almost that now, but Ellie had never been one for time-keeping. She'd think nothing of leaving her friends waiting for half an hour and she always seemed to have a valid excuse. Somebody had always called to the door at the last minute or she'd had to take an urgent phone call. When they were in Ireland, if Ellie arranged a meeting time of six, it was probably safe enough to aim for half past. Sharon was the opposite and a stickler for punctuality. She hated being even a minute late when she'd arranged a particular time. Still, she was used to Ellie and her ways, and it had stopped annoying her years ago.

She took the risk anyway, went into Starbucks in the lobby, grabbed two teas and sat down. If Ellie didn't come soon, she'd drink them herself.

A hugely obese woman waddled past and her mind wandered to her mother. This last week had been a bit of a revelation for Sharon. She'd spent years worrying about her mother, checking on her most days and making excuses not to go on holiday, just in case she was needed. But her time away had taught her that maybe it was *she* who'd been the clingy one – not her mother. Maybe she'd just liked being needed. She'd rung her mother every day and she was doing really well. She was increasing the time of her daily walks and had even joined WeightWatchers. Now she was counting the calories and points in everything. Sharon couldn't have been happier. To hear her mother so excited about losing weight made her heart soar. It also meant that Sharon could begin to look ahead to a future for herself.

Now it was hard to believe that telling Ellie she was seeing her brother had been Sharon's biggest worry until a week ago. Well, there'd be plenty of opportunities to break the news over the next couple of days when they'd hopefully be spending loads of time together.

Sharon spotted Ellie coming through the revolving door. Her face was flushed from the cold but she had a happy glow about her. She looked like a different Ellie from the one who'd been upset in the Oyster Bar the previous day. Perhaps things had gone well with Ann and the family. It was a really delicate subject and it had been difficult to gauge how they'd react but, judging from Ellie's smile, they must have taken it well. Sharon couldn't wait to hear about it.

Ellie rushed over to her. 'I'm so sorry I'm late, Sharon. My card got stuck in the machine at the station and I had to go and buy another ticket and then when I went back to the hotel I realised I'd run out of dollars so I had to get some more and —'

'Ellie, relax. I expected you'd probably be running late.' She handed her the tea she'd bought for her.

'So anyway,' said Ellie, taking off her coat and throwing it behind her on the chair. 'I'm *dying* to tell you everything but I want to tell you both together so I won't start until Matt's here. Where is he?'

Sharon had been dreading this moment. She honestly hadn't been sure how Ellie would take it. Would she be gutted or relieved? After all, *she* was the one pushing him away. She fiddled with the lid of her takeaway cup – clicking it on, pulling it off, clicking it on – playing for a bit of time.

'Sharon!' Ellie sounded alarmed. 'What's up? Where's Matt?'

Sharon looked at her friend and felt sad for her. 'He's gone, Ellie. Matt's gone.'

'Wh-what do you mean?' Ellie gave a nervous laugh. 'Gone where?'

'Home. He thought that was what you wanted.'

Ellie just stared at Sharon and, as realisation dawned, her face crumpled.

Sharon reached over and took her hand. 'Ellie, don't tell me you've changed your mind. You were so sure you didn't want to get married and that it was the end of the line for you and Matt.'

'I've been so stupid. I'm a bloody disaster area. I can't do anything right.' She began to cry – big heaving sobs which resounded around the lobby.

Sharon was torn between wanting to comfort her friend and mortification that everyone was looking at them. 'Come on up to my room. We can have a good chat there in private.'

Ellie let Sharon lead her towards the lift. 'And I told him I didn't want to marry him and that I didn't even want to be with him but my head was all over the place, and after I saw Gracie, Ann gave me a good talking-to and I can see clearly now that it wasn't my fault and – and –'

Sharon shoved her into the lift, away from the stares of the other guests. Bloody hell. Trust Ellie to have a mini-fit there in the lobby. Then, seeing Ellie's devastated, tear-streaked face, she softened.

'Come on, Ellie,' she said as the lift pinged at her floor. 'Let's get you inside and you can tell me everything.'

'I'm just hoping I haven't made the biggest mistake of my life.'

○

Ellie stared at herself in the mirror in Sharon's en-suite. She was a complete mess. Her hair was standing on end because she'd kept running her fingers through it and the tears had left streaks down her cheeks. God, she wouldn't have thought it possible to go through so many different emotions in one day.

All the time she was pushing Matt away, it had never occurred to her that maybe he'd actually listen to her. He'd been so determined to marry her, no matter what she'd said, that she'd mistakenly thought he'd always be there, waiting for her.

She took one of the hotel facecloths and wiped off the remainder of her makeup. Spraying a bit of Sharon's hairspray into her hands, she ran her fingers through her curls in an effort to tame them. She was looking marginally better but that didn't reflect how she was feeling inside. She unlocked the door and went back into the bedroom.

'Are you okay, Ellie?' Sharon had concern written all over her face. 'You had me worried there for a minute.'

'I'm sorry,' said Ellie, sitting on the edge of the bed beside her friend. 'I suppose I came to meet you on such a high and then it was such a blow to hear that Matt had gone. What happened? How come he went?'

Sharon leaned back on her elbow on the bed. 'Well, he was telling me about your conversation in the Oyster Bar yesterday. He said that he was starting to realise that you really *didn't* want to get married. It was the first time I saw him falter. He'd been so determined all along that you two were meant to be together. He'd never doubted it for a minute.'

'And he decided to get a flight home so he wouldn't have to see me?'

'Well, yes, I suppose that's how it was. But it was probably more that he thought you didn't want to see him. He was booking our flights for tomorrow evening and, on the spur of the moment, checked to see if there was any earlier availability for himself. Before I could talk him out of it, he had his own flight booked for this evening.'

'I've been so stupid, pushing him away like that.' Ellie shook her head at her own foolishness. 'I honestly thought I was doing the right thing.'

'But why, Ellie? That's the one thing none of us could understand in all this. You said you loved him but yet you didn't want to be with him. If your family and friends were finding it hard to get their heads around it, imagine how poor Matt felt.'

'I know, I know,' said Ellie, lying back on one of the feather pillows. 'It's hard to explain, but I wanted to punish myself. I thought I deserved to have my happiness taken away.'

'Why would you think that?'

'Because of Caroline. I didn't do enough, Sharon. I could have saved her but I was too scared to go in the water. Everyone thinks I was in there too and managed to get out but I was just too scared. Caroline died because I was a coward.'

'Of course she didn't die because of you! Is that what you've been thinking all this time? Why didn't you talk to us? Have you been bottling it up for the last few years?'

'It wasn't as though I was thinking about it every day. I'd managed to blot out the pain – to forget about how I really felt. It was only when I found that letter that things began to crumble.'

'But why? I don't understand.'

Ellie sighed. 'I began to think about how Caroline always wanted a big family. She'd been living for the day she'd meet her Prince Charming, get married and have a whole load of children. Then there was this little girl out there that she'd never met. It just seemed screwed up and it was my fault. And with all the excitement about the wedding, I got to thinking, why should I be so lucky?'

'I don't know what to say,' said Sharon, sitting up and looking at her. 'I'm really sorry you were going through all that and I didn't know.'

'You probably knew better than anyone, Sharon. You were always trying to get me to talk but I was determined to keep it to myself.'

'And what's changed now? I'm guessing from your reaction to Matt leaving that you came here today to reconcile with him?'

'Yes, I did. And I stupidly thought he'd be waiting for me. I've really made a mess of everything, haven't I?'

'Yep! As Lara would say, you've made a total arse of it! But you still haven't told me what made you change your mind.'

Ellie smiled, remembering her conversation with Ann. 'Well, we'd better get comfortable here because this might take a while.'

Sharon listened intently to every word as Ellie told her about the visit to the house and seeing little Gracie.

'It must have been so emotional,' said Sharon. 'Just knowing that Caroline played a part in her creation. It's amazing, isn't it?'

'Yes, it is. But what's even more amazing is Ann.' Ellie told Sharon about how Ann had made her see things clearly – how she'd talked to her about Caroline and convinced her that her sister wouldn't want her to give up her chance of happiness.

'I really wish you'd discussed it with me, Ellie. *I* should have been the one to give you advice, not some stranger.'

Ellie could see Sharon was put out. 'But maybe that was what I needed – a total stranger. Someone who didn't know Caroline and doesn't know me. Sometimes it's hard to talk to those closest to us.'

'I know, but I feel I've let you down. If I'd got to the bottom of it before now, maybe Matt would be still here and we'd still have a wedding to go to in a few weeks.'

Ellie moved closer to Sharon on the bed and hugged her. 'You could never let me down, Sharon. You're my best friend. I'll always be grateful to Ann for listening to me rambling on and for offering some sound advice but she'll never replace you.'

'Thanks, Ellie. That means a lot. But what are you going to do now? Do you think it might be the end for you and Matt?'

'I honestly don't know. How was he before he left?'

Sharon thought for a moment. 'He was sad. That's the best word I can use to describe how he was. He wasn't angry at you or anything. He just wished things had turned out differently. But you can get him back, Ellie. If you really want to, you can turn things around.'

'It's too late for that. And Mam has probably cancelled the wedding anyway. I don't know why I thought things would stand still and I could just walk back into my life. God, I'm an eejit.'

'Let's not jump to any conclusions. You can ring Matt

tomorrow or wait until we're home on Wednesday and talk to him face to face. In the meantime, let's get over to your hotel and pack your stuff. We've got one last night in New York and you're spending it here with me. There's loads of room.'

'Are you sure? I mean, I'd understand if you —'

'Shut up, woman! I'm sure. We're both exhausted so we'll order room service, watch a chick flick and have an early night. How does that sound?'

'Absolutely perfect. And, Sharon …' Ellie felt choked up again. 'Thanks for everything. You've never let me down – not once. You've always been there for me.'

'It works both ways, Ellie. You've helped me through stuff too. Now, come on. I think we've done enough talking for one day. There'll be a lot more to do when we go back to Ireland.'

As they headed towards the lift, Ellie thought about Matt and how much she loved him. She thought about the little things he did, like listening to her mother yapping on about wedding plans and pretending he was interested. She thought about his gorgeous smile and how it made a dimple on his left cheek. She thought about his kindness and his big heart. She'd been mad to want to throw all that away. She'd already lost one very special person in her life and she was going to do everything she could to make sure she didn't lose another. She only hoped it wasn't too late.

THIRTY-TWO

'Oh, God, oh, God, oh, God!' said Sharon, clutching the arms of her seat. 'I bloody well hate this bit.'

Ellie smiled at her, remembering Sharon's panic on their way over. It was less than two weeks ago but felt like a lifetime. So much had happened while she'd been in New York, and although there'd been some traumatic moments, she was definitely coming home a better, more content person. All she needed now was to sort things out with Matt.

Sharon grabbed a handful of Ellie's jumper as the plane took off and sat bolt upright. 'One, one thousand, two, one thousand, three, one thousand, four —'

'What in the name of God are you talking about, Sharon?'

'Sssh! I'm counting … eight, one thousand, nine …'

Ellie was half amused and half embarrassed by her friend, as the guy at the window seat beside them was watching with interest.

'Afraid of flying?' he asked as Sharon continued to count.

Ellie nodded. 'Yeah, she's terrified. I don't know what she's doing but if it keeps her happy, I'm all for it.'

'There! All done,' said Sharon, looking more relaxed. I read somewhere that the first twenty seconds after take-off are the most dangerous, and if you're going to crash, there's a good chance it will be then.'

'That's a load of rubbish, Sharon.' Ellie wished she would stop reading stuff about plane crashes because she was making her nervous too.

'It's not entirely rubbish, actually.' It was the guy at the window. 'Apparently, take-off can be the most dangerous time. Once the plane is in the air, it's stabilised and a crash isn't as likely to happen.'

'You see?' said Sharon, beaming. 'I know my stuff.'

Ellie rolled her eyes but was delighted that at least Sharon could enjoy the rest of the flight, knowing the worst was over.

The guy was speaking again: 'But some statistics show that landing is even more dangerous. That's the part that makes *me* nervous.'

Sharon looked at him. 'Really? I didn't know that. What time are we due in? I hope the weather isn't too bad over in Dublin. Oh, God!'

For fuck's sake. The last thing Ellie needed was Sharon to be stressing for the whole journey. She leaned over to whisper in her ear: 'Don't mind Dr Crash over there – I'd never trust anyone with a mono-brow.'

Sharon giggled and Ellie was relieved to have distracted her. The flight home was an overnight one so hopefully they'd get some sleep. It had been lovely to spend the previous night together, having some much-needed laughs and even shedding a few tears during *Love Actually*. Ellie felt fired up to go and get her man. It was funny how the tables had turned. It would now be *her* trying to convince *him* that they were made for each other.

'So how are you feeling now?' asked Sharon, flicking through the in-flight magazine. 'Are you ready to face everybody?'

'Ready as I'll ever be. But my head is clear now. The only thing I'm worried about is how Mam will react to the egg-donation thing. I think it will come as a real shock to her.'

'Do you? I think she'll be fine about it. Maybe even a bit excited about possibly seeing the child.'

'But I'm not sure she'll understand. You know how traditional she is. Sure she was almost having a coronary when I mentioned moving in with Matt.'

Sharon opened her mouth to say something, then closed it again.

'What, Sharon?'

'It's – it's nothing. It's just …'

'Come on, spit it out. Is it something about Matt?'

Sharon shifted in her seat. 'Not specifically about Matt. I was just thinking that maybe you're underestimating your mam. She may not be as prudish as you think. I'm sure if you and Matt had moved in together, she'd have got used to it.'

'I doubt it. You'd want to have heard the sniffs out of her when I broached the subject. There's no changing her mind when she has certain opinions.'

'Well, I think you'd be surprised.'

'So what's brought all this on? Since when have you been interested in my mam's morals?'

'Well … I may have a reason …' Sharon looked at Ellie.

'Ah, I see,' said Ellie. 'Well, it's about time.'

Sharon looked confused. 'It's about time what?'

Ellie smiled. 'I assume you and Mikey are moving in together?'

'Wh-what? You knew?' Sharon blushed a deep red and Ellie couldn't help laughing.

'Of course I did. I've known since Christmas. I'm not stupid! I've seen the looks between the two of you. You're going around the house making secret phone calls and Mikey is like a lovesick puppy most of the time. It didn't take a genius to guess you two were an item.'

'And you don't mind that we're together?'

'Of course I don't mind, you big eejit. I'm delighted for both of you. I've been playing your game with you and waiting for you to tell me. I couldn't quite figure out why you wouldn't say anything.'

'I've been dying to tell you, Ellie, but I didn't want to upset you. I thought you might be worried about the age gap, and you didn't need another stress coming up to the wedding.'

Ellie looked at her friend. 'Look, if there's one thing I've learned since I've been over in New York, it's to grab any happiness that comes our way. I think you two are perfect for each other.'

Sharon laughed. 'God, I can't believe you've known all this time and we've been creeping around in secret so that you wouldn't find out. I feel so silly.'

'Well, you can shout it from the rooftops now. And maybe you two will even make it down the aisle before me and Matt.'

'Oh, God, we're a long way off that, Ellie. It's only been five months. And, anyway, you two will sort it out, I know you will.'

'Let's hope so.' Ellie sighed. 'But I'm not taking anything for granted. As soon as I've spoken to Mam and Dad about things, I'm going to go after him and try my best to make him understand. The wedding may be cancelled but that doesn't mean our lives have to be.'

'That's the spirit,' said Sharon, beaming. 'Although it may be pushing things with your mam if both her children decided to live in sin.'

Ellie giggled. 'Oh, could you imagine? Well, let's take it one step at a time and hopefully we'll all get to where we want to be.'

The cabin lights had dimmed and they decided they'd try to get some sleep. It would be a long night otherwise. Ellie closed her eyes and thought about Caroline. She felt sure her sister had led her to that letter for a number of reasons. And she was sure she was with her now.

Come on, sis. I could do with your help. I know you want me to be happy so please don't let me lose Matt. He means everything to me and I'm sure we can make one of those happy-ever-afters that you so loved in your precious movies. Help me to make it happen.

○

Matt turned onto his stomach for about the tenth time. He just couldn't get comfortable in the bed. It was probably a combination of jet-lag and so many things going around in his head. He'd come home earlier, showered quickly and gone straight to the gym where he worked. They'd been great giving him time off, especially when he hadn't been able to tell them exactly when he'd be back. They'd tried to send him home, saying he'd probably need to sleep for a while, but Matt had just wanted to take his mind off everything.

Training clients made him happy. He loved pushing them to their limits and seeing the pride in their faces at their accomplishments. He'd taken a few bookings from the other trainers and had thrown himself completely into the job. For a full six hours, he'd managed to put all thoughts of Ellie and the wedding out of his head.

Now his mind was full of nothing else. He'd made a very rash decision about coming home before he'd even seen Ellie but it had been the right thing to do. Yes, he'd vowed not to come home without her and, yes, he'd sworn to everyone that the wedding *would* be happening, but sometimes it was necessary to admit defeat.

At least he'd stayed until he'd known Ellie was definitely coming back. He still cared about her deeply. He'd rung Jean at lunchtime to update her. She'd been surprised that he'd come home before her but had been thrilled that Ellie and Sharon would soon be in Dublin. Jean had said she and Andy would go and collect them. He wished things were different. He wished he was the one going to meet them and celebrate Ellie coming home – but it wasn't his problem or his business any more.

For the first time since all this had happened, he felt annoyed with Ellie. She should have talked to him before everything had got out of hand. He didn't understand why she hadn't told him about the letter. They could have discussed it and he could have helped her decide on what to do for the best. He could have helped her through whatever crisis she was having about Caroline. He was her fiancé – she should have trusted him – but instead she'd taken it all on her own shoulders and things had become very messy.

He turned onto his back and kicked off the duvet, which was getting increasingly twisted. The more he thought about it, the more he realised that maybe he'd had a lucky escape. If Ellie was so unstable – if she could go from a woman completely in love with him to someone who didn't want to be with him at all – it didn't bode well for a happy life together. It was probably better that it had happened now rather than when they were married. Or, worse still, when they had a couple of kids. The thought of kids made him sad too. They'd often spoken about the future and it had always included children.

It was already four a.m., which meant that the girls would be well settled into the flight and due at Dublin Airport in less than three hours. He'd give Sharon a ring later and make sure they'd got in okay. Despite everything, he wished Ellie well. He really wanted her to be happy – even if it wasn't with him.

The wedding was another issue that they'd have to deal with, not to mention the apartment. There was so much to be sorted and he didn't have the energy to think about it yet.

His eyelids were heavy but his head was still full of what might have been. He felt sad that he was losing not only Ellie but a whole new family. He got on well enough with his own mother but wasn't close to his brother. His dad was an alcoholic and had left when Matt was very young. He hadn't bothered to keep in touch. Matt loved Jean and Andy and what they represented. He loved their spirit and how they fought like cat and dog but still loved each other deeply. He'd been looking forward to being a part of that family unit and had hoped that, one day, he and Ellie would be just like her parents.

Just as he was drifting off to sleep, he was jolted awake by the ringing of his mobile. Middle-of-the-night calls always gave him the heebie-jeebies so he sat up and grabbed the phone from his locker.

'Hello!' He listened to the voice at the other end of the line and was out of bed in a flash. 'What happened?'

He pulled on his dressing-gown while still listening. He couldn't believe it. Jesus! That had been the last thing he'd expected to hear.

'Right, leave it with me. No, it's no problem. Yes, I'll sort it. Talk to you later.'

He sat down heavily on the end of the bed and put his head into his hands. Fucking hell! When was it all going to end? He felt as though he'd been thrown onto a merry-go-round these last few weeks and he didn't know how to get off. Damn Ellie and her bloody family. He wished they'd all just go to Hell!

But even as the thought flitted through his head, he knew he didn't mean it. He was just angry – angry with Ellie for all she'd put him through and angry with himself for still loving her so much.

THIRTY-THREE

'I'm scared shitless about going out there,' Ellie muttered. She and Sharon were in the queue for Passport Control at Dublin Airport and it had just hit her how much explaining she was going to have to do.

'It'll be fine, Ellie. Relax. Everyone will just be delighted you're home safe and that you're back to yourself again.'

'But there's so much to talk about – so much to sort out. And my mother is going to *kill* me!'

Sharon giggled at that. 'Ellie, your mam will run up to you and hug the living daylights out of you – then she'll kill you!'

'Ha-bloody-ha! But I'd probably deserve it after all I've put them through this last week.'

They reached the top of the queue and showed their passports before going on to collect their luggage. Ellie had been so positive earlier, but as she headed out towards her real life again, she was doubtful.

She'd pushed Matt away. How could she expect him to be ready to forgive and forget? She hadn't shared her thoughts and fears with him. She hadn't trusted him enough. She hadn't been honest. He'd said he still loved her but maybe he'd realised love wasn't enough.

For once, their cases came out quickly. There was no escaping the inevitable. They walked through the 'Nothing to Declare' channel and Ellie stopped suddenly before the sliding doors opened onto the arrivals hall.

'Are you okay?' asked Sharon, looking at her worriedly.

Ellie nodded, but she was breathing fast and her palms were sweating. 'I just need a moment. I feel as though I've been in some sort of bubble these last couple of weeks. It's like real life didn't exist for a while.'

Sharon linked her arm. 'I can understand that. But come on, it's time to face the music. Are you ready?'

'Ready as I'll ever be.'

They walked forward and the sliding doors opened. Considering it was still so early in the morning, there were a fair few people around. Usually Ellie loved this area of the airport. It was nice to see people's emotional reunions and to imagine what their stories were. But she was too stressed to think of that now. She scanned the crowd but didn't see her mam and dad.

'That's strange,' she said as they walked out past the sea of faces. 'You know what Mam's like. She's such a stickler for being on time – I'm surprised she hasn't had Dad here for hours, just to be sure.'

Sharon looked around too. 'Maybe they've gone to get a coffee. Or they could be looking for parking. Those car parks can get very full.'

'No, Sharon. Something's wrong. I can just feel it.'

They headed over to the seating area, sat down and continued to scan the crowd.

'Why don't you give your house a ring?' said Sharon. 'Maybe they've slept it out or something. It *is* very early.'

'Good idea.' Ellie pulled out her phone, switched it on and waited for the Apple icon to appear. When it sprang to life, she quickly tapped in her home number. She let it ring for ages but there was no answer.

'At least you know they've left. I hope they get here soon because I could sleep for a week. Why don't you try your mam's mobile?'

'She hardly ever has it with her but I'll give it a try.' She began to scroll down to look for the number when she heard Sharon's sharp intake of breath.

'Hi, girls. Sorry I'm late. Bloody Teletext was showing

the wrong time for arrival. It said you'd be half an hour late.'

'Matt!' Ellie couldn't believe he'd come. She was torn between delight at seeing him and fear that something was wrong. 'Wh-what are you doing here? I didn't know you were coming.'

'Come on,' he said, grabbing one of Ellie's suitcases and wheeling it towards the exit. 'We can talk in the car.'

Ellie was getting worried. 'What about Mam and Dad? I thought they were coming?'

Matt didn't say anything as he hurried outside, and Sharon spoke next: 'Is something wrong, Matt?'

'Oh, Jesus,' said Ellie, rushing to keep up with him. 'I knew it. I knew something didn't feel right. What's wrong, Matt? Tell me.'

Matt stopped at the pay-station and rooted in his pocket for the ticket.

'Matt!' Ellie swung him around with uncharacteristic roughness.

Matt's voice was gentle: 'Ellie, your mam rang and asked me to come and collect you. It's your dad.'

Ellie's heart began to thud. 'What about him? What happened?'

'He had a heart-attack a few hours ago. He's in the Mater Hospital, but your mam said to tell you not to worry. He's stable but they're monitoring him.'

Ellie burst into tears. 'Oh, my God! Why did that happen? He's really healthy and he's young – well, he's not really old – and he's always so calm and he's never sick and – and – and it's all my fault.'

Sharon put an arm around her. 'Stop that now, Ellie. Nothing is your fault.' She turned to Matt, who'd just paid for the parking and was ushering them towards the car. 'Do you have any more information, Matt? Is Jean there now?'

'She and Mikey went with him in the ambulance earlier. Apparently he's settled so they'll be heading home shortly. They said they'd meet you at the house.' He'd found a nearby parking spot so they were already at the car and he was hauling the cases into the boot.

'Can we go to the hospital?' asked Ellie, getting into the front seat. 'I want to see him. I want to make sure he's okay. Let's go straight there instead.'

Matt looked at her kindly. 'Ellie, you'd be better off just going home. They're not going to let you in to see him right now and, anyway, your mam wouldn't be leaving if she thought he wasn't okay.'

'I suppose.' Ellie was finding it hard to take in.

Matt continued: 'I'm sure you'll be able to see him a bit later. He's in the best possible hands. I assume you have your key if you're home before them.'

'Yes, it's on my key-ring. Okay, let's just go home.' Tears continued to stream down Ellie's face as they sat in silence for the journey home. Her mind was in turmoil about a lot of things. Had she caused her dad's heart-attack by making him stressed? Would he get better? The alternative was unthinkable – she adored her dad.

Even though she was worried sick about him, she couldn't help thinking about Matt. It had been good of him to come and get them, despite everything that had happened. But she'd also noticed that he hadn't hugged her when he'd met them or tried to comfort her when she was upset. Her heart felt heavy. Could it be that they were really over?

○

'Lara! What are you doing here?' Ellie opened the door for her friend to come in and hugged her.

'Matt rang when he dropped you off so I just had to come straight over. I'd been hoping to see you today anyway.' She pulled back from Ellie's embrace. 'Oh, Ellie, it's so good to see you and to have you back. But how's your dad? Is he okay?'

'Mam and Mikey are on their way back from the hospital now. He's stable but they'll have to monitor him closely and run some tests. Sharon's here – come in and join us.' She led the way into the kitchen.

'Hiya, Lara,' said Sharon, standing up to embrace her friend. 'You got here quickly.'

Ellie flicked the switch of the kettle to make more tea. 'Matt rang her. At least he's still thinking of me.'

'Of *course* he's thinking of you.' Lara looked from one to the other. 'Or have I missed something? Didn't he go over to New York to get you?'

'Did he not tell you?' Ellie put a cup of tea in front of her and sat down. 'What exactly did he say to you this morning?'

'He said he was driving so couldn't talk much but wanted me to know you were home and in your mam's because your dad was in hospital after a heart-attack.'

Ellie sighed. She didn't feel like having to explain everything that had happened. She looked at Sharon, who took the hint immediately.

'Did you not know that Matt came home without Ellie in the end? We all met up and they talked. Basically, Ellie told him that she hadn't changed her mind, and he eventually gave up and came home a day before us.'

Lara gasped. 'Are you serious? Ellie, is this what you want? Do you really not want to marry Matt any more?'

'That's just it, Lara,' said Ellie, rubbing her temples to try to get rid of the pounding in her head. 'I realised I *do* want to be with Matt. I *do* want to marry him and spend the rest of my life with him. But I think it's too late. He's realised I'm not worth the hassle.'

'Oh, you fucking eejit, Ellie!'

'Lara!' Sharon shot her a warning look. 'Ellie's upset enough without you wading in and making it worse.'

'No, she's right, Sharon. I *am* a fucking eejit. How could

I have let the best thing that's ever happened to me slip through my fingers?'

'I'm sorry for being so blunt, Ellie, but you tried so hard to push him away – did you not think he'd eventually get the message?'

'I know. I wasn't thinking straight. I – I just ...' Tears pricked Ellie's eyes and she couldn't speak. Just when she'd thought she was getting her life together, it was starting to snowball out of control again.

'Don't upset yourself, Ellie,' said Sharon, rushing over to her. 'You're just tired and emotional, and who could blame you?'

Lara shifted in her chair. 'I really am sorry for upsetting you, Ellie. I just care a lot for both of you and hate that things have turned out like this. What made you change your mind in the end?'

Sharon sat down again and began to fill Lara in on the last couple of days and everything that had happened. Ellie joined in with a word or two now and then, but largely left it up to Sharon to tell the story. Lara gasped and shook her head. Even Ellie found the whole thing hard to believe as she listened to it.

'So Caroline donated her eggs for this couple,' said Lara, when Sharon had finished. 'Wow! What a gutsy thing to do. She really was a great girl, wasn't she?'

'Yes, she was. And she didn't deserve to die.' Ellie's voice was small, and silence hung in the room as everyone took in the words. 'But I know now that it wasn't my fault and I can't blame myself and punish everyone else around me for the rest of my life.'

Sharon smiled at her. 'You've no idea how glad I am to hear you say that, Ellie. You deserve to be happy.'

'But it could be too bloody late now,' said Lara, never one to get caught up in emotion. 'So what are you going to do about it, Ellie? I assume you're not going to just accept that it's over.'

Ellie shook her head. 'Well, for now, I need to concentrate on Dad and make sure he's okay. And as soon as I can, I'm going to go and talk to Matt. It's too late for the wedding, but there's a tiny chance that it may not be too late for us. I'm going to do what I can to convince him that I love him.'

'Ellie love, are you home?' The front door banged and Jean rushed into the kitchen. 'Oh, Ellie, I'm so happy to see you.'

Ellie jumped up and ran to her mother, tears streaming down her face. 'Mam, I'm so sorry for everything. It's all my fault. I'm sorry for stressing you and Dad out and making you worry so much. If it wasn't for me, he wouldn't have had that heart-attack and he wouldn't—'

'Ellie, love. Sssh! Nothing is your fault. They've confirmed it was a minor heart-attack and your daddy admitted he hadn't been feeling well for months. Even last night we thought it was indigestion, but when he got weak, Mikey rang for an ambulance straight away.'

'And how is he now, Jean?' Sharon pulled out a chair for her to sit down. 'Is he any better?'

'He's doing fine, thanks, love. They're going to run some tests later today, but he seems to have recovered pretty well.'

'Thank God, Mam.' Ellie sat down. 'I can't wait to go and see him. And where's Mikey? Did he not come home with you?'

'I was just paying the taxi-man,' said Mikey, arriving into the kitchen at that moment. 'Hiya, sis, good to have you back.'

Sharon stood up. 'I think I'll head off home and get some sleep. Ellie has plenty to fill you in on so I'll leave you to it.'

'I'll come with you, Sharon,' said Lara, jumping up quickly. 'I can give you a lift home.'

'That'd be great, thanks. I hope Andy continues to recover well, Jean. I'll give you a buzz later on.'

'Thanks, Sharon love. And thanks for bringing Ellie home. This family owes you a huge debt for all you've done.'

'Don't be silly,' said Sharon, blushing. She glanced at Mikey. 'Sure I feel like I'm part of the family, to be honest.'

Jean nodded. 'And that's how we think of you, love. You've always been—'

'That's it. I'm not waiting a minute longer!' Everyone stared at Mikey as he jumped up from his seat and grabbed Sharon. He wrapped his arms around her and planted his lips on hers.

'Mikey Patrick Duggan!' Jean gasped. 'What the hell are you doing?'

'I'm just doing what I should have done a long time ago!'

Lara gave a big guffaw and Ellie giggled despite herself. Jean glared at them both. 'But Sharon already has a boyfriend, Mikey. You can't just go and —'

'Yes, I *do* have a boyfriend, Jean,' said Sharon shyly. 'It's Mikey.'

'Wh-what? You two? Together?' Jean looked from one to the other.

'Yes, Mam. We're together. And I know what you're going to say. There may be a few years between us but what does it matter? I love Sharon and that's the only thing that matters.' He turned and looked at Sharon's surprised face. 'I love her, Mam.'

'Well, instead of second-guessing me, why don't you let me have my say?' Jean looked furious.

Mikey sighed. 'Go on, then.'

'It's wonderful! Why in God's name did you think I wouldn't be happy? That's the best news I've heard in ages. Sharon love, our Mikey has really landed on his feet with you. I couldn't be happier.'

'Thanks, Jean,' said Sharon, beaming. 'We were planning to tell you all soon, but we just wanted to get the wedding over with first.'

'Yes, the wedding!' Jean sniffed, and Ellie guessed she'd be in for a tongue-lashing once the girls had left.

'Right, come on, Sharon,' said Lara, ushering her friend towards the door. 'Let's leave these people to chat. You can catch up with Lover Boy later.'

Mikey gave Sharon a wink. 'Go on, I'll give you a buzz in a few hours when you've had some sleep.'

Sharon went to hug Ellie briefly and whispered, 'Good luck. You'll be fine.'

Ellie hugged her back and felt blessed to have such a fantastic friend. She stood up and walked Lara and Sharon to the door. 'Thanks for everything, girls. I really don't deserve you two.'

'Sure I did nothing,' said Lara. 'It was Sharon who went over and Sharon who brought you back.'

'But the emotional support is just as important, Lara. Now, I'd better go in and have that chat with my mam. I'm just hoping I'll be able to explain this whole egg donation to her. I want her to look on it as a positive thing.'

Sharon nodded. 'She will, Ellie. As I said before, your mam is a lot more clued in than you think.'

'Thanks. I wanted to tell her and Dad together, but I think it's best if I speak to her on her own, under the circumstances. We can talk to Dad when he gets out, please God.'

'And then go and get your man, Ellie,' said Lara, wagging a finger at her as she hopped into the car. 'Your future is important. Don't forget about your own happiness with everything else that's happening.'

Ellie waved as they drove off and her heart felt heavy again. Right. She was going to have to face this. It would be emotional. She'd be bringing up lots of memories of Caroline and there were bound to be plenty of tears. She took a deep breath and headed back into the kitchen.

O

As soon as they had turned the corner and Ellie was out of view, Sharon burst into tears and Lara almost swerved off the road in fright. 'Jesus, Sharon. What's wrong?'

'I – I'm just – I can't –' She blew her nose but the tears kept flowing.

There was a lot of traffic on the road and Lara didn't want to be distracted so she pulled up. 'Come on, Sharon. Tell me what's wrong. Have I missed something?'

Sharon wiped her eyes. 'He said it, Lara. And he really sounded like he meant it.'

'Said what? I'm lost.'

'Mikey! He said he loved me.'

'Oh, for fuck's sake! I thought there was another major disaster I didn't know about. Jesus! Is that all?'

'Is that *all*, Lara? Have you no idea how much that meant to me? He's never said it before and just hearing the words was like music to my ears.'

'Ah, go on, ya big sap!' But Lara's voice was gentle. She was happy for Sharon and glad her relationship with Mikey didn't have to be a secret any more. 'And I assume you feel the same? Or is that a stupid question?'

'Of course I do. I love him to bits. But we'd both been skirting around it and never actually said it. I hadn't realised how much it meant to me until I heard him say the words.'

Lara indicated and pulled back out into the line of traffic. 'Well, I'm delighted for you. But moving on, what are we going to do about Ellie?'

'What do you mean?'

'Ellie and Matt. Don't you think they need their heads knocked together?'

Sharon laughed at that. 'I suppose you're right. But what can we do?'

Lara tapped the side of her nose with her index finger. 'I have a plan. Now let's go back to yours and get some coffee into you. There's no time for you to sleep just yet.'

THIRTY-FOUR

Mikey had gone back to bed for a rest and Jean was on the phone to the hospital. Ellie sat nervously in the kitchen, planning how to approach the subject of the egg donation. She took the now well-worn letter out of her pocket and smoothed it out on the table in front of her. There probably wasn't a better place to start the story than with the letter.

'Well, thank God for that,' said Jean, coming back into the kitchen, smiling. 'The hospital said your dad's doing really well. He's fasting, because they're going to take him down for a few tests shortly, and he's complaining that he's starving.'

'Oh, that's brilliant news, Mam. Can we go and see him soon?'

'They said to ring back in a couple of hours. It will probably be lunchtime before we can go in.'

'I can't wait,' said Ellie, relieved. 'But come on and sit down, Mam. I've made a fresh pot of tea. We need to have a chat.'

'Thanks, love. I'll turn into a cup of tea at this rate but, sure, go on. I'll have one more with you. I have a million questions to ask you and I don't know where to start.'

Ellie poured the tea into two mugs and pushed one in front of her mam. 'There's loads of things we need to chat about, Mam, and the wedding is one of them. But first I want to talk to you about something more serious.'

'Oh, Jesus, Ellie. Not more bad news. I don't think I could take any more.'

'No, it's not bad news, just unexpected.' She fumbled with the letter in front of her.

'What's that you've got there, love?'

Ellie took a deep breath. 'Do you remember when I was clearing out my old room a few weeks ago?'

'Of course I do, love. I know it was tough for you to do but you needed to face it.'

'I know, Mam. But when I was looking through Caroline's things, I found this.' Ellie decided she'd just let her mam read it and see how much she could take in. Then she'd explain. She handed her the letter.

Jean took her reading glasses out of her cardigan pocket and shoved them onto her nose. Ellie hardly dared breathe. She watched her mother's face carefully as she read down through the words. Eventually she took her glasses off and looked up, shaking her head. She had tears in her eyes.

'Mam?' Ellie wondered if she'd understood.

Jean's voice was a whisper. 'I never knew she got a letter. She didn't tell me.'

Oh, God, she hadn't taken in what was in it. She was probably too emotionally drained, with everything else. But there was no going back now. She'd seen it so Ellie would have to explain. 'Mam, of course she didn't tell you she got the letter. She didn't tell any of us. Did you read it properly? Did you understand what it's saying?'

'I know, love,' said Jean, looking at Ellie. 'The recipient of her eggs got in touch. She never told me.'

It was like a physical slap in the face for Ellie. 'You – you said that as if you knew about her donating eggs?'

'I did, love. I was the only one, though. I told your daddy, of course, because we don't have any secrets, but she didn't want anyone else to know.'

'I can't take it in,' said Ellie, sitting back in her chair. 'So you knew all along? Right from the beginning?'

'Yes. She spoke to me initially when she was thinking about it. I was a bit shocked at first by the idea, but Caroline spoke so passionately.'

Ellie didn't know what to say.

Her mam was still talking. 'So that's the address Matt found on your computer. I'm guessing you did a bit of investigating.'

'Yes, I did. But that can wait. Tell me about Caroline. Why did she do it and why didn't she tell me? Did you know about the child? I have so many questions.'

Jean poured fresh tea into their mugs and took a big sip of hers. 'Caroline and I were watching a programme on RTÉ one night about fertility and it really affected her. You know what she was like – she wanted to take the problems of the world on her shoulders.'

Ellie nodded. 'That sounds like her.'

'Anyway, about a week later, she told me she wanted to find out more about egg donation with a view to donating her own eggs. I thought she was mad because it's not an easy process, you know. But I didn't think much more about it. A few weeks after that, she told me she had an appointment with a clinic and asked me if I could come along with her.'

'I don't understand why she didn't tell me, Mam.' Ellie was near to tears. 'We were so close. Why didn't she want me to know?'

'I think she was going to tell you on a number of occasions, love, but she said that she didn't want you to talk her out of it.'

'Did she really think I'd try to do that?' Ellie shook her head. 'She mustn't have had a very good opinion of me.'

'Oh, no, you've got me wrong, Ellie. I tried to talk her out of it myself initially. She had enough of a job trying to convince me and didn't want to have to go through the same with you.'

'But what about afterwards? She could have told me after.'

'I think she planned to eventually. It was less than a year before she died that we heard the lady had had a baby. She was—'

'So you knew?' Ellie was astonished. 'You knew there was a baby!'

'Yes, love. There was very little information given back and forth between the donor and the recipient, but Caroline was able to ring up after a certain time to find out if the donation had been successful. The clinic told her a baby had been born but didn't say whether it was a boy or girl. I thought that was the end of it and we'd never hear any more.'

'I can't take it all in. I wish I'd told you now about the letter. I wonder why Caroline didn't.'

'I don't know, love. We'll never know now either.' Jean began to cry softly. 'She was a good girl, wasn't she?'

'The best.'

'She had to go through so many scans and examinations and even hormone injections to donate those eggs. And she never complained once. She was so happy that it all worked out – that she'd had a hand in giving that couple a baby.'

'She was brilliant, Mam – one of a kind. That's why I wanted to follow up on the letter. I wanted to see the child and to tell the parents how wonderful Caroline was. We'll probably never know, but I bet she'd intended to get in touch with them herself. Knowing how she loved children, I don't think she would have passed up an opportunity like that.'

Jean paused and looked at her daughter. 'And did you? Did you actually follow it up? Did you go and introduce yourself to those people?'

'I did, Mam.' Ellie began to tell her mother the story from the beginning, trying to make sure she left nothing out.

'But I don't understand, Ellie. Why didn't you tell anyone? You didn't have to do it all on your own.'

'I know, Mam. It was just something I felt I had to do by myself. The letter had really unsettled me and made me face things I'd pushed to the back of my mind.'

'What things?' Jean looked alarmed.

'I'll tell you about that in a minute. Let me finish about the visit to the house first.' She continued the story of how she'd gone there, followed Ann and made several attempts to tell her. Jean nodded as she hung on Ellie's every word. She ended by telling her about meeting Ann's family for the first time.

Jean gasped. 'So you saw her? You saw the little girl?'

Ellie nodded and, without saying a word, she reached into her bag and pulled out a picture. She put it down in front of her mother and watched her reaction. Jean's hand went immediately to her mouth.

'Jesus, Mary and holy St Joseph! She's the spit of our Caroline. The little pet.' It was all too much for her and more tears spilled.

'That's Gracie, Mam. They called her Gracie.'

'Ah, Caroline would have loved that. Imagine them calling her that.'

'That's exactly what I said. You'd swear Caroline herself had had a hand in picking the name. They're coming over to Ireland in the summer and they said you can meet her if you like. They're really lovely and open, and they want Gracie to know her history.'

'I'd like that.' Jean reached over and took Ellie's hand. 'You've done a good thing there, love. Caroline would be very proud that you did that for her.'

'I had to,' said Ellie, wiping her own eyes. 'You were asking me why the letter had unsettled me. I felt guilty about Caroline, Mam. I blamed myself. I didn't try to save her that day. I could have tried. She was such a good person – better than I'll ever be. She shouldn't have died.' Ellie buried her face in her hands and began to sob.

Jean was quick to go to her and put her arms around her. 'Ah, love, I didn't know you felt like that. You never said.'

'I – I just didn't want to admit it. I didn't go in the water, Mam. I didn't even try. I was too scared.'

'You listen to me, Ellie Duggan.' She pulled Ellie's hands

down from her face and made her look at her. 'Caroline's death is *not* your fault. I'm very thankful you *didn't* jump in to try and save her that day. If you had, I probably would have had two dead daughters and not one.'

'That's exactly what Ann said.'

'She spoke a lot of sense. And you're going on about how Caroline was such a good person. Yes, she was, but so are *you*. Look at how you kept this family going after she died. Look at how you put your own life on hold to help us through it. Look at all you've done in the last few weeks and the sacrifices you've made.'

Ellie didn't know what to say.

Jean continued. 'Well? And I suppose that's why you've been pushing Matt away. You kept saying you weren't good enough for him. So is this what it's all been about?'

Ellie nodded. 'I just felt unworthy. I thought I didn't deserve my happiness and now it's too late. I pushed Matt away and now he doesn't want me.'

'Ah, love, you don't know that.'

'Yes, I do. But I'm going to fight for him. I'm going to go after him and try my best to get him back.'

'Good girl.' Jean was beaming now. 'There's still a couple of hours before they'll let us in to see your dad so go and get your man. There's no time like the present.'

'Thanks, Mam,' said Ellie, jumping up from her chair. 'You're right.' She kissed her mam on the cheek and went to find some fresh clothes in one of her suitcases. Her heart was much lighter all of a sudden. Things felt like they were slotting into place.

She pulled out a pair of Levi's jeans, a Ralph Lauren T-shirt and some underwear. She couldn't wait to talk to Matt. The thought of life without him was unbearable and she was praying he felt the same. She'd have a lot of making up to do, but she was hopeful he'd understand that everything she'd done was for the right reasons. Of course he'd understand – that was why she loved him so much. But it wouldn't hurt to have a helping hand. She closed her eyes and had a silent chat with her sister.

THIRTY-FIVE

'I'll be up again later, Dad. I'm so glad you're okay.' Ellie hugged him gently and kissed her mam.

''Bye, love. And there's no need to come back. Sure I have your mam here to keep me company. You have enough to do.'

'I'll be here. It's the least I can do after disappearing for so long. Is there anything you need?'

'Not a thing. Your mam has it all covered.'

Jean beamed at her husband. 'Of course I have it covered. Sure what would you do without me?'

'Don't make me answer that,' said Andy, a smile forming on his lips.

Ellie smiled to herself as she left the intensive care unit. They were keeping her dad there for twenty-four hours for observation but everything seemed to be okay. They'd done a test and found that one of his arteries was blocked so they'd blasted it out there and then. It had only been a mild heart-attack – a warning. Her mam was already making plans to put him on a diet and get him out walking more often. It was good to see the two of them together again, her mam nagging and her dad rolling his eyes. And it was good to have a bit of normality after all the madness.

She checked her phone as she walked out of the hospital doors onto Eccles Street. Damn! Still nothing. She'd rung Matt a number of times and left messages for him. He was a light sleeper so the phone always woke him, and if he was in work, he always checked for messages between clients. He was avoiding her.

It was unusually warm for the time of year and she took her jacket off as she walked. She turned right onto Berkeley Road and headed for the North Circular Road towards home. She'd been so sure Matt would answer the phone that she hadn't thought past that. She'd imagined they'd be sitting down somewhere by now, talking things through and trying to get things back on track. As she reached the corner, she made a snap decision. Instead of turning right towards her house, she made a left and headed for Doyle's Corner.

She picked up her pace and turned down towards the

apartment she'd bought with him. She tried to shake off her nerves. Why should she feel like this? It was stupid. She was going to see Matt in their apartment – the one they'd bought together. Of course, she was entitled to be there just as much as he was, but in her heart of hearts she knew that there was a chance she wouldn't be welcome and she had only herself to blame.

She let herself in quietly, but the apartment was empty. It looked as though he'd been gone a while because the kettle was cold and Matt always kept it boiled for coffee when he was home. Ellie walked into the bedroom. They'd chosen the colour together – she'd wanted cream and he'd wanted something bold. They'd settled on cream for three of the walls and a dark red on the one behind the bed. He had left it unmade. Now she sat down heavily on it and laid her head on the pillow. It still smelt of him and she breathed in his scent.

This was where she should be – here in her new place with the man she loved. She began to drift off to sleep, thoughts of Matt filling her mind. Where was he? Was he thinking about her? Did he even care about her any more?

A shrill ringing jolted her awake and she sat up quickly. She saw from the bedside clock that she'd been asleep for more than an hour. God, she was exhausted. She reached into her bag and pulled out her mobile.

'Hi, Ellie.' It was Lara. 'Where are you?'

'Hiya. I'm just at … I've just left the hospital.' For some reason, she didn't want to say she was at the apartment.

'How is your dad? I hope he's improving.'

'He's doing great, thanks, under the circumstances. I'll chat to you more later on but for now I need to get home and get some sleep.'

Lara laughed. 'Sure you can sleep when you're dead. I have a much better plan for you.'

'What's that?' Ellie wasn't in the mood for doing anything.

'Can you come and meet me and Sharon? We're down at The Gardens so you don't have far to go.'

'Lara, I'm really not in form for a social evening. I just—'

'Come on, Ellie. We have things to discuss. You can sleep your brains out later.'

'But it's not just sleep, Lara. I have stuff to do. I need to talk to Matt and—'

'Look, I'll tell you what. Come down and meet us for even ten minutes. If you're fed up by then, which I guarantee you won't be, you can go home and I won't try to stop you. Deal?'

It would be easier just to give in to Lara. 'Okay so. I'll be there in ten minutes.'

She reluctantly left the comfort of the double bed and took a last look around the apartment. It was strange: she almost felt as though she was saying goodbye to it. She knew that sounded a bit dramatic because she and Matt were adults and would have to sit down and work things out either way.

As she headed towards The Gardens, she tried Matt's phone again. It was still switched off. He *never* switched his phone off. She felt like curling up into a ball and crying her eyes out. She wished she hadn't agreed to see the girls. Well, she'd just have one, then make her excuses and leave.

She saw them as soon as she walked through the door. Lara was talking animatedly about something and Sharon was throwing her head back, laughing. She felt completely at odds with the scene. She couldn't relate to them, nor did she want to.

'Hi, Ellie,' said Sharon, spotting her standing a bit away from their table. 'Come on, we've got you a drink in. And we've ordered you a sandwich. We reckoned you wouldn't have eaten since you got home.'

Ellie sat down and smiled weakly at her friends. 'Thanks, but I'm really not hungry. Look, I know I said I'd stay for ten minutes but I'm not good company at the moment.'

Lara patted her hand. 'Maybe just listen to what we have to say and it might cheer you up.'

'The only thing that could cheer me up at the moment is finding Matt and talking to him. I don't suppose either of you have heard from him since earlier?'

Ellie caught the look between them. 'What? What is it? You've spoken to him, haven't you? What did he say? What are you not telling me?'

Sharon laughed. 'Relax, Ellie. Now, I don't want you to get mad at us, but we've been doing a bit of background work today.'

'What do you mean?' Ellie was too tired to try to work it out.

'First of all, we've been to see Monique and we've arranged for a dress-fitting this evening.'

'But why would you do that, Sharon? She needs to be told the wedding's off. I don't understand.'

It was Lara's turn. 'And we've been to the florist to confirm the order and the singer is booked for the church.'

Ellie's head was in a spin. 'If you think by doing all this, it's going to help me get Matt back, you can stop now. I really appreciate your help, but I don't want to railroad him into something he doesn't want. Anyway, the main part of the wedding is the hotel and Mam has cancelled that.'

'We've just been out there and uncancelled!' The voice came from behind.

Ellie swung around and there he was, with a big grin on his face.

'Matt! Oh, Matt . . .' She couldn't say any more but jumped up and threw her arms around him. 'I've been looking for you all day. Does this mean that— Are we going to—'

'Put him down and sit over here,' giggled Lara. 'We have so much to do and so little time!'

Ellie reluctantly let Matt go, but kept a firm hold of his

hand as they sat down. 'I don't understand. What's going on?'

Matt put his arm around her. 'The girls contacted me earlier and filled me in on what happened after I left New York. They told me about the day Caroline died and how you'd been feeling. I'm so sorry, Ellie. I never realised.'

'How could you have? I kept it to myself. Nobody knew.'

Lara interrupted: 'Well, let's forget about that side of things for a minute and discuss the wedding. I don't know about anyone else but I'm madly excited about it. Not long now.'

'But how can everything be reorganised so quickly? I thought once the hotel was cancelled, that was that.'

Matt squeezed her hand. 'The girls made a phone call to them early this morning and they confirmed that your mother had cancelled but they hadn't yet got any other bookings for that day. They said if we went out with the next instalment of the payment, we could rebook.'

Ellie could hardly believe her ears. 'And you've done it? You've rebooked?'

'It's all sorted now, Ellie,' said Sharon, beaming at her friend. 'All you need to do is turn up for the dress-fitting tonight. I'd say Monique will have a job to do on yours with all the weight you've lost.'

'I … I don't know what to say. Sharon, I might have known you'd do something like this. I don't know how to thank you.'

'It was all Lara's idea. She came up with the plan this morning and we rang Matt. She's orchestrated the whole thing. She's been fantastic.'

'I totally agree,' said Matt. 'She's some woman for one woman.'

Lara blushed. 'Feck off, would you? I was only doing what had to be done. There was no way I was letting you two go your separate ways. You're meant to be together. And, besides, I didn't want to be the only one with some good news.'

Everyone stared at Lara and waited for her to continue.

'I got the email I'd been waiting for,' she said, beaming. 'The agent loves the book and wants to meet me.'

Ellie jumped up, went to Lara and threw her arms around her. 'Oh, Lara, that's brilliant. I'm thrilled for you.'

'Me too,' said Sharon, going to hug her friend.

Ellie sat down again as tears formed in the corners of her eyes. 'God, I don't know what to say to you all. You're wonderful. I probably don't say it enough but you're such fantastic friends. I really don't deserve you all, and I've been so upset all morning about the wedding and then I was even more upset that I was upset about the wedding because I should have been more upset about my dad and then I couldn't find Matt and I know you all think I'm stupid but ...' Everyone was laughing. 'What?'

'Mini-fit!' they said in unison.

'Feck off!' Ellie was giggling too. 'But, Matt, are you sure about this? I mean, I don't want you to feel railroaded into it if you're not sure about us or —'

He put a finger on her lips to silence her and pushed the table forward. Ellie's mouth dropped open as he got down on one knee.

'Ellie Marie Concepta Duggan, will you marry me?'

'Oh, that's so romantic.' Sharon was in tears now.

'You big sap,' said Lara, laughing at Matt.

Matt wobbled on his one knee. 'Come on, I'm not staying here for ever!'

'Get up, you big eejit,' said Ellie, half laughing, half crying. 'Of course I'll marry you. It's all I've ever wanted.'

They kissed and everyone else melted into the background. Ellie's happiness was now complete and, more importantly, she knew she deserved it. Her friends were great, but she was convinced that one person, more than any other, was responsible for everything coming together.

I know you want me to be happy so this is for you, Caroline. I can't thank you enough. She raised her glass. *Cheers!*

ACKNOWLEDGEMENTS

Right, since this is book three and you've had to endure pages and pages of acknowledgements for books one and two, I'll make these short. Ha, got you there, didn't I? Do you honestly think I can do short? But bear with me – I owe so much to so many people who've helped me along the way and I need to let them know how much I appreciate them.

Sometimes I think I have the easy bit in this writing process. I just sit in my office when the children are at school or when everyone is in bed and I spew out all the words and ideas that have been building up in my head. The most difficult part of the process is shouldered by my wonderful, long-suffering husband, Paddy! Paddy is the one who comes home from work in the evening and, seeing that I'm still buried in my computer, rummages in the fridge for something he can throw together and call dinner. Paddy is the one who'll close my office door when he sees I'm under pressure. When I have a deadline to meet, I don't even have to ask him. He'll iron, clean, kiddie-juggle – whatever needs to be done, he'll do it and without a word of complaint. He's the love of my life and my best friend, my superhero. So thank you, Paddy, for everything you do. I love you more than you'll ever know.

Then there's the fantastic four: Eoin, Roisin, Enya and Conor – my gorgeous children. When I can't find any cups in the kitchen, I know that they have a collection behind the sofa. When the laundry basket is suspiciously empty, I know they have a mound of dirty clothes under their beds. When there's no milk left, I know one of them has used the last of it on their cereal without a thought. They drive me mad at times but I love them more than they'll ever know. Whether it's a cheeky smile or an unexpected hug, every single day is worthwhile because of them.

I owe a huge thank you to my lovely parents, Aileen and Paddy Chaney. They've always been supportive of everything I've done but they've been amazing during these last few years. They haven't complained when my visits were scarce but accepted I was just bogged down with work. I get regular updates from them about where my books are displayed in their local Tesco and rumour has it they've been known to lurk around the aisles, politely recommending the AMAZING author Maria Duffy to anyone looking at the books! So thank you, Mam and Dad, for everything. Also, I should say a huge happy birthday to my mam, who's about to celebrate a big one (I'm not telling you which one because she'd kill me but it's not fifty, sixty or seventy!).

Thanks to my lovely brother, Gerry Chaney, for all his support, his picture-taking and especially for photo-shopping my wrinkles! Thanks to his wife, Denyse, who I've adopted as my sister and who's always there when I need her. I'm also very lucky to have lovely in-laws and I want to thank them for their support – especially my mother in law, Mary and my sister in law, Marena, who's always ready with her make-up brushes to work her magic on me.

I have to say a huge thank you to the wonderful team at Hachette who are such a pleasure to work with and make my job so much easier. Firstly, to my editor, Ciara Doorley – thank you for your unwavering support and your wonderful instincts that make my books so much better. Thanks to Joanna for always knowing the answer and for giving it with a smile. Thanks to Ruth for putting up with my incessant talking for hours on end as we make our way around the Dublin bookshops. You have my husband's sympathy! Thanks to Breda, Jim, Bernard, Siobhan and the rest of the team for all their hard work and support. I want to say a special thanks here to Margaret Daly who retired from Hachette Ireland recently. I hope you have a wonderful retirement, Margaret, and thank you for looking after me so well over the last couple of years. And as for the newest member of the team, Edel, I look forward to many more meetings in the future – hopefully some will involve wine!

I know you've heard me say it a million times, but I owe a lot to my lovely agent, Sheila Crowley. She believed in me right from the beginning and I'm very grateful for her continued support and friendship. Thank you also to Becky, Sophie and the rest of the hard-working team at Curtis Brown UK.

Thank you to all the wonderful booksellers in Ireland for their continued support. I've been overwhelmed by the lovely displays and I'll never get tired of seeing my books on the shelves. Independent bookshops are going through a tough time at the moment so I'd like to say a special thanks to Aideen Brady from Abtree Books in Lucan. Aideen and the rest of the staff at Abtree have been a huge support to me and my books, and have ensured that as many people as possible in the local area know about me!

Writing can be a very lonely process and it makes me all the more grateful for the wonderful friends I have. Thank you to my longtime friends Bernie and Dermot Winston, Lorraine Hamm, Angie Pierce and Sinead Webb who are always there with a glass of wine when I emerge from my writing haze. Thanks to my lovely friend Niamh O'Connor for the well-timed phone calls that keep me sane, to Vanessa O'Loughlin for all the help and advice and to Michelle Jackson and Denise Deegan for a night of champagne, gossip and laughter just when I needed it most. Thank you to my partner in heels, Mel Sherratt, for the laughs and ridiculously long emails! Thanks to Hazel Gaynor for all the coffees and chats and to the other girls who lure me to Avoca regularly for cakes as big as my face. Thanks to Colette Caddle for generously giving of her time to read *The Letter* and for giving me such a lovely quote. Thank you to Niamh Greene, who also gave of her valuable time to do the same with *The Terrace*. Thank you to all my other lovely author friends who are always there for advice, chats and some brilliant nights out. I apologise for not naming everyone individually but I'm so afraid of leaving any of you out.

When *The Terrace* was published, I spoke a lot about

my neighbours. I feel so lucky to live in such a wonderful community where I'm surrounded by friends and I know I'll never be stuck for anything. I want to thank all of the Larkfield gang from the bottom of my heart for being so wonderful. When is the next party?

If you've read *The Letter* by now, you'll know it deals with some fertility issues. I'd like to thank Dr David Walsh from the Sims IVF clinic for all his help and advice. The Sims Clinic is one of Ireland's leading fertility clinics and they can be found at www.sims.ie.

You'll be glad to know I'm almost done, but I couldn't finish up without mentioning one of my favourite places. Yes, I'm talking about Twitter! Thank you to my Twitter friends for always knowing the answer to my research questions or knowing somebody else who does, for making me laugh, keeping me company and keeping me sane.

I'm going to finish up by saying a huge thank you to the most important people in this process – you, my lovely readers. Without your support, I wouldn't have the privilege of being able to do what I love. I wish I could say a personal thank you to each and every one of you for taking the time to read my books. I'd be delighted to chat to you if you'd like to contact me either on Twitter at @mduffywriter or through my website at www.mariaduffy.ie. I hope you continue to enjoy my books and I wish you all the good things life can bring.

Maria x